1411172

THE NIGHT HUNTER

THE NIGHT HUNTER

Caro Ramsay

Town of Vail Public Library
292 W. Meadow Drive
Vail, CO 81657 / 970-479-2184

This first world edition published 2014
in Great Britain and the USA by
SEVERN HOUSE PUBLISHERS LTD of
19 Cedar Road, Sutton, Surrey, England, SM2 5DA.
Trade paperback edition first published in Great Britain and the USA 2015 by
SEVERN HOUSE PUBLISHERS LTD

British Library Cataloguing in Publication Data

Ramsay, Caro author.
  The night hunter.
  1. Anderson, Colin (Fictitious character)–Fiction.
  2. Costello, Detective Sergeant (Fictitious character)–
  Fiction. 3. Missing persons–Investigation–Fiction.
  4. Murder–Investigation–Fiction. 5. Police–Scotland–
  Glasgow–Fiction. 6. Detective and mystery stories.
  I. Title
  823.9'2-dc23

ISBN-13: 978-0-7278-8422-0 (cased)
ISBN-13: 978-1-84751-525-4 (trade paper)

All Severn House titles are printed on acid-free paper.

Severn House Publishers support the Forest Stewardship Council™ [FSC™],
the leading international forest certification organisation. All our titles that
are printed on FSC certified paper carry the FSC logo.

Typeset by Palimpsest Book Production Ltd.,
Falkirk, Stirlingshire, Scotland.
Printed and bound in Great Britain by
TJ International, Padstow, Cornwall.

For there is no friend like a sister,
In calm or stormy weather;
To cheer one on the tedious way,
To fetch one if one goes astray,
To lift one if one totters down,
To strengthen whilst one stands.

Goblin Market, Christina Rossetti

PROLOGUE

I am sitting at the kitchen table, waiting. I know he is coming and all I feel is a sense of relief. I am past being scared.

The only movement is the tapping of my fingernails on the top of the oak table. This could all go wrong. I check everything again. Then again. My eyes are sore with staring and looking, counting and measuring.

But I wait.

Mum's kitchen, her comfy and cosy kitchen, in our nice detached house in our nice little village. Who knew it was all going to end here? The worktops are tidy, the knives neatly in their block in the corner, just out of reach. The matching jars of pasta, coffee and sugar are stacked up at the window ledge beside a tired peace lily fringed and curled with brown. The old balance scale sits near the door with its weights lined up in size order, each equidistant from its neighbour. They look like a set of Russian dolls. This is how I like it. This is how I have arranged it. The heaviest weight is nearest the door. I look at it again, counting, measuring; the distance from the weight to the door handle, the distance from my hand to the corner of the worktop. I make sure it is within my reach. Just in case.

My phone is lying near the sink. The ticking of the clock is loud in the night air but I am listening beyond that, listening for the quiet rumble of tyres on gravel. I told him to bring the car round to the back of the house where it will not be seen.

He liked that idea. Because he is stupid.

As the hour hand clicks its way to three, I realize I am getting cold but try to stay focused on the weights, the distance. Nothing has been left to chance. Then I hear it, a gentle purr, a gear change, the familiarity of a car in the drive. The engine dies.

Silence; the click of a car door opening.

More silence. This time it is full of expectation.

He is walking up the back path. I can sense him at the other side of the kitchen door where he hesitates, composing himself. I don't move. I can afford to give him the small pleasure of his anticipation before the shock of my reality.

The knock when it comes is surprisingly soft and unobtrusive. Polite, even.

I get up and turn the handle. Immediately, he pushes the door open and walks in without a word, without giving me a second glance. He forces me to sidestep so he can pass. I resume my position as my eyes check the distance to the end of the worktop, ensuring I can reach.

It's fine.

He is a tall, rather ugly man. He has an air of confidence that borders on arrogance. He is starting to run to fat. His after-shave smells like pine disinfectant, cheap and nasty. It sums him up.

I hate this man for what he has done to my family.

He turns slowly and stares at me, standing close as he studies my face. He is trying to make me feel small and vulnerable in my own mother's kitchen. He is trying to make me feel like a victim. This is how he operates. He nods his head, gesturing that I should close the door. I am happy to oblige. I kick it with my heel so that I do not break eye contact with him. He reaches round me to turn the key in the lock. That was unexpected.

'Nobody in?' he asks. As if he doesn't know.

There is no point in lying. 'No. We're on our own, nobody about. Even our neighbour is away.'

He smiles. I do not smile back. He picks up my mobile phone from the worktop, glances at it and then scrolls through my messages, my calls. He puts the phone down and regards me with circumspection. 'When did you last speak to Sophie?'

I fold my arms, steadying my nerves. I will not tell him anything about my sister.

'Did you hear me?' There it is again, that politeness. But his eyes are desperate and that makes him dangerous.

I nod. It is up to him now. He will do either the right thing, or the wrong thing.

He laughs slightly, shaking his head. I don't understand

that. He leans on the worktop looking at me. Lifting the weights for the scales, he starts moving them around, placing them on the plates, watching the pointer swing from one side to the other. Then back again. The weights move like chess pieces. I watch like a grand master. He smiles at me; he finds this amusing. He puts the heaviest weight down in the wrong place. I have to put that right so I lift it and put it back in line, putting the scales back in balance. This is the way it *has* to be. He thinks he is one or two moves ahead. I am three or four.

He draws his fingertip slowly along the edge of the worktop, speeding up as he reaches the edge where he pauses, his fingertip twitching like a dying fish on a line.

Our eyes lock. I can see the flecks of fat collecting on the folds of his lids. I wonder what his arteries are like. He stretches out his arms and grips me by the shoulders. We are so close we could kiss. I can smell vinegar on his breath. I focus on the blocked pores on the end of his nose. He grips me harder, squeezing my flesh. It hurts.

I am not scared. I will not step back.

'I need to talk about Sophie.'

When I speak I do not recognize my voice; it is thin and raspy. 'Then you'll be here a long time.'

He tightens his grip and my head tilts back, forcing me to look at the plaster on the kitchen ceiling. A fine cobweb dances on a draught; it's not like Mum to miss that kind of thing. I am thinking that I must mention it to her as I feel the joints at the top of my neck grind together. In my peripheral vision I see him slowly raise his other hand; he is going to punch me. I reach out for the weight; my fingertips touch the heaviest one.

I smile.

I have my weapon.

Just in case he does the wrong thing.

FRIDAY, I JUNE

I once had a self-help book that started with the words *Today is the first day of the rest of your life*. I threw it in the bin. My life changed yesterday. I might be unsure as to how I am going to make sense of it all but I know that a book by some Botoxed TV psychoanalyst isn't going to help me.

A month ago my doctor suggested that I attend this meeting. I would rather juggle with razor blades but I have to show willing.

So it is two o'clock and I am waiting outside a grimy building near Bath Street. The city centre of Glasgow is lazy, enjoying rare summer sunshine. I go through the doors of the hall into the darkness and have a wee read at the noticeboard as my eyes adjust. There's all the usual crap – loads of self-help groups for folk with no sense of responsibility.

My sister Sophie says that I have no empathy. She's right.

A middle-aged woman in a heavy white jacket gives me a sweaty smile as she shuffles through the double doors. I catch a glimpse of the room beyond. No matter how many reinventions this place has gone through, it still has the dull, musty smell of a church, stagnant as if nobody ever opens a window to let any hope in. I slip into the room carefully so that the door makes no noise on closing.

There are about thirty people milling around, aimless. Are they all drifting in private purgatory, haunted by the memories of a loved one who walked out the door never to be seen again? Are they, are we all, suffering from the Not Knowing?

It doesn't seem to bother them. This could be a Bowling Club outing to Largs enjoying a mingle with a free cuppa and a chocolate Hobnob before shuffling towards the main feature, another monthly instalment of a real-life soap opera.

I didn't think I would ever be in this position.

Did any of us?

I steel myself not to leave, settling for avoiding eye contact.

I am supposed to be here as some kind of therapy. The doc says it is good to bond with others in the same situation but people like me do not bond. We don't see the point.

A youngish man with a ridiculous fringe covering his eyes says hello to me. He has that sugar-coated soft focus kind of hello deployed by ministers and bereavement counsellors. The Fringe waves a bony hand over his little crowd of acolytes. The audience are mostly women, mostly old enough to be my granny. There's one man about my dad's age, dressed in a checked jacket. His hair is Brylcreemed back like an oil slick and he is two decades too old for his jeans. There's another couple of younger men with the same earnest expression as the Fringe who nod a lot. One much older man stands at the back of the hall, and as I am watching he kicks off one plastic slip-on shoe and rubs a grubby sock on the calf of his other leg. His zippered jacket struggles to support his beer belly, and his grey hair sticks up at the back of his head like a spring from an old mattress. His jogging bottoms are baggy at the knee, making his legs look misshapen. He catches my eye and flicks me a look of dislike. I return it with knobs on.

Checked jacket has taken his seat, a few others have nodded to him but nobody sits beside him. Slip-on shoes is ignored by all as he wedges a Hobnob between his teeth while his hand rifles in his pocket for something. Or he might be having a little play with himself. He looks the type. He stares out the window, and a nicotine-stained hand rises to flatten the unruly hair. I rather admire his stance. It says, *Do not speak to me.* I can use that. I watch and learn.

The Fringe hands me a cup of water, a film of grease dancing on the surface. I don't catch Fringe's name, I'm not that interested. He wants them to be quiet so he takes a deep breath while looking high into the rafters, waiting for God to intervene. God doesn't, so the Fringe coughs once, twice and the audience take their seats and settle. He smiles at me, gesturing that I should come and sit beside him.

I do, tugging down the sleeves of my black Rohan jumper, curling the cuffs into the palms of my hands. The old guy in the jogging trousers is taking his time about finding a seat.

The Fringe introduces himself as Danny but the audience feast their eyes on me. He runs through what he calls the *usual housekeeping points* accompanied with enough scratching to intrigue a dermatologist. He calls me Elvira, which is my name, but I never tell anybody that for obvious reasons. They chorus *Hello, Elvira* like we're at a friggin' pantomime. I do not hear the voice of Slip-on Shoes, but somehow I know it is raspy and thick with nicotine.

'Elvira has come today to share her story with us. Her story is challenging.' Danny nods in solidarity. 'We all have these challenges. Elvira is at the start of a long road, a road that everybody in this room has walked.' His voice quivers a little. 'I know that we will support her in any way we can.' He sits. The silence goes on. I see the dust motes dancing in the sunshine, then I focus on their sad, pathetic faces.

'My name is Elvira. My dad was an Elvis fan. I get called Elvie.' There is a mutter of *I knew it was her.* The words float up to the rafters to escape through the open window and into the sunshine beyond. 'My sister Sophie went out for a run on the fifth of April. It was a Thursday. She left at six p.m.' I pull my sleeve in a little tighter. 'She never came back.'

I last thirty-two minutes, then escape.

Elvira has left the building.

By quarter to three I am hiding on the stone steps in Bothwell Street, my back against the railings, deep-breathing to calm my nausea. As experiences go that meeting was up there with tooth extraction and biopsies. After my little speech they had decided to 'engage' me. The Fringe had kicked that off, of course. *Do you and your mother have a positive dialogue about Sophie?*

She's never sober long enough.

I escaped as fast as I could to the sanctuary of the steps; they put it down to me being upset. I am trying to sit still, aware of that feeling again. The blood in my veins is turning to ice and the impulse to move is overpowering.

Sitting by my car, I debate if I should jog round the city streets to loosen up or just sit here and wait for it to pass. I need to let go the stress before I go out to Eaglesham and endure the weekly drama of family dinner. Later I will drive up to the tranquillity of Argyll. Strange that I now feel more at peace at work than I do in the house I grew up in.

I glance at my watch, calculating how long I can leave it before I need to head home, where Mum will feed us in silence while Rod, her boyfriend, answers her questions for her like a translator for the pathetic. Grant, my younger brother, will start ranting. He's seventeen now, he has the looks of a Greek god and the personality of a spoiled six-year-old. His passions are himself, exercise and eating in any combination. Just to annoy Mum, he will probably be wearing a vest and mirrored sunglasses. He will flex his muscles while picking cheese off his pizza with his fingers. He thinks he's Travis Bickle; he's obsessed with *Taxi Driver* and sleepwalks round the house keeping everybody awake. The absence of table manners is usually the trigger for Mum crying, the absence of gin is the trigger for her screaming, the absence of Sophie is the reason for her pain. Rod will open a good bottle of red to pour wine on troubled waters.

At no point will anybody mention that Sophie is believed to be missing, and has been so for fifty-seven days.

Nobody is comfortable in that house any more. The sideboard is constantly set with coffee and biscuits for Avril, the police liaison officer who calls frequently with her offerings of sightings, partial and bogus. I used to pay scant attention to her. I might have to pay more attention now, though.

Everything has changed since Sophie left. I have deferred my medical studies at Glasgow uni for a year. I used to live in my own flat in the West End of Glasgow, and now I am a nanny of sorts and live in the middle of nowhere. I used to look at MRI scans and contribute to important decisions. Now I eat breakfast with a five-year-old with a Coco Pops addiction. Grant's hopes of his sports scholarship at Texas University are shattered because of a knee injury and he savours his resentment as if it were delicious. Avril, the plump cop with nice fingernails, is only helping us because she worked at the Vulnerable Victims Unit and knew Sophie through her work at the Boadicea project for victims of domestic violence.

But Sophie has never been a missing person in the eyes of the police, not officially, and I do admire the textbook logic that Avril quotes at us. Sophie took money with her, therefore she had planned her disappearance. A married man called Mark Laidlaw had met her through Boadicea and he has not been seen for fifty-one days now. She was a blonde with a wide smile and huge blue eyes like a china doll, a young lawyer with a fierce social conscience. Mark was a bit of rough. Their conclusion was obvious and the police will need evidence of foul play before they will do anything to find Sophie.

And until midnight last night that was fine with me.

Now I need to rethink.

My mother has spent the last eight weeks cooking but refusing to eat, a remnant from her days as a model. Sleep is a shadow she chases. It was Rod, Mum's boyfriend, who decided to start the Find Sophie Campaign to alleviate the pain of sitting doing nothing. He was the man of the house now, he told me; he owed it to my dad's memory. At that time I knew that Sophie was not 'missing', we just had no idea where she was, and all I could do was go along with it while trying to stop them spending real money or too much time as my bedroom evolved into a mock office with letters, posters, envelopes and boxes all over the place. I was guilty of omission and nothing else.

The campaign grew like the heads of Medusa. Sophie was pretty and charismatic so the press got involved and created a mystery where there wasn't one. I used to think that wherever Sophie had gone to ground was well chosen as nobody had set eyes on her. Now I hope to God there isn't another reason.

I look at my watch, time is moving on. As soon as dinner is over I can get back to Ardno and the Coco Pops kid. I need to time it right; lying to my mother is very tiring. Drunks can sense evasion and have no intuitive sense of when to back off. She will ask me at least forty times what is wrong, then ignore whatever I say and go and cook something.

I am stretching out my calves when a nicotine-scented shadow falls over me. It starts to cough, a deep phlegmy cough that rattles through inflamed tubes as it splutters and cackles up from the base of the lungs. The coughing stops with a huge spit then there is the wheeze of laboured breathing. That cough belongs to a sixty-a-day man.

I open my eyes to see a pair of slip-on shoes.

'Jesus,' he rasps. 'You left sharpish.'

'You shouldn't smoke with a cough like that.'

'And you would know, being a medical student.' He waves the cigarette around. 'Before you dropped out.'

'I deferred,' I correct him, cupping my hands to my eyes to catch the sun while I try to focus on his face, but he remains a fat, wheezing silhouette. 'And who are you, exactly?'

'Billy Hopkirk. Private investigator.'

'If you're looking for business, forget it.'

He does not answer but fishes about his pocket, bringing out something that he balances on the palm of his hand like he's checking the denominations of a foreign currency. 'Sophie? Sophie went out running in a nice posh place like Eaglesham and vanishes. No forensics, no blood. No nothing. Just her parked car and a big fat pool of nothing.'

'You seem very well informed.'

'Charismatic, no money problems. A highly qualified lawyer who chose to live at home. A lawyer who worked for a pittance in a practice that specialises in legal aid for battered women.' There was another bout of coughing, another spit. 'Bet your mum was well chuffed, spending all that on her education to see it thrown away for the benefit of the great unwashed in the dole queue.'

'You seem very well informed,' I repeat, admitting to myself that he had my mum down to a T.

'The cops are doing nothing. DI Costello is a shrewd cookie and she takes the official line – Sophie has done a bunk with Mark Laidlaw.'

'Mark Laidlaw?'

Mark Laidlaw. Cheap piney aftershave. I resist the temptation to look up.

'He hasn't been seen since Sophie went missing.'

'Soph went missing on the fifth of April,' I correct him. 'He was seen on the eleventh.'

'OK, but his wife hasn't seen him since Sophie went. Nice-looking girl, Sophie. Him a married man. How well did she know him?'

I'm not good at these *shades of grey* questions; I only do black and white. 'What's it got to do with you?'

'Nothing if they went away together. Everything if they did not. My card – I'll pop it under your windscreen. Save you getting up.'

I wait until he walks away. I want to ignore that card but it flickers in the wind, making a clicking noise that is both persistent and annoying. I think he might be as well. Rod makes a point of making sure the house looks the same; he likes to maintain its *kerb appeal*, as an estate agent would say. The two conifers in the front garden are perfect examples of topiary balls on stalks. Mum's Octavia and Rod's Focus are sitting in the driveway, waxed and polished. At least the Focus is back from being repaired after Grant bumped it and Mum went bonkers.

I grew up in this detached box on the far side of Eaglesham but moved out four years ago. The village is the same as all villages; small, gossipy. Eaglesham sits high on Fenwick Moor well within the Glasgow commuter belt, but when we left school Sophie and I bought a flat in the West End with the money Dad left us. It was handy for the university but Sophie never got round to moving in with me, and in the end I stopped asking. The flat is empty now that I've moved sixty miles north to Ardno. My new job thwarted Mum's hope that I would return home to help her with Grant's increasingly fragile mental health when Sophie left. My brother's mind was fractured when Dad died then blew apart when Sophie disappeared. When Dad collapsed on the golf course, Grant reinjured his knee, and that injury meant he failed the medical for his sports scholarship in America. The echoes of those events resonate long and loud in this house. We all seem in limbo, can't move forward or backward.

Last week I didn't get home until midnight and I was locking my car door when Eric the neighbour called to me, indicating Grant was in the back garden again. We found my brother sitting naked on the grass sobbing his heart out. The security lights from the house glistened on his sweat, making his skin shine, which made him look like a young gladiator. Except for the tears streaming down his face. He said one word when he saw me.

Sophie.

Eric and I helped him back into the house. It was the only time I was tempted to tell him that I knew Sophie was safe and well. Thank God I didn't as it might not be true. I have kept quiet for fifty-seven days. She asked me to keep her secret and I will. It is black and white. For some reason that I still do not know, she had told me she had to go away – those were her exact words, *go away*. Not run away, just go.

Tonight the house is quiet but tense. The dark blue Axminster and Regency stripe seem oppressive after the light summer evening. The smell of garlic and basil drift out to meet me; I can hear Radio Four chat from the kitchen. I drop my rucksack and catch sight of myself in the mirror. The physical changes are gradual so I don't notice them but Mum always recoils a little when she sees me. My acne is worse, there's a little more growth of hair under my chin. The whites of my eyes are still clear, the irises still the colour of Bournville. Small reminders of the girl I used to be. I was never the prettiest of children, I was never going to be a Sophie. Dad said I had the face of the Mona Lisa, enigmatic and alluring. But then my dad always lied to make up for all the times in my life when I didn't get the joke, when I didn't see the point. He made sure that I didn't feel different; he made me feel special.

Mum appears from the kitchen wiping her hands on her apron and we hug. Beneath the garlic, I can smell juniper. She stands back, looking at me, then drops her eyes. She witters her usual rubbish about the weather and the drive up north – was my car OK?

My responses are the usual and I go upstairs to see my old bedroom, 'the office', to see if there are any developments. I do this every visit, but this time my interest is genuine, because since yesterday Sophie *is* missing.

There's nothing new, so I go into Sophie's room. I need

to focus my feelings and see if anything has changed, if I have missed something. I think of the room the way it was when Soph was around: a complete tip with clothes piled on the floor and her bed looking like the linen table at a jumble sale. Now it is very tidy, the duvet cover millpond smooth. The empty hook of her graduation photograph is still stuck on her bedroom wall, a faint dust mark outlining where it had been. Like Sophie, it has gone but has left a trace.

Everything else is the same. The room is the familiar blaze of colour born of her infamous impromptu painting party – three pizzas, two huge tins of paint and some drunken friends from uni. It took Rod hours to clean it up.

After Sophie 'disappeared', Avril had asked us all to look carefully at this room and she watched me intently as I was the only one not crying. Mum told them I was 'like that'. Avril used all her police training but I am not easy to read. I know I see things with a clarity that other people can't, and that clarity comes from lack of emotion. Under the scrutiny of Avril, I had to point out that Soph's gym bag was missing, the new Calvin Klein one that was too good to fill with sweaty running kit. Then Mum had a moment of sobriety and pointed out that Soph's favourite Cossack boots had gone. Then Rod, for some reason, asked about the expensive VB jeans Soph had bought in New York. Those were also missing. And so the police started to draw their own conclusion; Sophie had gone of her own free will. So nobody was sending out search parties or wasting police time. I was relieved about that, partly.

There was no harm done. The small silver locket that Gran left her was gone, of course. She wore it all the time, even when running. In that locket was a picture of Mum, Dad, Grant and me. Wherever she is, I like to think that she has us with her. In the drawer are her graduation presents, the good watch from me and the gold ankh from Mum.

Her bedside table is free of clutter, the alarm clock is upright. Sophie would always slam it face down the minute it rang. There's a small pile of books, her usual romantic Victorian stuff and her copy of Christina Rossetti – it falls

open at *Goblin Market*, of course, our favourite poem. I recall
her laughing at me in the way that those who possess a good
imagination can laugh at the pedantic nature of those of us
who do not.

We were very drunk when we found the petrified forest in
Victoria Park, hidden behind an ugly fence that we climbed
over. We found the path and descended into the old quarry
where somebody found the remains of an ancient forest. Sophie
found goblins. We sat at the bottom, the stone walls stretched
high above us, right up to the canopy of leaves that hang on
to nothing. Sophie stuck her toes in the lily pond and watched
the dragonflies and the ferns that danced in the air currents.
She told me to imagine goblins squatting out of sight in the
shadows, watching us watching them.

It became 'our place', our Goblin Market.

I think of the times that Soph and I spent there, laughing
and drunk, she reciting and me not quite getting it. *Goblin
Market*. Soph and Elvie. Laura and Lizzie. Rossetti's poem
was alive, it was written for us and only us. Laura, the sister
who loved life and got into trouble with the pleasures of the
goblins, and Lizzie, the one who was sensible and came to
Laura's rescue.

I pointed out that goblins didn't exist.

She said the whole poem was allegorical. She held my
shoulders and stared into my face. 'But you are Lizzie and I
am Laura. This poem was written for us and this is our Goblin
Market.' It's something important to Soph, and therefore
important to me. I read the poem again, pages of it, but it is
the last verse that speaks to me now. *To cheer one on the
tedious way, To fetch one if one goes astray.*

Sixty-three days ago, Soph had stood in front of me and
held my arms in hers, forcing me to look at her face. 'Elvie?'
she said. 'Listen to me. I think I'm going to have to disappear. I
have to go away.'

I hear the radio being silenced and Mum shouting down the
phone. I think I'll stay up here for a while, the drama will
wait.

I pick up the picture from the window ledge, a photograph

of Sophie and three pals red-faced with cold, standing on the side of a mountain. Soph has her blonde hair in twin plaits that run from her temples back to a single plait at the back, a style she picked up from Eric's wife. This photo would be taken on one of her working holidays when she promptly charmed her way out of doing any work. She is hugging the other girls in the picture but I don't recognize any of them. Soph was a magpie, the way she collected friends. She was the most open person I have ever met, yet recently she felt she could tell me nothing. With the benefit of hindsight, she had not been herself for months.

Deceit changes people.

I look out the window and note that Rod is digging in the back garden, trying to work off Mum's cooking. Oddly, Grant is with him, sitting on the wall. He looks muscled and fit as he yells down his mobile. As he stops, Mum starts downstairs. This is typical of our family, one in the kitchen and one in the garden and they communicate by shouting on the phone. As I watch he cuts the call and pulls his baseball cap from his head to reveal that he has shaved the hair off one side of his head, but that's better than the barcode beard he had before. My wee brother has been developing his own special psychosis since he was thirteen. It was a long, slow drift but the drift is now gaining momentum.

Grant waves over at Eric, our next-door neighbour, who has wandered into his own garden. A little chat over the fence, which I read as a sign that Eric engages him more than Rod does. No surprise there. Eric loves his garden; he almost lives in it when he's down here and not up north in his 'country retreat'. It's majestic, from the fine lawns near the house to the oriental pool at the bottom, with its huge flower beds, statues and the marble pillars that he has just had engraved. It is surrounded with shrubs and the centrepiece is the waterfall that drives the water clock. I raise my hand and the movement catches his eye. He gives me a little wave. I owe Eric a lot; he got me the job at Ardno looking after the Coco Pops kid. He thought he was helping his boss out; in fact, he was throwing me a lifeline that saved my sanity. He turns and points out something of his latest project to

Grant. Grant is pristine clean while Eric is a shambling teddy
bear of a man, dirty jeans tucked into muddy boots, standing
in his garden and loving every minute of it. They are still
deep in conversation when I hear the door open at the bottom
of the stairs. That will be Mum about to call me. Dinner is
ready.

I take a deep breath; this is not going to be good.

And so I go slowly downstairs for another meal of badly
cooked pasta with a huge side portion of angst for dessert. In
the dining room Rod is already sitting in his chair, caressing
a bottle of wine with his head tilted back, eyes screwed up as
he tries to read the label through his varifocals.

'Your face will stay like that if the wind changes,' I say. I
am not good at humour.

'Hello, sweetheart, how are you?' He does not raise his
eyes from the label. 'Your mum said you'd arrived. Have you
seen this, half price at Waitrose? Tempranillo. Do you fancy
a mouthful?'

I shake my head. 'I'm driving straight back.'

He nods. 'You enjoying it, being nanny for the filthy rich?'
He makes no eye contact; he is listening to the kitchen where
Mum is angrily banging plates around. Rod drops his voice.
'Eric doesn't know of any other jobs, does he? Digging or
labouring? Grant needs something to get him out and about.'

'I clocked the new haircut.'

'Grant is . . .' He stops as the door opens. Mum comes in,
cradling hot plates with her oven gloves. Rod places a mat near
to her. She goes into this strange catering mode when she is
reluctant to talk about 'it', whatever it is. Sophie's disappearance,
Grant's problematic mental health or my physical health.

This meal will follow its usual pattern. At some point Mum
will smile at us and say, 'This is pleasant.' Then Grant will
come in, sit down and sigh his way through the pasta. Mum
will tell him that he might get on better if he ate his broccoli.
At this point Rod will start a monologue as no one can bear
the silence.

There is a bang at the back door. I get up to see what is
going on but Rod puts his hand on mine. Mum's voice is the

banshee screeching of a mad woman. *Look at the mess! Can you not take your shoes off?* Rod looks at me with a raised eyebrow. This is not the first time.

'It's not that I ask you to do much, just take your shoes off at the door!'

'Get a fucking job and a fucking life! Don't ask for fucking much . . .' Grant stomps past the dining room door, limping slightly. He does not look at us.

'I'd just be happy if he got out of his bed before three in the afternoon, and into his bed before three in the morning,' mutters Rod in a conspiratorial whisper.

Grant slams into his seat, pulls his baseball cap down and folds his arms, his perfect features set in a mask of bitterness.

'Good evening,' I say with some sarcasm.

He ignores me.

Mum comes in with a huge dish of burned lasagne which would easily feed twelve.

'That looks very nice, Nancy,' says Rod, as he always does.

Grant sighs with boredom at the family pleasantry. So far the meal is following its usual plan.

Mum then sits, lifts a serving spoon and starts again. 'I mean, it's not as if I ask you to do anything. Just make a bit of an effort, get a wee job. It's been a year now. And your hair is a disgrace. Who will employ you with hair like that?' The spoon swings about a bit.

'Somebody employed Elvie with a face like hers. So tell it to the hand . . .' Grant's palm blocks Mum's face. The serving spoon stops in the middle of the béchamel sauce backswing. ''Cause I ain't listening. You're screwing Dad's mate and this . . .' the finger points to the lasagne, '. . . stinks.'

'Elvie is . . .'

'Elvie is, Elvie is . . .' He mimics Mum's voice with uncanny accuracy. 'Elvie is a fucking freak.'

Suddenly Mum stabs the serving spoon at him, swinging it round so fast that the sauce whiplashes and splatters the wallpaper. She loses her grip and it bangs off the sideboard before coming to rest on the carpet.

Grant stands up, his chair tumbles and hits the wall behind

him. He sticks his face right in my mother's. 'Fuck you.' He holds her gaze, then slowly walks out. Then he pops his head back. 'Fuck the lot of you.'

'Grow up,' I say quietly.

'You talking to me? You talking to me?' He points his finger at me. I stand up, our eyes lock. He senses something and backs down before strutting off without the charm of De Niro.

Mum gets up from the table and wipes her hands on her apron before dabbing the stains on the wallpaper with it. She then returns to the kitchen and we hear the chink of the gin bottle coming out of the cupboard.

I realize that Rod's hand is over mine. I pat the back of it. 'Not exactly the Waltons, are we?'

It's going on for half ten by the time I manage to escape. Mum wanted to talk and Rod let her. The lasagne lies congealed and uneaten in assorted locations in the dining room – the serving dish, the plates, the carpet, the wall. Mum wanted her hour of happy families and it was a small price to pay.

So by the time I hit Loch Lomond side it's nearly eleven. The Polo is nippy round the sharp bends. Clever engineering might have smoothed out the corners of the road but God made the geography of the place. Get your road position wrong with an HGV coming round the corner and you're either crushed under its wheels, smashed into the sheer rock face or drowning in the freezing waters of the loch. The rolling peaks of Ben Lomond lie as a dark shadow, watching, barely visible in the night air. It is a very pretty road. But deadly.

I am listening to some old Elvis on the CD player, thinking that he would get nowhere on *The X Factor* nowadays. *Elvie is the name of my greatest flame*, my dad would sing to me. The music of Elvis seems an odd passion for a headmaster, yet I feel it is the strongest link I have to him, a link to a past where life was easy because Dad sorted things out. All these songs hold a memory in a way that nothing else does. The irony is that now I look a bit like Elvis. In his younger days.

Darkness surrounds the car in a thick soup, as 'Way Down'

hits the CD. I have to keep switching from full beam to dipped. At Arrochar I turn off to head up the Rest and Be Thankful. The mountains sit in the distance, their black peaks sharply silhouetted against the indigo sky. I concentrate as the 'The Rest' is a full-beam-all-the-way kind of road. There are often rockfalls and landslides, webcams now warn of trouble. They are still working on the stability of the east bank after the most recent fall and rumours abound that they are reopening the old drovers' road at the bottom of the glen because it has never been blocked in a thousand years. When I drove down this morning there was temporary traffic control so I proceed with more caution than usual as the road follows the contour of the Glen Croe Alps. The landscape has switched again, the hills rise up to the right now, dropping steeply down on the left. I can see two headlights ahead but they are not moving. Maybe there has been a further rockfall, boulders escaping from their wire cages and smashing on to the concrete, or cars, below. Automatically I lift my mobile and make sure it's on as I pull up to the red light. I am suspicious, as any woman on her own would be. It's never safe being forced to stop a car in the middle of nowhere.

In particular, I am suspicious of the man dancing in the road in front of me.

A green Prius is stopped on the far side yet his light must be green if mine is red. I flash my lights at the dancing figure and he gestures that I should get out of the car. Then my full beam catches his warning triangle. I move the Polo forward on the narrow cordoned lane, pull up and memorize his registration. Then I see what he is pointing at.

There is something lying on the bonnet of his car. The impact has crazed the windscreen and blood gives it the appearance of raspberry ripple sorbet. Deer are notorious for being stupid and a hazard to cars on this road. I drop my window to tell him to drag the body off, leave it at the side of the road and punch out his windscreen. Then drive on. It happens, and he can claim it against his insurance.

But the man is now a dancing demon, pointing at his car. I pull on the handbrake, cut the engine and stick on my own hazards. There is no one else around, which is just as well, as our two cars are now blocking the road completely.

He rushes to my car and opens the door. There is no doubting his distress.

'She fell. She fell,' he is saying, pointing his fingers at the Prius as if he can't bear to look. I step out, looking at the blood smeared on his face and hands. He is shaking, tearful with shock.

'OK,' I say. I am calm. I look over and see the reason for his distress and the use of the word 'she'. On his bonnet is a lump of flesh and bones, human bones. Her face is to the sky, her arms flung outward like she was sunbathing under the moon. Her hair hangs down the side of the car. She is slim. Very slim. And very naked.

'Have you called the police? An ambulance?' I ask as I jog across.

He trots behind me like a dog, saying *Oh God Oh God* over and over again. 'I didn't hit her, she fell.'

I place my finger on her neck and find a faint pulse. Just an irregular flutter. I look at her legs. She has a black swollen injury on the back of her calf. The widest part of her leg is her knee joint, a sign of anorexia. She has marks on her ankle as if her socks were too tight. 'When did you call the police?' I look at my watch as the pulse fails under my fingertips.

'Five minutes ago? Ten?' He looks into my eyes, wanting me to make the situation right.

I calculate that she might not last until help gets here. I reach my hand under her neck; the vertebrae move too far and too easily. I move round the bonnet of the car and scrape my thumbnail on the sole of her foot. Her reflex is wrong. I have a decision to make. It might not be the right one, but to do nothing will definitely be the wrong one. 'Help me,' I say to the dancing man. 'Let's get her on to the road.'

He moves, glad to be active. I take my jumper off and try to cradle her head and neck. I pull the man towards me, place his hands on either side of her and tell him to use his fingers like a cradle. 'I think she's broken her neck, you must hold her steady.'

He stands and looks at me blankly.

'Come on.' This time he responds very slowly. He is in shock so there is no point in shouting at him. 'Brace her neck while I slide her to the ground and try to keep her straight. After three.' We pull her from the bonnet of the Prius. She slides easily in her own blood. She is no real weight, her body sags as if it has no strength to hold itself together. She is nacreous in the beam of the headlights. Then a slight change to the colour of her skin reflects that the traffic light has changed to green again. It makes her look dead already.

We lower her on to the ground. He is on his knees holding her neck as if it is the most precious thing in the world. I press on her chest and the palms of my hands fall through her ribcage like a stone through a wet paper bag. There is no compression here, there is no structure left in her ribcage. I sit back on my hunkers.

'What's wrong?' he asks.

I place my fingers on her carotid. Nothing. Not even the faintest flutter. I look at him and shake my head. He looks down at her face, caressing her with his eyes. But his hands are still clamped tight. He is holding on, even though she has let go. I reach over and pull his fingers free. Her head rolls a little, comfortable in the pillow of my jumper.

He looks up at the rock face above us, working out where she came from; it doesn't make sense. We sit there for a minute. I can hear the munching of sheep down in the glen, the odd bleat. Somehow it helps to know that we are not alone out here.

I pull the hair from her face. She looks my age. Her lips are bloodied. I smooth the matted hair which spikes across her cheek. She smells of decay already. I look at her face; it is barely human but . . . I feel I know her. She is a mass of blood and swelling. Mentally I fill in her features, in my mind she is smiling. I hear the voice of Avril, our police liaison officer, in my head. I hear her asking my mother if she knows her, asking if Sophie might have known her. Avril slipping the picture to me across the dining room table, keeping her fingertip on the photograph. I remember thinking what nice nails she had for a cop, French manicure or Shellac.

The face on that photograph is lying in front of me now.

* * *

The police arrive in a flurry of flashing blue neon. Sitting in the back of their car, I listen to the radio chatter in the night air. It is getting cold now; my jumper remains under the head of the woman lying on the road, a woman I think is Lorna Lennox.

The car stinks of vomit and Dettol so I get out and close the door. Two officers stop their conversation. The older one with chubby grandpa cheeks walks towards me, slapping the other cheerily on the back as he passes. Even I think it strange that a man should be happy in a situation like this.

'Miss McCulloch? Elvira?'

'I think we've established that.' What is it with cops and their uncanny ability to state the friggin' obvious?

'PC McAndrew. And you were driving . . .'

'To Ardno, up beyond St Catherine's.'

'Why? Bit late to be out and about.'

'Going back to work. I'm a nanny, paid companion, child minder, call it what you like.' I give him the address and the phone number. Then the address of Mum's house. And the address of my flat in Glasgow. Grandpa Cop looks at me. It's complicated.

He writes slowly, I can almost see his brain trying to spell without him moving his lips.

'And what did you see? Did you see the woman in the road?'

'No. I saw a man in the road. Panicking. I saw the woman on the bonnet of his car. At first I thought he might have hit a deer, then I got closer.' I look across at the driver. His name is David. I know that he is thirty-six. Another cop is walking him up and down the grass verge to calm him. He has been sick twice already and he isn't finished yet.

'Brave. Stopping in the middle of nowhere like that. At night, lady on her own.'

'The light was red.' I stare him down. He is in his fifties and is still on traffic patrol or sheep patrol or whatever it is they call themselves up here, so I judge that he is not attending Mensa meetings on his night off. My story seems to be confusing him. 'I am taking a year out of uni, I'm studying medicine. I stopped because the light was red. I got out because I thought I might be able to help. The woman was haemorrhaging internally, her pulse was weak and failing. She had a broken neck.'

He nods, making a few more notes. I see David bending over, his hands on his knees, more retching. He straightens up and wipes his mouth with the back of his hand then starts pacing across the road again. As he turns our eyes meet, he looks lost. I give him a wan smile. Tough call.

'You didn't see him hit her.' Grandpa Cop moves in front of me, blocking my line of vision. Maybe he's not so daft after all.

'He didn't hit her.'

'We are well aware what he's saying . . .' he says in that tone that cops use because they think their uniform means superiority.

I take a step closer to him, invading his space. I'm tall and broad, not a pretty sight with my acne. He takes a step back. I speak right in his face. 'I stated a fact, he did not hit her. Why would he say something so outrageous unless it was true? If he just ran into her, why not say so? But he said she fell out of the sky. You can tell by the lack of skid marks on the road that his vehicle was stationary at the time of impact. If he'd been moving when he hit her then she would have come sideways off the bonnet. If he'd been moving fast she would have gone over the top. But she dropped on top of him.' I look down at the Prius. 'It's parked right at the sign that says *Wait here when the light is red*. So he was waiting . . .' Grandpa Cop snorts so I carry on. 'One look at the lack of damage on the front of his car says that she didn't impact there; even a skinny woman like her would leave some kind of dent. So he is telling the truth.'

He lifts his pen, hoping that I have stopped.

I haven't.

'Look up there.' I point up to the wire-caged cliff above us, its rocky teeth jagged and treacherous. 'Imagine she was running over that hill, not realising she's so close to the edge. She's tired, she stumbles into the downward slope of the landslide. She drops off the edge like a stone. Your question should be why. And why naked?' I realize that I am trying to make some kind of connection, the same connection between Lorna and Sophie that Avril had already made.

Grandpa Cop throws me a look like I have crawled out from under a stone then his radio crackles, sounding loud in the dark night. The glen seems darker now with the metronome illumination of the blue lights. Lorna is still lying on the road, covered by a plastic sheet. I think how long she had been missing, three months longer than Sophie. I recall Avril shrugging, being non-committal. There were similarities; both went out running and neither came back. The police had mentioned another name at the time, another woman, missing for a much longer period. It is in the back of my brain, beginning with a G. Gillian. Gillian Porter. I can see her face in my mind's eye. There is something else about her still hiding in my brain. It will come to me eventually, it always does. I might be slow but I am never, ever wrong. I try to recall it, thinking about the pictures Avril had placed in front of me. I remember Mum answering her questions, me shaking my head. I did not know this other woman. Of course, there should have been no connection as I believed then that Sophie had gone of her own free will. But now?

Grandpa Cop has turned to look at me; his radio has told him something that he does not like. Then my mobile rings, the number displayed tells me it is Alex Parnell, my boss. The cop is on his radio, I am on my mobile. A brief look of fear flicks across his face. I realize that Alex Parnell, the millionaire builder, is someone in these parts. His child's nanny has been involved in an incident. I can sense Grandpa Cop backtracking. Parnell does not do conversation; he issues instructions. 'Elvie? Eric's up at his croft, he'll pick you up and bring you to Ardno. The police are impounding the Polo. Don't worry.'

The call is ended and I am not sure that I have spoken at all. Grandpa Cop's expression has changed. He says, 'I'm sorry, the name Elvira McCulloch meant nothing to me.'

'But the name Sophie McCulloch does?'

'Of course it does.' His voice has softened, I can see the

granddad now. He smiles at me. 'I think her photograph is on the wall in the office. A bonnie lassie.' He puts his radio away without saying *you look nothing like her.*

'I think I should tell you something.'

'Yes?'

'I recognize that woman.'

'You know her?' The notebook comes out again.

'I don't know her, but I was shown a photograph of her. A woman called Lorna Lennox. I've had a picture of every woman missing in Glasgow over the last two years put in front of me. That woman went missing on January the fifth.'

He is looking at me, a suggestion of patronising humour flirting with his lips.

'I am right.' I add, to make it perfectly clear, 'Read a bit further down on the MisPer list. There's a picture of a woman with long dark hair, and someone standing behind her is hugging her.' I demonstrate. 'You must have seen the picture. She looks a bit like Ali McGraw.'

'Ali McGraw?' He nods to himself; that has sparked off a memory in him. He flicks the notebook closed. 'Did I hear you're being picked up?' He stands to one side as a small queue of traffic goes past in convoy, all gawping at the Prius and the body covered in its plastic bag and wondering how the car came to hit a pedestrian out here. I look down the road to where David is sitting in another cop car, his face hidden.

'Eric Mason is coming to get me,' I say. 'He works for Alex Parnell.'

'Oh, Eric from the croft up at Succoth?' he says. 'The water clock man?'

So he knows him. 'We live next door to each other in Glasgow. I need to get my stuff out the car?'

'Of course.' He walks over with me, his boots scuffing the gravel as he chatters about Eric. He seems to know him well. 'Better to wait up at my car. Eric can pick you up from there.' He raises his hand. 'No doubt we will talk again. You take care now, Miss McCulloch.'

I watch him walk back to the body and say something to another officer. They lift up the top of the sheet and examine the face. There is a brief discussion then Grandpa Cop stands up, talking animatedly down his phone as he connects the chain of events. My sister is missing, then another missing woman falls from the sky just as I happen to pass. I look at the small bump lying on the ground like a traffic calming device. She has been missing for six months. Lorna's family will now have closure and resolution. They will move on.

Their not knowing is over.

SATURDAY, 2 JUNE

J ust after midnight, I hear a sound reminiscent of a World War Two bomber struggling with a difficult take-off. The echoing roar is quickly followed by pinpricks of headlights through the dark, accompanied by a sudden gust of cold wind. Death must feel like that, a chilled breath of ice.

Grandpa Cop claps his hands together. 'It's getting a bit nippy now. But here's Eric in that old rust bucket of his. He'll have you back up at Ardno within twenty minutes. Out the cold, nice brandy for shock.'

A Land Rover, hazards flashing, is driving on the rocky verge, slowly overtaking two waiting cars. It stops beside me and as the door opens the smell of sheep and damp dog wafts towards me. Eric leans over, says nothing but pulls a filthy blanket from the hammock-like seat. He offers me a troubled smile.

'Make sure that she gets back OK. Miss McCulloch, someone will probably want to talk to you tomorrow. You'll still be here, won't you?'

'Yes.' Can't think I would be anywhere else.

Grandpa Cop chats to Eric like they're old pals. 'How are things up at the croft? You got enough water to play with?' He nods up into the hill. So the croft was up there somewhere. *Up there* is hundreds of square miles.

'More than enough. I'm pumping out the basement. Again.'

The cop looks up to the sky, chuckling at the dark rolling clouds. 'Well, good luck with that one. There's no end to this rain, you know.'

'Tell me about it.' Eric waves and attempts a U-turn. The Land Rover takes a few goes at it, back and forth as the turning circle is so poor. We drive off in silence. He's a man of few words at the best of times.

I like that about Eric. Even when Sophie and I were kids and he was in his late teens he kept himself to himself. He

was born in the house next door to ours and stayed there after
his mum died, even after his wife left him. Eric is nothing
like his mother: he is large and lumbering; she was small and
powerful, a nippy wee bird of a woman. Eric worshipped her.
He was a mummy's boy. He wouldn't have survived if he
wasn't. Once she died he tried being married, but it didn't last
long, and once his wife Magda had scarpered he started
spending more time at the croft and neglecting the house in
Eaglesham. Rod casually mentions the state of the house next
door every time they meet as he believes it will eventually
affect the resale value of ours, and in Rod's eyes that is a
hanging offence. I used to think that was strange for an architect, letting a house go to ruin, but Eric is also an artist. He
is great at designing buildings and rubbish at maintaining them.
I understand that. I like diagnosing illness in patients, I like
the puzzle, but anything beyond that is tedious.

Once we're on the straight road I feel Eric relax. Sophie
would want me to make small talk, so I have a go. I need to
think about it so I turn in my seat to rearrange some boxes of
groceries that have worked free from their restraining straps
and are rattling against each other.

'So you were up at the croft?' I try as an opener.

'Yes.' He adjusts the sound on the CD. It is something Gaelic-y,
a soulful fiddle with a breathy female vocal drifting above the
engine noise, ghostly music on a night for long-lost souls.

It makes me think of Magda, the beautiful woman who ran
off with another man and caused a scandal. Sophie might have
nicked her hairstyle but as people they were miles apart. Soph
was full of life and laughter whereas Magda was silent and
aloof. But they have both gone. Maybe that's why Eric has
shown such empathy in the last few months. I am only here
because Rod and Eric had a chat over the garden fence about
getting me away from all this stress. It was obvious to both of
them that I was not well, not coping, not sleeping. Even before
Soph went missing, I was losing concentration at uni and my
running was becoming obsessive. They were worried about me,
having witnessed Grant's slow mental decline, and were scared
the same thing was happening to me. They should have been
worried about Sophie.

In April Eric had said his boss was looking for someone to spend the summer at his new house at Ardno with his wife. Someone responsible and young. When Rod spoke to me about it, my first instinct had been to laugh. Why would I want to babysit a spoiled bitch of a woman old enough to be my mother? Then he said that she lived in the middle of nowhere and I thought – why not? It was a great excuse to stay out of the house until Sophie came back. And I could do some real running.

Eric changes gear and watches the road ahead intently. The deer are moving down from the hills, he explains, driven down by the rain. He seems happy chatting to me in a way he never was talking to Sophie. Maybe because she spent her life teasing him in that way pretty women can. When Magda left, Sophie said that she was probably stuck in the attic somewhere, tied to the bedstead, screaming in the night to get free. I'm not sure she was joking. Mum's only comment to that was that she was surprised the marriage had lasted so long, Eric being about as attractive as old slippers. Magda was a shock to the neighbours with her generous curves, her white-blonde hair, scarves and long gypsy skirts. She would saunter past, hips swaying, with a nod, never a word, as if she knew she was too good for us. But when Magda left, legging it to London with some builder bloke, she broke Eric's heart.

Two days after Eric had talked to Rod, I had a brief interview with Alex Parnell at the Eaglesham Arms. Parnell was either a self-made man or a cowboy builder, depending what paper you read. He might have owned property worth six million but the broad Glaswegian in his voice was still detectable. Good nutrition and an iron will to succeed in life had got him where he was today, yet his thick neck and broad shoulders showed he was only two generations away from the Glasgow docks; he wouldn't be past sticking one on you if you crossed him. His fringe reminded me of Hitler but he looked much younger than his fifty-three years. Like Eric, he was a man of few words. He looked at me, my black sweatshirt, my Rohan trousers, my trail boots, my small rucksack slung over my shoulder. Five eight, about ten stone, acne, different. I could see him calculating. He offered me the job

there and then but gave me no idea of what I was supposed
to do except a casual mention of a new wife who was lonely,
a young son, Charlie, and a house in the middle of nowhere.

That meeting was the start of the chain of events that got
me here, being bounced around in a Land Rover at one in the
morning in a remote glen, because a woman had fallen from
the sky.

'How is Charlie?' asks Eric, his own attempt at small talk.

'He's a bright wee kid. He would benefit from going to
nursery, being with kids his own . . .'

'Alex will not allow that.'

'True,' I say. 'But he is illogical.'

'And you are "best practice" at logic.' He laughs. 'Was it
bad, the accident?' He changes gear.

'It was not good. She died.' I know I can sound callous,
Soph has warned me about it. 'It was so weird; that guy was
stopped at the light and she just fell on to his windscreen.'

He snorts with incredulity.

'No, really. She died from an internal haemorrhage. No way
back from injuries like that.'

'And they have no idea where she came from? Can't be
from round here. Was she flung out a car or something?'
Another noisy gear change.

'Not that I recall, and I would.' My eyes sweep over the
barren landscape; I'm thinking out loud. 'If they threw her
out a car they must have known this place well. She fell to
her death, in the middle of nowhere, naked. She was brought
here and abandoned all right.'

He nods, conceding my point. 'You make sure you tell that
to the police tomorrow.'

'I did recognize her though.' I say the words into airspace;
it still seems unreal.

'That would be bizarre.' He takes his eyes off the road for
a minute and looks at me. He is pale and red-headed, bald at
the top. The unruly curls round the side dance as he moves
his head.

'I am sure she's a woman who went missing before Sophie
did.'

He is dismissive. 'Really?'

I nod.

'Maybe in your circumstances – with Sophie and everything – you might see things that are not quite there.'

I stay silent and look out the window.

'What I mean is, when Magda left I thought I saw her everywhere – a mere turn of a head or a glimpse of a figure. Yet every time I took a closer look, there was no resemblance at all.'

'She was very pretty; the wee lassie across the road thought Magda was a princess.'

Eric smiles, recalling that story. Magda was a rare exotic creature in Eaglesham, which was probably the reason she legged it. 'What I mean is, I think some small antenna of the brain is always on the lookout. It becomes more sensitive, it sees what it wants to see.'

'That was Lorna Lennox,' I say. 'I never forget a face and I was holding her head in my hands.'

'And she died in your arms.' He changes gear again, the engine growling at the effort. Eric has not shaved, his cheeks are black hollows in his face.

He opens his mouth to say something, hesitating slightly. 'I was going to ask if there was any word. About Sophie?'

'Various sightings that all lead nowhere, so Mum gets pissed, Rod sobers her up. But then my brother would drive anybody to drink.'

'Their way of coping. But if the police still think that Sophie left of her own free will, then you might be better to accept it. Maybe she drove to the reservoir to meet somebody and left. She was an exotic creature too. Maybe, like Magda, she just wanted a life that she wouldn't get if she stayed. That's the hardest thing to accept. I mean, Sophie can't have just disappeared; that's too difficult to do in a city. There'd be a trace. Or a body.' He ducks his head slightly and looks up to the hills. 'But it's easy to disappear here.' He turned the CD up slightly, having said all he had to say.

I sit back in my uncomfortable seat and look out the window, admiring a view that I tend to miss as I am driving. We are following the road across the glen heading south before we turn west. I can see the flashing lights on the other side. The landscape above the incident site is a steep slope and there is no road up there that I know of. When the Rest is blocked the detour takes an hour. So the logical question is – where did Lorna come from?

The glen between is a dark abyss, the sky overhead is dense, cold and threatening. It could be another country, another lifetime. A different lifetime to the velvet warmth of the Goblin Market. Even the weather has agreed that the world is a darker place today. When Sophie said she had to go away, she promised to come back. She held my arms and stared me straight in the eye. *'I'll be back, midnight, right here at Goblin Market. Last Thursday in May. You remember that.'* Like I would forget. She had that same fear in her eyes the day she told me Dad was dead, a feral fear. As if the real world had intruded on her perfect one.

Last Thursday was the last Thursday in May.

She didn't make it.

The house is hidden from the loch road by a long, high beech hedge. The roll of the hills and the tall trees suggest there should be some great Gothic mansion behind the eight-feet high wrought-iron gates, but in reality there is a modern white concrete box with glass panels the full height of the west side making the most of the view of Loch Fyne at the front, and views of the bens of Argyll National Park at the back. This road is single track and dangerous for a few miles round the loch before it meets the main road out to Dunoon and the ferry, or a long drive round the head of Loch Long to get to Glasgow. It is breathtakingly beautiful and deathly quiet. The silence is glorious.

But the house does not fit the landscape, and Mary and Charlie don't fit the house. It is not a home. There are early Peter Howson originals: stark images of religion and violence. There are classic marble statues. The furniture is minimalist and the house itself was designed with blunt concrete edges on all stairs and shelves. The only soft feature is the smooth curves of the single porthole window. It is all Alex. Everything shouts money and an interior designer's taste; there is nothing personal about it at all.

Mary doesn't care for it. She once picked me up outside Mum's house, and she sat in the car entranced by the kids playing on their bikes in the street as two neighbours chatted in their front garden, one with a white wine, one with a coffee. She was fascinated by humdrum life in a rural Glasgow suburb.

When I first arrived here, I thought the woman who opened the door was the outgoing nanny. I had heard lock after lock being opened behind the glass panels, then she and I stood in awkward silence, staring at each other. I was uglier than she expected. She was as young as I had expected. She was slim and pretty, raven black hair pulled into an elastic band; a few wisps had come loose and fallen down over her face. But her huge blue eyes regarded me with all the warmth of anti-freeze. The hall behind her was a huge space, as if she had opened the door in a cathedral – a vast, empty interior in pure white plaster. Soulless marble statues hung around, as if waiting for the door to open far enough to let them out. The arches of the ceiling went high into the roof space, stretching the whole height of the house. On the wall was a series of multi-coloured glass pipes, as if that was art. It was like a Hollywood film set.

Mary was icily polite, nervous, a little shaky even as she tried to welcome me. Then a shock of unruly brown hair appeared between her ankles followed by a jam-covered face. There was no need for a DNA test to confirm who his dad was. The child pulled back to hide behind her Ugg boots then asked who I was, pointing at me. He was as unfriendly as his mother.

'I'm Elvie.'

'I'm Charlie. You have a strange face. Are you a monkey?'

Mary was about to admonish him for being cheeky but I answered, 'Well, I can swing from trees and I eat bananas.'

He sniffs. 'Are you here to sort me out?'

'I'm here to tell you that sniffing like that is bad for you.'

'Good luck with that,' laughed Mary, and even then I sensed that she did not have a lot to laugh about. Charlie offered me a Kinder Egg penguin as some kind of key to the kingdom. Mary gestured that I go into the front room where there were white sofas, a designer coffee table and a strong smell of money. I hesitated at the door, eyeing the Chinese rug, then I pointed at my trek shoes.

'I spend most of my time in the kitchen,' she said as we both stood at the doorway, looking at the big room, the huge window with the trees and the loch and the mountains beyond. It seemed a very wild world out there.

'Kitchen then?' I suggested.

Mary was the young mother of a hyperactive four-year-old stuck miles from nowhere. We gelled quickly and soon found common ground. She was keen to tell me that she had walked away from uni too. I mentioned I was going back, she said I was lucky. She had been doing English literature. I told her about Sophie's love of Christina Rossetti and she actually got excited. Her old life came back to her like a train.

'Can I ask you a question?'

'Sure.'

'What is your actual name?'

'Elvira. If the second kid had been a boy he'd have been Elvis, so I took the hit so that my brother could be called Grant.'

She suppressed a giggle.

We also liked silence. We could walk down the road to the loch to sit on stones, saying nothing but perfectly happy in each other's company. I began to sleep, began to rest. I began to eat. The running became joyful, not punishing. The stress decreased, the adrenaline rush in my veins less frequent.

I realize, as the majestic house rolls past, that I have been better since I came here.

The crunch of another bad gear change breaks my train of thought and I register that Eric has been talking to me. 'Pardon?'

'I said, it's an impressive house, isn't it?'

'Yes.' My radar had a moment to tune in this time. He had designed the house and I should be complimentary. 'It's a work of art. Where is your croft from here?'

'Building site, you mean. It's miles back, way back down the Rest, past Succoth and up the other side, the Loch Lomond side.'

He drives carefully up the narrow lane. The gates of the Ardno house are big and forbidding, but all I see are the strange shadows, and their secrets.

I notice that Eric has the same keypad to open the electric gates as me. His is much more worn than mine, but his code is different. So not only does the gate computer note 'when' but also 'who', such is the security needed for a millionaire's wife.

He does not pull up at the front of the house but drives round to the entrance to my flat, which sits above the formal dining room. I can make all the noise I want doing my exercises because the dining room is never used. The headlights flash on the western perimeter wall that still bears the scars of the last storm; it looks like a gap-toothed smile. The builders haven't been for days, and the last time I saw them they were too busy talking to Mary about building Charlie a tree house to be bothered fixing the wall. I notice that the Shogun is not here.

Eric sees me looking. 'Mary is at the flat in Glasgow with Alex.' He pulls the Land Rover to a halt but keeps the engine running as his fingers drum on the dashboard. 'Do you need any help?' he mutters.

'No, I can manage on my own, thanks.' A few spots of rain start to dot the windscreen.

He looks at the sky, a look of concentration on his face. 'If you need to chat, in the next few days? I mean, Mary will be in Glasgow a lot. Call me if you need anything. I mean, after tonight. Not that . . . Well, you won't, will you . . . What about a bit of dinner, Loch Fyne? I might even show you round the croft.'

It's quite a speech for him. I nod and thank him.

I go up the stairs and press the buttons for the entry code to my flat, dumping my stuff in the hall before I turn to wave goodbye to Eric. He's been watching me, making sure that I got in OK. He waves back and I close the door before picking my bag up and nipping upstairs to my kitchen. Before I unpack I press the button on the instant water heater and put some fresh coffee into a cafetière. Five minutes later I'm sitting on the outside step, high up over the garden with a soft blanket draped round my shoulders, sipping a mild Colombian blend and letting myself get wet in the summer rain. I think back on the day and the previous night, wondering what other

Goblins are shadow-dancing in the garden, what else is going
to happen before I can make sense of it. Everything is unreli-
able. Dad died, Grant blamed himself. If I'm honest, I blame
Grant too. Did that stress spark my illness? Do I blame Grant
for that as well? Grant certainly blames us for the mild knee
problem which has become the root of all the evil in his
universe. My mum gets lost in a bottle and Rod and I pick
up the pieces.

Where does that leave me?

I should be here sitting with nothing on my mind at all,
except my missing sister and what she might be going through.
And what the woman who fell from the sky had already been
through.

At moments like this I yearn for the times when I had things
to think about apart from Sophie. If that makes me selfish then
so be it. Tomorrow will start a whole new round of interviews
and I must stay one step ahead. Maybe if I'd said something
earlier, maybe if I'd told them the truth straight away – that
Sophie had gone of her own accord – if I had not kept Sophie's
secret, then she might be back here with us now. But I didn't
have a crystal ball. I sat for hours at the Goblin Market, on
the log by the lily pond, from midnight right until the dawn,
waiting for her before I gave up and drove here.

I have no idea what has happened to her.

I have no idea what to do.

I look round at the hills, the rolling summit of Ben Ime in
the distance. The closer pointed crag of Ben Lochain. Right
on the back doorstep is Cruach nam Mult lying like a sleeping
puppy. It makes me think – the hills are unchanging but I am
not. I am a transient in the world; we all are.

It is gone six o'clock when I finally crawl into bed. Every
night before I go in search of sleep I look through my photographs. These are just for me, not for the press or the police
or the Facebook page where everything is food for public
digestion. I have seen these images so many times, but I relish
them as others enjoy seeing a close friend. There's the one of
me and Dad digging the garden. Another of Soph and me on
a swing, she's about ten or so. Then again on the same swing

aged twenty, very drunk. Second last is an informal shot at someone's wedding with the family as it is now. Rod at the helm, Mum holding on to him, Grant looking blond and blue-eyed, Sophie his female double at one side, me the raven-haired geek at the other. We are like bookends. Then three of us at Soph's birthday meal for the family – that was the twenty-ninth of March – the week before she disappeared. Hindsight focuses the mind but I now realize that Soph hardly ate anything that evening. Grant acted drunk long before he was, and Mum acted sober long after she was drunk. I ignored both of them. In a paper clip I have two pictures that Belinda from Boadicea had taken at Soph's party on the thirty-first. I wasn't there. Soph only invited me to her social events safe in the knowledge that I would never go. I'd rather put staples in my toes than sit and listen to her pals talking about nail extensions and child protection orders. Soph loves company whereas I don't see the point of other people.

I didn't need all that, I had Sophie. We had each other. We were Lizzie and Laura.

I put the photos back in the drawer and lie back, staring out the windows waiting for sleep. When I do close my eyes, the dream is waiting. The little night-time goblin that comes out from the shadows to mess with my head is now showing me a film of Sophie in the bath in my flat, bleeding. Her head turns away as I try to speak to her, then she dissolves in the water, laughing, then screaming. Sophie is there one minute, gone the next.

It's me screaming, of course. I wake myself up and a glance at the clock confirms I have been asleep for all of five minutes. I crawl out of bed to go to the toilet, where my stomach retches and retches, trying to get something out of nothing. Just bile. I need to eat to be sick. I need to go out for a run; my veins feel like they are bursting.

I open the bathroom cabinet and look at my medication. I should be taking it to control these symptoms until the tests are complete, but I've cancelled the appointment because I'm not taking any of this stuff; I need to be strong. In the mirror the changes are obvious. I should face the fact that I need help.

But Sophie needs my help more.

To fetch one if one goes astray.

I pull on my running socks and trousers, my top and my Nikes, then head out down the road to the loch side where I can watch the seals bobbing their heads through the water as I run. On a good day I'll tackle the lower slopes of Cruach nam Mult but today is not a good day. At the water's edge the air is deathly still. It is cool in my lungs and my legs loosen as I wind through the bracken on the lower slope. I feel weightless and supercharged. This is what it does for me; I become another being when I run the hills in the early light. Everybody else is somewhere other than here.

One hour and fourteen minutes later, I come out of the shower and sink on to the sofa with a strong coffee and a Pro Plus. The TV is on with the sound turned down low. I like looking at the moving pictures. It's like having company without having to listen to any crap.

I watch a rerun of some cop show with subtitles as the sun creeps its way across the carpet. I am in a dwam rather than asleep, the adrenaline is melting. The cop show ends and the two leads drive off in their car having caught the bad guys. It freezes on a still of them doing a high five. A subtitle comes up to tell me that there is music playing now. The TV screen changes to the seven-thirty news bulletin, the doom and gloom economy and a bit of football gossip. Then the Scottish news. Alex Salmond is the lead story. Some blue-haired coffin dodger is jabbering on about her pension, her mouth moving nineteen to the dozen while her teeth try to keep up. The colour of her lips matches her hair colour, a sure sign of insidious heart failure, so by Christmas she'll no longer be dodging her coffin, she'll be lying in it. Then I recognize the Rest and Be Thankful in a long panning shot. A library picture of the rockfall site. I flick up the volume a little . . . *expect delays, an incident related to a missing person.*

I lean in closer. It doesn't say how the body was found. There's that same picture of Lorna Lennox, smiling her Ali McGraw smile.

The newsreader is an eternally optimistic girl with black hair and a bobbing head. She's trying to tone down her lust for life as the picture of another woman fills the screen; she says there might be a link to the disappearance of Gillian Porter. I used to think women who went missing were stupid and should have taken more care, but that was before last Thursday, before Sophie failed to turn up at the Goblin Market. They show old footage of a press conference, a long table, Gillian's mother tearfully reading a statement. Gillian's husband leans over to the microphone to add something he has written, his hands trembling. He's appealing on behalf of their two kids. The four people at the table are showered in the flashlights of a hundred cameras. Then the camera pans out and I see him sitting on the far side, wearing an ill-fitting suit, speaking into a microphone with a voice that could grind concrete; a granite-faced man who has seen everything and been impressed by none of it. His hair was darker, shorter then. The skin was still pink so this was before his liver packed up with the drink. The sign underneath him says DCI W. Hopkirk of Strathclyde Police; he was the chief investigating officer in the missing person enquiry.

The Private Investigator.

Mr Slip-on Shoes.

An hour of Googling William Albert Hopkirk tells me he achieved some kind of status when he found two missing children. Another link to a picture of a girl with dark, corkscrew hair, her murder unsolved. I recognize her: she was killed while she was at Glasgow uni the year before Sophie went, which means she must have been there about the same time as Mary. I recall her name before my eye catches the small print. Natalie Thom. She was murdered as she walked through a Glasgow park at midnight. I thought then that it was a stupid thing to do.

I still think it now.

The voice that answers the phone is raw Woodbine. It's half seven in the morning. He says one word.

'Hopkirk.'

I say, 'McCulloch.'

He doesn't miss a beat. 'How are you doing, hen?'

'Sorry to call you so early.' Sophie always says politeness opens doors.

'I don't sleep. I bet you don't either.' I'm listening for the
sounds behind his voice – he's not at home, he's outside
somewhere. 'We need to talk, you and me.' Then he asks
me if I'm still up at Parnell's house. So he knows that much
about me.

'Yes, I am.'

'Can you get away?' There's a muffled tap; I guess the
phone has been moved from one hand to the other to check
the time.

It's a Saturday, Mary is in Glasgow. There won't be a problem.
'Yes.'

'Can you meet me today? What about Dunoon? I can get
the ferry over, you can drive round. About one?'

'Yes.'

'Do you know the Henry the Eighth Tearoom?' He hears
my snort. 'So you do.' It's his first show of humour.

'The Henry the Eighth Tearoom is full of old gits with
bladder issues.'

'Yeah, I know. That's why I blend in.'

By a quarter to two I am sitting outside the Henry Eighth
Tearoom in Dunoon. The little resort town sits right on the
Cowal peninsula and is reputed to have the second most vulnerable economy in Scotland. A scabby seagull picks at the left-
overs of a fish supper and gets a mouthful of newsprint which
has more fibre than any of the locals ever get.

I park Mary's two-seater silver Merc on the opposite side
of the road with the window open slightly. It's conspicuous
but the Polo is still with the police and the Shogun is with
Mary in Glasgow. Mary won't bother; she hates the Merc as
much as she hates all the cars Parnell buys her. It's five to
when Mr Slip-on Shoes comes waddling round the corner in
his disgusting baggy jogging bottoms, which are four inches
too short so the world can see his white socks. The waist
elastic is still fighting to contain the swollen belly that protrudes
and flops as he waddles. He's wearing a faded Fred Perry shirt
and the bobbles on his burgundy fleece are visible from the
opposite side of the road. The scent of old nicotine carried on
the wind might just have been my imagination. He looks like

a jakey just out the hostel and looking for a bin to rake through. As a disguise, it's a good one.

If it is a disguise.

At the door of the café he drops his cigarette, stubbing it out under his toe before grinding it into the ground with a foot motion that reminds me of my dad doing the twist. He waves. He has known I was here all along.

This is a lesson for me. Never underestimate him – he is a clever man. He just hides it well.

I get out the Merc, lock it and wait a minute for the traffic to pass. The Henry the Eighth Tearoom used to be a small department store but now it is a Thornton's and a bakery on the ground floor and the café on the first. There is a gallery of overpriced prints of little girls with unfeasibly large eyes looking at lambs under a sky the colour of an engorged spleen on the stairway. Little wonder there is such a high level of drug abuse in the area.

The café smells of damp and chip fat, and the ancient Artex on the ceiling is stained with circles of water damage. Slip-on Shoes is sitting at the fake coal fire, which is on full blast despite the fact that it is the middle of summer. As I walk towards his table, I feel I am walking uphill. The building seems to be slowly sliding into the Firth of Clyde.

'Take a pew,' he says, without looking up from the menu.

I slide into the seat opposite him.

'The latte is good, 'cept it'll be cold or in the saucer before you get it.' He sucks air through his teeth; it sounds like someone clearing a blocked drain. 'But you do get a nice wee biscuit.' He flicks the menu with his thumb. 'I'll have a Coke, chips and cheese sauce.'

'Classy.'

A waitress with peroxide hair and five chins is hovering. Both her black jumper and matching skirt are in need of a good wash. Her face powder has sprinkled over the front of her jumper, making her bosom look like a dusty shelf.

He orders.

The waitress turns to me. 'And what do you want, son?'

I say nothing. Then ask for a black coffee, folding my menu over and giving it back to the stupid cow.

'You'll get that a lot, with a face like yours,' he says as he watches her waddle away, her worn shoes scuffing the carpet as she goes, leaving a dual trail in the pile like a jet engine. I watch him watch her, his tongue playing around his lips. His face is red and swollen, with flecks of dry white skin around his nose and mouth. The whites of his eyes are red-veined and yellow-tinged. I could write him up for a case study at uni and list his disease processes alphabetically.

His eyes are still on the waddling figure as he says, 'So you phoned me because . . . let me guess, you saw me on the news?'

I nod.

'And you are wondering if it was pure chance that I was at that meeting?'

I nod again.

'Do you know how many meetings like that one I've sat through, listening to all the shite of the day? Listening for anybody with a story like Gillian's?'

'You were lucky you picked that meeting.'

He winked. 'Not called Billy the Fox for nothing. Your dad put it on Facebook.'

I say, 'He's not my dad.'

He drops his eyes from mine the way folk do when they touch a raw nerve. I pick up a small envelope of sugar from the bowl and squeeze all the contents up to one end. I have only one question for him. 'Can you help me find Sophie?'

'Can you help me find Gillian?' He chews on his lip.

I stare him out. He blinks first.

'I was in charge of the Gillian Porter case and I failed to find her. She went missing in the first week of March 2010. It was a Thursday night, her usual running night, but she went out later due to the rain. Stop me when this sounds familiar . . .'

The reality of it hits me; the simplicity of his words exaggerate the similarities.

'We failed to find any trace of Gillian. Your lot failed to find any trace of Sophie.' He pauses a little, he is making sure that his words are sinking in.

'She was a teacher?' I ask. 'A PE teacher? Something like

that?' Rod used to be a PE teacher, that's the thing that has stuck in my mind.

He nods. 'Well remembered.' He sits back a little as the coffee is put on the table along with a can of Coke and an old-fashioned thick glass. My cup is small and chipped, with a little band of gold that doesn't quite go all the way round the top. I turn it until the chip is furthest away from my mouth, placing the handle directly towards me. It might look clumsy but at least it is infection-free.

A plate of chips arrives in front of him, like oily dead worms. A lake of vinegar swirls round, adding to the aroma. A yellow paste of cheese sauce sits to one side in a ramekin, a nod to sophistication. He picks up the ramekin and slaps it heavily on the bottom, making the sauce splurge on top of the chips. He picks up a long chip, scoops up some sauce and stuffs it in his mouth, chewing noisily. He eats like a starving pig.

'Chips are great.' He pulls the can of Coke towards him, opens it and the noise goes round the room like sniper fire. 'It was not my biggest case, but it was my last one. I've spent a long time looking round for any others.'

'Others?' I hold my cup to my lips, moving it back and forth under my nose, smelling the coffee, breathing in caffeine.

'Others. I don't think whoever took Gillian stopped. People who are good at doing things like that don't come out of nowhere; they've been around and they've practised.' He waves a chip in the air before it disappears between those fleshy blue lips. 'Problem is, if these women were loonies or lezzies or druggies or whores, the cops would be all over the place, searching.'

'I presume you were kicked off the force before you could sign up for political correctness class?'

'You bet your bottom dollar, sweet cheeks.' He waves another chip at me. 'It's more likely that young, clever women from decent homes decide to leave for their own good reason. They're also more difficult to take and that makes me suspicious. Why would Sophie go away with a stranger?'

I can't tell him that. Ex-DCI Hopkirk is staring at me, waiting for an answer. 'Do you think the same man took Soph?'

'Do you?' He stuffs another chip in his face, sideways. 'I'm a private detective and I'm working this case. Unhampered by the force, I can take a more free range approach.'

'The case you started and didn't finish because of the drink?'

His glass of Coke pauses slightly between his mouth and the table; he regards me again with eyes of warm, faded cornflower blue. 'It was the drink that finished my career.' He smiles a little. 'It was that case that drove me to the drink.'

He calls the waitress over with a nod and a wink. She is putty in his hands as he asks for two lattes. She smiles back at him, the bright red lipstick cracking open to reveal nicotine brown teeth with a gap where she balances her fag. They would make a good couple, these two. They share the same rank body odour.

As she ambles away her buttocks roll like a strolling elephant. Billy stares after her, his eyes narrowing slightly as he struggles with a thought. He looks like a fox scenting the night air, a sleekit, sly, canny old fox. 'So tell me about Sophie. What about the clothes missing from her room?'

'How did you know about them?'

'I didn't but I do now.' He nods to himself; he does not seem to gain any pleasure from outwitting me. 'I knew Costello had good reason not to investigate it too seriously.'

'I think that there's a fine institution looking for them. It's called Strathclyde Police. I think they're doing all that needs to be done.'

He looks at me, his face incredulous. 'And I think that most people will agree that the NHS is a fine institution but it does not do all that can be done. It does all it can do and that is not the same thing. Is it? So anything you can tell me, anything at all, will be good.'

I consider that for a moment before I say, 'There was something up with her. She said nothing to me, but according to her friend Belinda, Sophie got upset at her birthday party.'

'That was the thirty-first of March?'

'She was a bit quiet but she had a lot on at work. On the fifth of April she went out for a run and never came back. I was busy so she went out on her own. I went over later when Rod phoned me to say she was very late; he'd already phoned everybody he could think of. My brother was frantic, he'd just come in from looking for Soph; my mother was on her third G and T.'

'And you then went out and found her car parked down by the dam, locked? Like she'd walked away and left it.'

'As I've said before, you seem very well informed.'

'Friends in low places. You got nothing else to tell me about the car?'

'No.'

His eyes flash over mine, he does not believe me. Tough. 'And then?'

'Rod reported it to the cops. Sophie and Avril Scott . . .'

'The PC? Giffnock?'

'That's her, they knew each other personally, so Avril has been going above and beyond for us, but the official line is that Sophie went of her own free will.'

'Because of the clothes taken, the affair with the married man, the money? Understandable.'

'She is missing,' I say. 'Rod got the Facebook campaign going. Avril said that was the best thing to do. A whole load of people have responded – school pals, uni pals, running pals, the gym, men she liked, men she'd never even looked at, her teachers, clients, and staff from Boadicea. I think Rod has been every-where and spoken to everybody.'

'Boadicea? The refuge for battered woman?'

'For victims of domestic violence,' I correct him.

'Why were you not doing that stuff?'

'I'm not good at it.' I deflect that question. 'But nobody has heard from her. That means that something's happened to Sophie.'

'But Rod had all those conversations one to one.' Billy seems to mull this point over. 'And what happened last night?'

'You're the one with friends in low places; you must have friends in the force that can tell you that.'

'I use my natural charm.' He wiped some snot from his nose on the back of his sleeve. 'It's been confirmed it was Lorna Lennox.' He does the trick with the sideways chip again, and globules of fat gather at the side of his slavering mouth.

'I knew it was her,' I repeat. 'I don't get things like that wrong.'

He looks over my shoulder and sighs. 'So Sophie left about dusk, she had been waiting for the rain to go off. There was a vehicle track close to the path where she ran through the trees. The track itself is isolated. And she was young, slim, smallish. Clever. Of a type. As was Lorna. And Gillian.'

'All that is true.' All that is perfectly true, and I'm chilled by the way he has connected these words, these cases. 'You think that Gillian is still alive?'

'Lorna has been missing for six months and she was alive until last night. No reason to think that Gillian is dead.'

'She's been missing two years.'

'Two years and three months, to be exact. But Lorna was held somewhere, held prisoner.'

Suddenly I am short of breath.

He nods, acknowledging that he has struck a chord. 'But they were all taken from different locations within a ten-mile radius by someone with the means to hide them. It's not easy to hide a human being. You need property, isolation.'

'There are loads of places like that up here.' I am thinking of every house that I go past as I drive up here, every remote light on a hillside.

'But now we know where one of them ended up. My ex-colleagues with Strathclyde's finest are spending most of the day today going through all those wee crofts dotted around the Rest, every garage, every outhouse. Including your pal Eric's.' He smiles at me. 'They're trying to puzzle out where Lorna came from, if she really did come over the top of the rock face.

'Eric thinks she was dumped from a car.'

He nods at me thoughtfully, as if agreeing with Eric's thought process. 'What was your opinion of Lorna, when you saw her? Physically? Medically? What do you think had happened to her?' He gives me that encouraging nod again. I can see that he would have been a good interviewer.

'Well, she was thin, her skin was poor, she had an injury to her left calf.'

'Left calf?' he repeats.

'Yes. She was covered in scratches and scars – they were recent – but the injury to the leg was much older. She was pitiful. When I see her in my mind's eye I think of those scenes from Belsen. Those long limbs, skeletally thin.'

'And?' he prompts.

I think, picturing her in my mind. The Henry The Eighth Tearoom recedes, and I am out there on the road again. I can feel the tarmac through my trousers, hear the sounds of the animals down near the water, feel the chill in the air. The weight of her head is on my knees, and there is a peculiar noise rattling from her. I take my jumper off, I roll it up, I look down the length of her . . . 'Ankles,' I say.

'Ankles?'

'They were discoloured.' I try hard to think. 'At first I thought they were marks from socks being tight but there were changes to the skin, as if she had been chained or shackled.'

'OK . . .'

I find the thought shocking. Billy is made of harder stuff and crams another chip into his face and nods as though he finds this noteworthy.

'Anything else that you've forgotten to tell the police about Sophie? And don't lie to me, you're rubbish at it.'

'They know her gym bag was missing too. She always kept some stuff in it.'

'Stuff for going to the gym or for going away for the weekend?' He has spotted my omission. 'With someone like Mark Laidlaw. They met through the refuge.' He is thinking deeply now, staring into the middle distance. 'She ever mention him to you? He is a person of interest, as they say.'

That is a black and white question – did *she* ever mention him to me? 'No.'

'Really?'

'No.'

He gives me a long, hard look but I do not waver. He continues, 'I've had a chat with the cop in charge of Gillian's case although it's barely active; the finding of Lorna might get it fired up again. I want to know the results of the PM and I do have my friends in low places. You need to talk to the new SIO.'

'Why doesn't he talk to Rod? He's the one who knows all this, he's in the middle of it all. I've lived up here since May.'

Billy sniffles slightly. 'Look, Elvie, I need to clarify if Sophie is part of my case or not. Maybe she left of her own accord, maybe she has reasons for not getting in touch with her family. Maybe she was running from one of you. Sophie is a very attractive young lady, and Rod is your mum's boyfriend. Maybe you should ask what was in that house that she wanted to get away from.' He drains his coffee cup, puts a twenty on the table to cover the bill and leaves. I stare at the cold, glutinous chips sitting on his plate.

Billy knows as much about Sophie – my smiley and lovable big sister, cute as a box of pink peppermints, as adorable as a bunny – as there is to know. He is wily like a fox. I like the idea of sending the fox after the rabbit.

I am still mulling the conversation over in my mind as I take the Loch Eck road back to the house. Something runs in front of the car and I slam my foot on the brake to avoid a flash of red fur and fluffy tail. A red squirrel stops in the middle of the road, perches up on his hind legs with his front paws raised as if he's about to go three rounds with the bumper of the Merc. After a little whisker twitching, he bounces on his way to the undergrowth at the side of the road where I follow the ripple trace in the foliage until he reappears, bolting up a tree. He sits on a branch, hands on hips, looking at me. The message is clear – *what do you think of that then?*

I am still smiling as I pull into the driveway at Ardno. The timer on the gates says four thirty-five and as they swing open I can see the Shogun abandoned in front of the house. I park the Merc beside it and walk round the back where the patio door is open a little. Something is not right. The door is ajar but Charlie is sitting on the swing at the bottom of the garden, on his own. Parnell's big rule: Charlie is never to be left on his own. He is the only son of a millionaire and all that, but here the wee guy is, sitting, not swinging. He does that when he's feeling out of sorts. I can tell that he has been crying by the way he turns his head, defiantly looking away from me. I wave at him to let him know that whatever huge issue is troubling his little mind, I am OK with it. We have already agreed on many occasions that it is sometimes a bit tricky to be four, but being four is shitloads better than being three, or a grown-up, or a monkey.

As I walk to my flat, it becomes very clear what is troubling Charlie Parnell, aged four. I hear his dad through the patio doors. They are in the kitchen, and the white voile curtains are blowing in the wind slightly, making them twirl through the gap. I hear gentle birdsong, the clunk-clunk of Charlie making circular patterns with the swing and the forceful, unpleasant voice of Alex Parnell coming from within. He is interrogating his wife, the tone hard and persistent. I can make out the question, *So where were you then? Where?*

I can't make out the words of Mary's mumbled answer but there is fear in her voice. I've heard her sound like that before. Before the bruises appear.

I hear her say something about Charlie as she appears as a dark shadow at the curtains, her clumsy hands pawing them to get through. She is so desperate to escape, she is halfway across the patio before she realizes I'm standing there. The expression on her face sears into my mind. The same expression was on Sophie's face. Shame, fear, relief. Somewhere in there are the words, *help me.*

'I'm back,' I start, as though I have heard nothing. 'I've left the Merc at the front. Do you want it in the garage or . . .'

The curtain is nearly ripped from its track as Parnell pulls it to one side. 'Don't you . . .' Then he stops when he sees me. My mind fills in the unspoken words: '. . . *walk away from me . . .*'

'Oh, Elvie, glad you're here. Maybe you can shed some light on a matter I'm concerned about.'

'If I can,' I say cheerily. Mary wants the patio to open up and consume her.

'Last Tuesday. Can you recall what Mary was doing?'

Now I do look at her but I keep the expression on my face to one of mild amusement. 'Tuesday? Her book group and then some yoga, I think.' I shrug.

'She didn't go out again? In the Shogun?'

'No.'

We share a brittle silence. Charlie's swing is quiet and motionless. Even the birds seem to have stopped singing.

'There's some mileage logged on it that we cannot account for,' says Parnell. His tone is more than accusatory. He waits for an answer.

Out the corner of my eye I can see Mary looking past me to Charlie. She is scared and humiliated. I keep my gaze focused on Parnell. 'I had it.' My voice is simple, a bit confused.

'Really?'

'Fifty miles from here to Dunoon, does that account for it?'

'Just about,' he says, jangling his change in his pocket. Uncertain.

'Sorry if I shouldn't have, but I did shout on Mary and tell her.'

Mary looks at me, lost.

'You might not have heard, you were doing your yoga thing. I didn't want to disturb you.'

'I didn't hear.' Her voice is almost a whisper.

'Not surprised,' I say cheerily. Contrary to popular belief, lying can be easy when folk think you incapable of it. 'You had your whale music on and I didn't shout that loudly. I knew I would be back before you noticed.' I make my voice stern and nod towards Charlie who is watching us, still sensing the tension. 'There was an urgent need for large chocolate buttons. Ears for teddy bear cupcakes.'

'There were chocolate buttons in the cupboard.' Parnell's stare is challenging.

'And none of them were left by the time we turned the oven off.' I force him to look away.

Mary looks puzzled then the penny drops. 'Oh, those cupcakes . . . I was wondering.'

I move towards the door of my flat, as if I consider this conversation over. 'Your son is a keen baker but gets a bit rattled if the ingredients aren't exactly right. He was a wee Gordon Ramsay heading for a five-star strop.' I smile at Parnell. 'So I nipped out to Morrisons in Dunoon, got a few things while I was there. Was that OK?'

'Why not take the Polo?' Parnell fires the question at me.

'No booster seat,' I reply.

Now he smiles at me, his melting smile. 'Oh, I see, that's fine. Just that the accountant was wanting to know about the mileage.'

'Well, if it will help I'll get a notebook. I can stick it in the glove compartment then you'll know where I've been.' I nod my head in a fair-enough kind of gesture. 'Or I can get a booster seat for the Polo.'

Mary swallowed. 'The notebook might be a good idea, Alex. I couldn't remember what I was doing, thought I was going doolally for a minute.' She looks at me closely. 'Elvie? How are you after last night?'

Now Parnell joins in, hands out of pockets and outstretched towards me. 'Oh, for God's sake, Elvie, we'd forgotten. Come in and have a coffee. You must be exhausted.'

'I'm fine. I'll go up to the flat if you don't mind. I've just had a long chinwag with some cops. I'm coffeed out. I'll be down in half an hour to let you away. You're going out to dinner, aren't you?' Now I am the nanny talking to a normal married couple again.

'Anytime that suits you. So, any news on last night?' They move to stand together. He has his arm round her shoulders.

I do my shrug thing. 'The dead woman was Lorna Lennox right enough.'

Mary takes two steps forward and hugs me. 'Oh, you poor thing.' The hug is for more than witnessing the death of a young woman. She stands back.

'Well, let us know if there's anything we can do,' says Parnell. 'And, oh yes, if you need time off, Mary can look after the boy.'

'But you have that fundraiser in Glasgow on Monday night.'

'I don't need to go,' mutters Mary.

'Yes, you do.' Parnell is abrupt. 'It will be a late one and we'll stay over.'

I nod. 'No problem, I can take Charlie to my flat if you want.' I turn to Mary. 'If you're thinking about that navy blue dress, you know it's still at the drycleaners.'

Parnell smiles, now full of good humour. 'And while you're

at it can you make sure my dinner jacket is clean as well, Elvie? It's formal black tie. I'll see you later.' He goes back in through the curtains and leaves the two of us on the patio. The sun beats down on my back, the sweat makes my acne prickle.

Charlie has clocked that Mum and Dad have stopped arguing. Mum did not get hurt. In his wee world all is well.

'Shall we go and give him a push?' I ask.

'Why not?'

We walk away from the open patio doors across the expanse of lawn. She whispers *thank you* out the corner of her mouth. Any more than that and Parnell might hear, any gesture and Parnell might see.

I act as if I have not heard.

I have no idea where she was or what she was doing, but whatever it was, it is something that she needs to do and something that Parnell cannot find out about. And if it makes her happy, that's enough for me.

I pluck Charlie's baseball hat from his head and place it backwards on my own. Mary pulls him back on the swing and I stand in front to make him feel secure. He knows that I will catch him. We chat about everyday stuff. The weather. What it's like to be an astronaut, and the big topic of the day – do you get Coco Pops in space? I let Mary deal with that one. Alex Parnell is behind that curtain watching every move we make – I ignore the temptation to turn round and wave at him.

MONDAY, 4 JUNE

'Hi, I didn't want to bother you yesterday, you seemed busy,' Mary says, standing on the doorstep of the flat. 'You went for a very long run.'

'I had a lot to think about. Come in.'

She hesitates. 'I just wanted to return this book I borrowed.'

'You didn't borrow a book.'

Her eyes flit sideways down to the patio. The message is clear: Parnell is out and about, having a quick smoke and a coffee. I lean forward, pulling my hair from my eyes so I can see him. I wave. He waves back. He could be in Marbella sauntering around enjoying the sunshine in his shorts and T-shirt, but he's at business. It's half seven on a Monday morning and the mobile is already glued to his ear, a look of intense concentration fixed on his face.

'Ta,' I say, playing along, and take the book from her. *Catch-22*, anniversary edition. 'Have you read it?'

'Bits of it, but it's not worth the hassle from Alex, he doesn't like me reading. I think he's a bit threatened by anybody with an education.'

'Why?'

'Why?' She mimics me slightly. 'Oh, Elvie, you are a tonic.'

'I mean, why are you giving me this?'

She turns to look behind her, checking on Parnell, then taps the book with her forefinger. 'I was given it by . . . a friend to see if Rachel wanted to do it at book group but I think it's a bit beyond them. Thought you might like it.' Her eyes wander past me up the stairs. 'Can I talk to you a minute about the arrangements for the week?' she asks rather formally.

'Come on up.'

She gestures to Alex. I do not see his response but I presume that his watch has been flashed at her. *Don't be long.* There is already heat in the air and she is wearing a new long-sleeved shirt, the shade of blue matching the bruise on her wrist.

Once in the flat she collapses on the sofa and swings her
feet up in a way she's not allowed to in her own house. 'Sorry
you had to witness that on Saturday.'

'He was giving you a hard time.' I place the book on top
of a pile on the coffee table before going into the bedroom to
get my running shoes.

'He has a lot on at work and he gets so stressed about it
all.' Her voice drifts through the hall to me.

'Why does he take it out on you?'

She never answers that question.

'So, are you going to this thing tonight?' I notice that she
still has not told me where she really was that afternoon.

'I have to.'

'Well, I've to go to Glasgow today to sign a formal statement.' I tap the copy of *Catch-22*. 'I'll take that and read it
tonight in the flat; Charlie can watch Sponge Bob.'

'That'll work,' she nods, then looks at me. 'Elvie? Do they
think last night had something to do with you? That poor
woman?'

'How can it? Nobody knew that I was going to drive past
that place at that moment in time, did they?'

She shrugs. 'I don't like the idea of anything happening to
you.' She rubs her arms with the palms of her hands, easing
the itching of new bruising. 'How's your mum?'

'Mum doesn't want to talk about any of it until she does
want to talk about it, then she blows her top. Or she gets
drunk.'

'Everyone has their way of coping, I suppose. It would be
so much easier if they knew that your sister was safe.
Somewhere.' She looks out the window, echoing Eric's
thoughts. I think they have been talking about me. I wonder
when she last saw her own parents. I'm pretty sure Parnell
has annexed Mary from them as he has annexed her from all
her friends. 'Poor Grant, he must have been very close to
Sophie for him to fall apart like that.'

I shrug. This is a theme of Mary's; the relationship between
siblings holds fascination for an only child. 'They were, once,
but he just gets on her nerves now. Grant has always been
self-centred, he loves winding Mum up. He was close to Dad,

I suppose. Things change. We are all diminished without Sophie, every one of us.' I tug the lace of my shoe really tight, tying it in a knot. For a minute I don't look at Mary. 'But nothing is going to happen to me, I am invincible.'

She shakes her head. 'Nobody is invincible.'

'Your son thinks he is when he's on that swing.'

'Oh God, he's awful, isn't he?' She sighs. 'I wish we weren't going to this thing tonight, I really don't feel like it. I never feel like it.' She leans forward to the coffee table and pulls *Catch-22* off my Krav Maga manual.

'Is this the weird thing you do in the garden? It keeps you very fit.' She flicks through the pages. 'Oh, it's self-defence. Is it vicious?'

'It is the way I do it.'

She raises her eyebrows, then sees my battered *Complete Poems of Christina Rossetti*. 'You never tire of reading this, do you? *Goblin Market*?'

'I'll never tire of it.'

'They were lucky girls,' she says. 'Lizzie and Laura. To have each other.'

We were lucky girls.

'I gave up my degree before we got to the Romantics. Alex got me a first edition of her collected works just because I mentioned this poem to him. Then he gave me a telling-off for reading it in case I mark it. It is *that* valuable. He bought it as an investment, so it has to sit on a stand in the living room and be admired, not read. He knows the cost of everything and the value of nothing. He thinks I'm bored up here.'

'You are.'

She stands up and gives me a wry smile. Her hand goes to the top of her left thigh, another little rub, another little bruise. She walks towards the door, reluctant to leave.

I say, 'I need to go to Glasgow now, so I'll let you know once I'm free then we can hook up and I'll take Charlie. I might even take him to the Goblin Market if we have time.'

'So he gets to see the secret garden and I don't?' Her anxiety has passed.

'He'll like it.'

'Tender Lizzie could not bear to watch her sister's cankerous

care, yet not to share . . .' Her hand sits on the handle of the door, her fingers curl round it and she looks down the stairs in that abstract way she has. 'And I know that you do care. For Sophie. She's very lucky.' I cannot read her expression, there is nothing I can reference.

'I feel a bit guilty that you're paying me to look after him when I'm caught up in all this.'

'I wouldn't worry about it. Alex didn't employ you to look after Charlie; he employed you to spy on me and he thinks you're good at it. He likes the way you rarely let me out of your sight. He thinks that you can't tell a lie because you lack imagination.'

'Shows what a bad judge of character he is.'

Billy Hopkirk seems to be an expert at parking illegally and not being seen. First he double parked as we dropped Charlie off at the flat in Park Circus. Mary was back from a stressful trip to Buchanan Galleries to buy a new dress, one to cover the bruises, no doubt. I spent a couple of minutes reassuring Mary that the dress – a long, swirling black number – was fabulous and she believed me.

Now Billy is stuck in the car park at the Western Hospital, without a ticket. He keeps looking at his watch. He wants us to be a bit late so that 'Jack' will be in a hurry and want rid of us, but not so much of a hurry that he'll blow us out altogether. So far he has refused to enlighten me about who 'Jack' actually is.

Billy is wearing the same clothes as yesterday and he smells as though he hasn't washed them for a month. His perfume is chip fat and vinegar with a top note of fag ash.

We've been sitting here for about twenty minutes, stewing in the old Vectra with the sun beating in the open window, listening to the noise of the busy street. For the umpteenth time I lean forward in the seat to pull the sweaty shirt from my back. The heat is making my acne boil painfully. I am in a mood and the wait is not helping. I've already lied and told him that I have to be back at Park Circus at two. All he said was that we had better get on with it, without telling me what 'it' is.

'Oh, look, we might be in business. Keep your gob shut, hen. If you can.'

I get out the car to stretch my legs. Billy eases his beer belly from the driver's seat then waddles towards a grey-haired man in a grey suit with matching face. He is carrying a brief-case and a load of files under his arm.

'Jack? Jack, just the man.'

The man stops and turns his eyes towards the sky. I'm not convinced that he is feigning his horror. 'Well, well, Billy the Fox Hopkirk. How are you, you old . . .' He stops when he clocks me. That look again, this time with a degree of medical assessment. 'Fox?' he finishes. His mind is moving quickly, I can see him making connections. 'What do you want?'

'You've just done the PM on Lorna Lennox.'

'Maybe.'

'That wasn't a question, that was a statement. I was going to pull the old pals act so you can tell us what you found.' Billy spreads his arms in mock endearment.

'As a cop you were always just on the line, but as a retired cop you are now on the wrong side of it. No can do, even if I wanted to. And I don't want to.' The man in the grey suit with the grey hair reaches out to his car door. His grey car door.

'Well, I'm now working privately for Gillian's mother.'

'And God forbid that the time ever comes when I have to deal with her. But if I have to, then I will.' He tries to walk round Billy, who puts his beer belly to good use.

'Oh, I know that.' He is civility itself. 'But at least you can let me know what you cannot tell me and let me draw my own conclusions. We've done that often enough in the past, you and me.' He looks up at the man in grey, almost fluttering his eyelashes at him.

I stand in front of the car door. 'When the times comes?' I repeat back at him.

The grey-haired man stops his little dance with Hopkirk. 'Sorry?'

'You said, "When the time comes". Which means when they're dead. Lorna was still alive on Friday.'

He drops his briefcase down to rest at arm's-length and looks away.

'This is Sophie McCulloch's sister,' Billy mutters out the corner of his mouth. 'She has issues.' He touched his temple indicating that he thought I was *not all there*. 'And if you don't fall for the emotional blackmail, think about the rant she's about to give to the press. You won't come out of it well, Jack.'

'I don't give a f—'

'Language in front of the lady!' Billy turns to me. 'Sorry, sweet cheeks, I was using the term loosely.'

'No offence taken.'

Jack is wrong-footed by the familiarity of our exchange.

'So come on, Jack, be nice, for old times' sake.'

'For Sophie's sake . . .' I keep my voice calm.

'So, Jack, a wee favour, an off-the-record chat between old colleagues.'

'He kept Lorna alive for a long time,' I add for effect. 'He might still have Sophie alive. You will help us.' It wasn't a question.

'Do you hear that certainty in her voice? She knows you'll help eventually, so you may as well tell us now and save time.'

The pathologist turns to Billy. 'Why don't you take it up with the SIO? My report is in the post to him.'

'Why should we, when we can hear it from the horse's mouth?'

Jack breathes in deeply; I think he'd like to punch that foxy look from Billy's face. 'I don't think I can help you,' he says to me directly. 'There are proper channels.'

'Lorna died in my arms.'

'Yes, I know. I read the report. It will be public soon enough. The cage webcam on the rock was activated by her falling past it.'

'So she was up on the hill.' I take one step forward, invading his space. 'I need to know if the same thing is about to happen to my sister.' I sound as if I blame him. And he is intelligent enough to know that my logic is sound. He bites his lip slightly, unsure. The dead he can cope with. But whether Sophie lives or dies might be up to him now. I read his discomfort so I push the argument home. 'The more knowledge we have, the more chance we have.'

'I am sure you will be informed in due course.'

'I want to be informed now.' My voice is steady but insistent.

'So where had Lorna come from?' asked Billy, nonchalantly. He could have been asking who dived for the penalty.

'Well, that's in the public domain. She came from the top of the moor. She was naked and barefoot, and got caught in the lie of the land where the ground level dropped because of the landslide. She was exhausted, it was dark. She headed towards the cliff where she fell.'

'No idea what she was doing up there?'

'I'm a pathologist, not a cop.' Jack looked at me. 'But I don't think they have any idea about that.'

'Any evidence where she was running from?' Billy asks.

'She couldn't have gone far, not in that state. She must have been taken by car and thrown out, which is a good theory except there's no road.'

'Could I have done anything to save her?'

'Not at all, Miss McCulloch. She was bleeding internally. Keep that to yourself.' His voice is quiet.

Billy speaks out the corner of his mouth. 'She's a medical student. She'll get the big words and all the patient confidentiality stuff.'

'She had an injury?' I persist. 'On her leg?'

'Yes. A clean excision but badly healed.'

I nod. 'Like a tattoo or something had been cut out? Or a birthmark, maybe?' I am not looking at him. I am simply thinking out loud. 'And she was so thin, emaciated.'

'Undernourished but not starved in the medical sense of the word.'

'Sexual assault?'

'There seems to be no sexual motive,' he said carefully.

'Lorna's fingertips were bloodied to the bone like she'd been scraping to get out.' Now I put my fingers on his chest. His shirt is cool to my skin. I keep my eyes on the back of my hand. 'Was there anything, any trace under her nails? Anything that might help us locate her?'

'You are very observant. So you will also have noticed that she was clean. And there was nothing under her fingernails, what there was left of them. And she had been deprived of sunshine. Now, I really have to go.' He casts me a look of pity, I step to one side. 'And one more thing. Was that your jumper under her neck?'

'Yes.'

'Do you have close contact with a dog?'

'No.'

He nods to me, grateful that I am going to ask no more.

Billy slapped his arm. 'You see, fair exchange.'

Jack gets in his car and I think he is about to drive off. Then there is a slight turn of his head, as if he has caught sight of me in the rear-view mirror. The window drops with a funereal hum. 'You should talk to DCI Anderson.'

The words were said to me but it was Billy who answered. 'Colin? At Partickhill?'

'One and the same.'

'Is he working this case now? Anderson and Costello?' Billy was leaning in at the car window, as if doing that would stop the pathologist driving off.

'They were not on the Lennox case, were they? And I wasn't speaking to you.'

'We're a team. I have the charm and she has the balls.'

'Why do I not doubt that?'

'So should I go and speak to this Anderson?'

'He will find you when he's ready.' Billy is sitting in the car with two coffees and four jammy Yum Yums. 'I'll drink this coffee. Don't touch yours if you're not going to drink it, then I can have it.' He slurps at the lip of his cup noisily. I begin to get that surge of uncontrolled adrenaline; the ice is starting in my veins. The frustration is getting to me. I'm going to be sick or hit Billy if I don't get moving.

'Do you mind if I go for a run?'

He frowns as if I have just asked him if I can shit in his car. 'Whit?'

'It's when you put one foot in front of the other, quickly. Not a concept you'll be familiar with. I need to get out of here. You smell.'

'Well, I will sit here and enjoy my coffee and Smooth radio. And my Yum Yums.' He sniffs annoyingly. 'Then I'll stick the car up that lane and go for a wee snooze, OK?'

'I need a run, I need to think.'

'You're off your fucking head, but on you go.' He looks straight ahead and sniffs again. 'You up to anything tonight?'

'Babysitting. That is my job now, technically.'

'Why? Where are they going, Parnell and the lovely Mary?'

'The Action Medical Research do, I think. At the Hilton.'

'Oh that, I've been stung for that one myself a few times.' He wipes his nose on the sleeve of his jacket. 'Off you go then, you have ten minutes. Remember to run in a circle. I'm not coming to get you.'

I slide out the car, peeling my jumper off and tying it round my waist, clipping my phone to my waistband. I warm up on the jog past the Kelvin Hall to the park, and then I run free. I switch off everything but the thoughts in my head. I hear no traffic, only the slap of my feet on the path. I run easily, breathing effortlessly. The pain in my limbs eases with the movement, the blood flowing, my joints are fluid. It feels good. Air floats in and out of my lungs, infusing me with energy. There is nothing like this feeling in the world. My mind focuses on Lorna running through the dark, scared and naked. She is someone that I never knew, yet in a strange way she has become more significant than Soph. Her death was shocking, it really happened. It happened to a human being called Lorna. Lorna laughed and loved and danced and worked, and I owe her something to make it right. I try to empty my head, looking at the trees in full green, verdant and luscious. The oldest trees, the sentinels of the park, stand tall and silent, reaching into the sky. They have stood there for nearly a century, there is nothing new. The autumn will follow the summer, there is death after life. This cycle that we worry about so much is nothing to them.

A jogger runs past the trees on the lower path. She is out of condition, overworking her lungs. She jogs down on to the flat path towards the fountain and I slow my stride so that I don't catch up. I am watching her but seeing Lorna. Further down the grassy slope the grey stone eyes of Thomas Carlyle stare out across the path. The returning glance of the soldier at the war memorial meets Carlyle's gaze with a look of complete indifference. The infantryman looks at the philosopher, as they have looked at each other for three generations, and nothing at all passes between them.

A sleek, muscled Rottweiler sniffs the grass behind the war memorial looking for the scent of a squirrel. I look around for my jogging pal and she runs into view on her second circuit. The man with the Rottweiler clips its lead on its neck chain and starts back up the slope to the high path, his hand raised in some acknowledgement to the jogger, who replies with a slight wave and crosses to the other side of the path. The dog pulls hard on its lead, head down, powerful shoulders straining. It opens its jaws as it gets a knee in the guts from its owner. But I have a mental picture of those jaws now. I slow my pace, imagining a dog coming up behind me, thinking of wolves and how they bring down prey.

My calf twitches again. I know what Lorna was running from.

Back on the road I run smoothly, getting a bit of a kick on before slowing to jog up behind the Kelvin Hall and the Transport Museum towards where Billy had vaguely indicated he would be parked. My mobile rings; it's Rod. He asks me how I am, then tells me the police have been back at the house. More questions but nothing new. The visit upset Grant, who has now locked himself in his bedroom. Rod wasn't aware that he had put a lock on his door. Rod is scared Grant will harm himself. I reassure him, thinking that it might be the best thing that he can do – then Mum would have to wake up and get him some help. I offer to kick the door in if he needs me to. Rod chuckles, thinking I am joking. We cut the call. I walk into the lane. A metal spike in the road prevents vehicle access. I hear a voice, Billy's, telling someone to *fuck off* really loudly. I consider the tone – anger? But there is something else. I run round the corner of the block of flats and the Vectra is there, doors open. Billy is wrestling a teenager in a tracksuit. Another boy is rifling through the car. I nearly fail to see the third one who is right beside me, standing guard at the mouth of the lane. Luckily he totally fails to hear me, a benefit of silent footfall. I run past the first ned and kick the one who has Billy in the crotch. I sink my heel into the back of his knee and push hard. As he falls I spin so that my knee comes round and smacks him in the throat. I leave him to fall grunting and spluttering to the ground and tell Billy to get in the car. I jump over the bonnet while the second ned is still thinking what to do. Junkies do not think quickly. I slam the door on his arm; it bounces back and he falls to his knees. I give him a kick in the throat as I go past. I see Billy's phone on the tarmac. The third junkie is on his way towards the car, a slim blade shining. I walk up to the skinny wee runt. His acne is not as bad as mine, and that incenses me more than anything. I am not scared of the knife in his hand. I walk up to him and bat his arm away from me so hard the knife goes flying, bouncing across the tarmac with the melody of a tubular bell. I grab him by the hair and slam his face into the wall of the flats. He is a featherweight. I hear his nose break, then his cheekbone. I stop. I pick up the knife and walk back round the car.

'Just drive,' I say.

'But he's in the way.'

'Well, go over him or round him. Do you want me to drive?' Now that I can see Billy's face I know what the other intonation in his voice was: he was scared. He is quivering. He is an old man now, an old man who has had a bad fright. 'You've hurt your wrist. Better go to the Southern and get it checked, old guy like you.'

'We are driving past the Western,' he says, pointing.

'We need to go to the Southern because they will go to the Western.'

'Did you hurt them that bad?'

'Yes.'

'You a black belt or something?'

'No, just angry.'

'You were expertly angry.'

'Krav Maga. Israeli self-defence. Kind of. Go for the eyes, the throat, the knees. If they can't see, breathe or run then they're fucked, aren't they?'

'You're bloody good at it.'

'My dad sent me when I was wee, he thought I had aggression issues.'

'Remind me not to get you angry.'

* * *

Billy wants to ask me something but can't quite find the words. This is what Soph would call an awkward silence, but I can't think of anything to fill it.

But Billy does. 'You know, hen, if you ever decide that medicine is not for you, you could be a great addition to the SAS. I'd just reverse-parked the car up that lane so I could pretend I was driving out if the traffic proles appeared. I got out to use the phone and the wee skinny one jumped me, spilled my bloody coffee – well, your bloody coffee to be precise. Now is the point where you ask who I was phoning that was so important I got jumped.'

'Consider it asked.'

'Mr Parnell.'

'You phoned my boss?'

'Indeed. You don't have to look after Charlie tonight.'

'Is Mary OK with that?'

'Mary does as she is told.' He presses a button and the window drops.

I look into the footwell where my rucksack was. The wee toerag had rummelled about but everything was still there. 'And why am I not looking after Charlie tonight? What am I doing instead?'

'I told him you were needed on police business.'

'Did you buy something off those guys before they tried to mug you?' Now I put the window down, the flow-through drifts caffeine past my nose.

'And now we need to speak to someone.' His voice is a little clipped.

'Who, specifically?'

But Billy is talking to himself, thinking as he goes along. 'I bet the whole case has come up now for review. That's why Anderson has been brought in. Jack gave us a heads-up about that one at least.'

'So where are we going?'

'The next best thing.'

'We're going to the hospital first.'

Two hours and three coffees later we are driving through a housing estate near Glasgow's most desirable postcode. Spelled

Milngavie, pronounced Mill Guy to separate those who belong there from those that just think they do. The phrase 'Near Milngavie' raises the value of any property by ten grand, Billy tells me as I drive. He left hospital with an X-ray, a strapped wrist and a prescription for Tramadol.

'Pull in here,' he says, pointing to a neat bungalow in Balvie Road, brown roughcast with a newly slabbed driveway.

'Nice gaff,' I say, more to annoy him than anything else. I was still thinking about that mark on Lorna's leg. And Jack's question about a dog. I needed to chat with this Anderson.

'Do you think you can be nice in here and only speak when you think it is appropriate? And not hit anybody?'

I tell him to fuck off.

'Watch your language, sweet cheeks,' he winks at me.

A thought strikes me. 'You're not going to lie to them, are you? If you're going to impersonate a police officer, I am . . .'

'Oh, I spent my whole friggin' life impersonating a police officer, so I'm not likely to stop now, am I?'

He rings the bell and the door opens so quickly it's obvious we're expected. Was this lady the reason for his distraction when he was jumped? She is a small woman, roughly the same age as Billy, with blonde hair dulled with grey, pulled back and twisted into a bun. She looks the sort that would do an Open University course or paint watercolours to amuse herself in her retirement. She is as unlike my mother as you could get, except for the restless look in her eyes. She too is looking for a loved one. I recognize her face from the news clip on the TV, and there is no mistaking the warmth in her eyes when she looks at Billy; their formal greeting has some false restraint about it. I retreat a little, not feeling part of this togetherness. They remind me of a pedigree poodle meeting a stinky mongrel. Billy introduces me as his associate and her smile slips a little when she sees me.

'Oh, you have an associate now?'

'Yeah, I use her to scare people,' Billy says, moving into a narrow hall with a laminated floor and a lot of doors. The glass doors at the bottom end are half open; I can see beyond to the new extension. I can see she has a porthole window like Mary has. The shelves on this one are full of spider plants.

'Christine', as she is introduced, smiles at me and has the good grace to keep the smile when she notices the acne and the hairs on the side of my face as I walk past.

'Now that the door is shut I can tell you who she is,' says Billy as he walks purposefully into the living room.

Christine sits down on the chair by the window, looks at Billy and then back at me. I stay quiet, I have to speak only when appropriate.

'This is Sophie McCulloch's sister.'

Christine's expression changes to one of five-star sympathy.

'Sophie? I'm Gilly's mother.' She extends her hand for me to shake; her hold lingers.

Billy was the head of the investigation into her daughter's disappearance, so these two have a professional history that has developed into something personal.

'Please have a seat.' She sweeps her arm out like BA cabin crew. 'Sorry, what is your name?'

'Elvie.' I sit down on her coffee-coloured leather suite, pulling my tracksuit bottoms underneath me. She can't help but glance at my trainers and her spotless carpet. Another thing she shares with my mother.

'How are your parents coping?' she asks.

I notice that Billy has sat down and made himself at home, leaning back with his legs crossed. 'Just my mum.'

Christine nods.

'I think she's OK,' I lie.

'Every time I get a knock on the door I think that this might be it.' Christine shudders slightly, and her forefinger caresses her chin as she looks at the photographs on the wall behind my head. I turn to look at the family portraits. Gilly has curly brown hair and a pretty smile. She's wearing an open-collared white blouse revealing a small gold dolphin leaping on her breastbone. 'But now the knocks on the door are getting fewer and fewer. And that feels so much worse.' She starts to well up. 'I can't stand the waiting. I had to do something. She went missing on Thursday night, the fourth of March 2010. Not a night I am likely to forget, ever.' She turns to Billy, her hand outstretched across the arm of the chair to rest on his knee.

Billy has the good grace to look a little embarrassed but pats her hand. 'Christine, have you seen the news?'

'Not that woman found in Argyll? Gilly?' Her hand goes up to her throat. 'Oh, please, no.' She shakes her head.

'No, no, no,' says Billy quickly, taking her hand in his. 'Christine? It was not Gilly.'

Christine bites her lip, her free hand wipes a tear from the corner of her eye. She takes a deep breath to compose herself.

Billy twists in his seat to take both her hands in his good one. 'But I do think that woman was taken by the same person that took Gilly and I didn't want you reading the details in the papers. There was a body found, that's all you need to know. We're going to have a chat with the Senior Investigating Officer and that might move the situation on, get us closer to finding Gilly.'

Christine glances at me and then back to Billy. 'So if the woman at the Rest and Be Thankful was alive until Friday night . . .' Her eyes look straight into Billy's. 'There's a chance that Gilly is still alive?'

Billy has the confidence to nod; Christine looks at me bleary-eyed and I smile. 'Every chance she is alive.' I am sitting on my hands so that she does not see that my fingers are crossed.

'You need to see the room, it might help.' She is suddenly on her feet and moving. 'There might be somebody there that you recognize, somebody your sister knew. You must look.'

'Was her husband abusive?' The question flies from my lips, and Christine looks stunned.

'Pardon?'

'No,' said Billy to me sharply before turning to Christine. 'There's a battered women's refuge that has come up twice in the investigation, that's all.'

'Refuge for victims of domestic violence,' I correct him.

'Gilly was happily married,' said Christine, sitting back down. 'Very happily.'

'Something we needed to ask, that's all. Can you think of any other reason for Gilly to come into contact with the refuge? In her role as a teacher, perhaps?' asks Billy. 'Needn't be anything personal.'

'I can't think why she would. But she wouldn't have told me.' She smiles at me. 'Do you want to look at the room, just through there?' She points.

'Just leave her to it, Chris. Come on, we'll put the kettle on . . .' says Billy.

She shows me through to the room across the hall, a dining room converted to a murder room. Just the same as we have at home, but with Gilly instead of Sophie.

'You found anything?'

I jump. They're both standing in the doorway and I think they might have been there for some time. 'Sorry, I was miles away. I've looked at the pictures, read the articles, but I don't see any link between them, except running. They were not the same kind of people.' I stop and check my radar that Christine is not offended.

Her pursed lips suggest that she might be. 'Gilly was married young to her childhood sweetheart. She loved her children and her family life. She liked working with the kids at school.'

'Whereas Sophie liked to live the life of a student. Gillian ran with the Milngavie Mummies? Did they have a trainer or a coach or something?'

Christine shook her head. 'Nothing so formal, they went out jogging on a Tuesday and Thursday night and there was a babysitter provided so they could all go out together. Afterwards they went for coffee. That's all.'

'But she must have been on her own the night she went missing.' I look at Billy for confirmation.

'Yes. She was late home from school that night, the weather was terrible. Rather than not go she went out on her own.'

'Did she run the same route?'

'I think so.' Christine shudders. 'She was down by the Baldernock Linn. That was where she was last seen. Graham said it was their favourite summer run.'

'Was she having an affair?'

Christine pursed her lips. 'No. Why, was your sister?'

'Probably,' I replied. 'She normally was.' I look at a little map, photocopied and folded many times. 'So she was along this route somewhere. The person who abducted her knew where she would be.'

'Or came across her?' asks Christine.

Billy shook his head. 'He couldn't get that lucky twice. He knows where these women will be and when.'

'Do you know any really big dogs – or anyone with a really big dog?'

Christine shakes her head.

'OK, Christine,' Billy says. 'We have another idea that might help.' As if on cue his phone goes; he smiles and accepts the call. 'Do you think that might be a flyer?' Absent-mindedly he rubs his nose, just where the skin is cross-marked with fine red veins from his drinking days. Then he listens. 'Well, you can take credit for it. It's your jurisdiction, your idea.' He progresses to scratching and turns to look at me. The scared old man has gone, the fox is back. 'Yeah, she'll do it. She can go out hunting in the night. It's something that she does. Yeah, she'll be glad to . . . no, I don't need to ask her. The body nearly fell on her, remember? And her sister is missing. She already is involved.'

TUESDAY, 5 JUNE

It's a simple plan. Find out where Lorna came from. We know where she ended up, so all I have to do is retrace her steps. I look out into the darkness. Same place, same time of night, same type of woman. It's the best that they can think of as the dogs can't find a scent with all this rain. Billy says that we don't know what it will achieve until we try. I console myself with the fact that even if Lorna was chased by the Earl of Hell her feet still hit the ground and somewhere up there was a footprint that might take us to a track, to a road, to a tyre print. To a CCTV camera. A number plate. An ID.

I couldn't say no.

So now I am running over the moor. Two crime lab technicians are standing in the glare of a very powerful arc light, huddled against the rain and poring over a plastic map. They have already calculated the radius that Lorna could have covered in her state of dehydration and weakness. One of them has factored in that I am fitter, well nourished and not injured.

'But I am not scared,' I said and jogged away to warm up. Lorna would have a runner's eye for the contour of the land, she would know roughly where she was trying to get to – the Rest. There was no sign of her being chased, and only her footsteps were at the top of the landslide, nobody else's. She was simply trying to get away. Didn't matter if that was uphill or downhill, she would run towards where she thought she would get help. The emptiness up here – hundreds of square miles of it – would focus her mind.

It's certainly focusing mine.

They talked me through it. I will be followed, and they will check for any evidence that Lorna also passed this way. I will have a camera on my skip cap to record what I'm looking at. Later they will clarify the images to examine any *places of interest,* as they put it. Sounds a load of cack to me.

At twenty past midnight we are still gathering on the hillside.

I'm dressed in my usual black leggings, wearing trail-running boots to protect my ankles from the clumps of heather. I feel good as I jog past the Land Rover that dropped me off, past the huddle of people taking notes. They are looking up at the sky, looking at their watches and wondering why their phones have no signal. It's going to be a very wet and windy night. Sipping my water, I head off down the track, loosening up my limbs, wishing these men would get their finger out so that I can get on with it. It will take us an hour or more to walk to where Lorna fell before I can start to run. I jog on past a police tape that separates nothing from nowhere and look back, they're still milling around. I go on, waiting for it to happen, getting my anger up, my own little roid rage. I roll my neck and shoulders until I feel it creeping along my arteries and I move away from the lights, into the dark shadows. I have no fear about the run; the bigger fear is that we might miss something.

Something moves in the darkness; I hear the breathless wheeze of unfit lungs behind me. I turn round quickly, he puts his arms up to protect himself. He is an older man, wearing a coat ill-matched to this weather.

'What's going on?' he asks. 'I know she was here.'

Of course she was or we wouldn't be here. I take a minute to read his body language; he is no threat. Not only is he scared of me, he's trying to hold back the tears.

'Please?' His hand reaches out towards me, shaking. His skin is red with exposure to the cold and the rain as he holds a creased piece of paper in a clear plastic folder out towards me. That Ali McGraw smile. It's a million miles away from the face that lay in my lap and ceased to breathe, so thin that the skin looked painted on her bones. His thumb grips the photograph tightly in case the wind should catch it and take it from him, as fate had taken Lorna.

'Mr Lennox? We will find the man who did this.'

'So what is happening? What are you looking for?'

'Whatever we can find. You should go home.' I can't tell him that his daughter spent her last hours on earth in this dark, lonely, desolate place.

'Three days shy of six months.' He shakes his head. For a minute his face is impassive, then he nods. 'And it comes down to this.' He coughs. I think that might be to hide a tear. 'Just tell me if she suffered.'

Tell me if she suffered. I recognize that type of question; he does not want to know the answer. 'She was doing her best to get back to you,' I say. We have been spotted, someone shouts to us. I say quickly, 'I'm Sophie McCulloch's sister . . .'

His head jerks up at that. 'Oh?'

'Can I ask you a question?'

'Aye? Whit?' His eyes narrow, I have his attention.

'Your daughter's running schedule?' It comes out as a formal question but he answers it.

'Well, she'd been up for the marathon, but she injured her foot. She got a pool thing built at her house so she could run in water. Nothing like that in our day. But she was fit enough when . . . when she was taken.'

I smile what I hope is an understanding smile. 'She went missing on a Thursday night, out running?'

He nods. None of this is news to him.

I nod back, he thinks we have empathy. 'I'll let you know how this goes.' I can say that confidently as I know Billy will know all about Mr Lennox. 'I'll do my best.'

'God bless you, hen, mind how you go.'

And I trot away.

A team of six of us set out to walk to Lorna's last known point, the point where she fell to her death.

An hour and ten minutes later. I am running, thinking that Lorna, marathon fit with all that muscle memory, could have run here from bloody anywhere, no matter what state she was in. She was tough.

The first part is almost a clamber up a few rocks, and it's easy to see where Lorna had come down. I have the camera fixed to my hat, a small flat torch clipped to my waist and two big clunking brutes of men behind me. I try to find a rhythm, ignoring the discomfort of the guy behind me trying to talk down his radio, his lack of breath giving his speech a staccato arrhythmia. My instructions were to go and to keep going, so I ignore him and push on. From the point where she fell, the natural path is upwards. She would have run down this gully, not realising she was being funnelled into the landslide and the sheer drop to the road below. Half a mile north or south she would have had an ungainly clamber down, but not here. Because of the heather I look down as I run and the torch finds the footprint before my eyes register it. A crescent moon of toes embedded in the mud on the bank of a stream that gurgles loudly in protest at all the rainwater pouring into it. So Lorna jumped it here coming the opposite way, this was her take-off point. The torch finds her landing footprint just beside my own take-off one. One of the cops takes a photograph of them, they look so slight, so inconsequential – just small imprints of a bare sole and toes. I am on the right track. So where she ran up, I run down. I feel she's talking to me, guiding me.

I look behind me along the grey outline of the tops against the dark sky, and see a gap. She must have seen it too, must have thought that was her way down on to the road, her way to safety and sanctuary. I slow my pace and move on, searching for any signs that she passed this way, then quicken my pace when I realize I'm on a hillwalkers' path. If she found it she would stay on it, conserving her energy. She would have had the gap in sight and she would move towards it just as I am moving away from it. I run on, heading north, not watching where I am going but running faster as I gain confidence that this path will meet a track of some kind and spark a chain of evidence that Billy is hopeful of.

Suddenly I am airborne, there is a pain in my ankle and the torch catches a sky full of rain and clouds, then grass, then mud. I fall straight into the soaking, spongy earth which does its best to swallow me up. The ground beneath me is giving way, and I stumble into a roll. The landslide flashes in my mind and I grip on to a clump of earth that yields and tumbles until it and I both come to a halt.

I hear one of the cops behind me say *Fuck*, the other say *Oh my God*, then one of them starts to retch and a terrible smell floats to my nostrils. The smell of dead flesh. I think I have tripped over a dead sheep. I lie there looking at the sky, at the huge dark clouds chasing each other, shape shifting the landscape, some so low I think they are snatching at my feet. The footpath has gone, the gap in the hills has gone, I have no idea where I am. The landscape has lied to me as it lied to Lorna.

The beam of light from the cop's torch bobs around me and I raise my head to examine my ankle which feels both hot and numb. I look around me, frowning as the rain and wind sting my eyes. The cop calls my name, nods to me then beams his torch to the ground where my hand is, where the remains of another hand lies in disturbed earth, its fingers entwined in mine.

The arc lights of the police team cast bright beams of white, catching the dance of the summer heather rippled by the wind. The crime scene officers are silent phantoms, no point in talking when the wind cuts the breath from their lungs and the words from their lips. The plateau of the Ben is its own little world; all actions are accompanied by the patter of the rain on nylon shoulders and the high-pitched whisper of the wind somewhere beyond the darkness.

At three-thirty I am in a four-by-four at the nearest point of vehicular access, having followed the professor, O'Hare, off the hill. I'm not sure that I am invited but I don't care. The sweat has dried and is salty on my skin, making me feel colder now than I was before. O'Hare immediately switches on the ignition and the heater before he starts struggling to get his jacket and plastic trousers off in the confined space. Grandpa Cop sits in the passenger seat, blowing on the palms of his hands. O'Hare reaches into the footwell, lifts up a small thermos flask and pours two coffees. He hands one to Grandpa Cop and offers the other to me but I shake my head.

I let them enjoy it, let them warm their veins. I've already reminded them that I have just found another body hidden amongst the tuffets of grass. Should they not be doing a wee bit more about it than sitting in this car and drinking coffee? Now I think if I am quiet then they might forget about me and talk a little more.

*   *   *

They are indulging in chit-chat about the endless rain when a figure in a white crime scene suit ghosts into sight looking like an overweight Teletubby.

Grandpa Cop mutters something about being glad that the coffee has warmed his brain up a little, he's getting too old for this game. O'Hare agrees. I deduce from this that the person approaching in the CSI suit is important, someone I should get to know.

O'Hare pumps the horn lightly and the Teletubby hurries towards us, hand up to hold a plastic hood in place, jogging clumsily. The Teletubby opens the back door and clambers in, and the hood is pulled down, accompanied by a vicious curse about the weather as small teeth pull quilted gloves from cold hands fingertip by fingertip. The same fingers then work through crushed, short blonde hair. She looks at me. 'God, this is fucking awful weather.'

'Good evening, DS Costello?' asks O'Hare, his tone drier than anything else in the vehicle.

'I've had better.'

Grandpa Cop twists on his seat to introduce himself like this is a tea party.

'Is it Sophie?' I interrupt.

Costello glares at me, annoyed at being spoken to.

'This is Sophie's sister,' says O'Hare quickly, warning Costello that any comment should be guarded. 'She's persistent.'

'By that you mean a pest.'

'Well, is it? Sophie had a silver locket on . . . here . . .' I put my fingers at my neck, round the top of the blanket. 'Right here,' I say.

O'Hare says quietly, 'That body up there is of a woman much taller than your sister. Off the record, five feet nine, at least,' he adds, keeping his gaze fixed through the front windscreen.

Sophie is five foot three. I recall my first sight of her Fiat at the reservoir where she disappeared, noticing that the seat was too far back. Somebody else had driven it, someone taller than five foot three.

This is not Sophie. The unspoken question has been on my lips since I felt that cold, rubbery flesh under my fingers and the beam of that torch had passed over hair. Stringy, matted, dark hair. Dark. Not blonde.

Grandpa Cop passes his cup back to Costello, offering a sip of his coffee. She declines with a vigorous shake of the head then opens a small folder of Polaroids and hands them to O'Hare. She leans forward, and her jacket squeaks as she angles her head and shoulders between the front seats. O'Hare switches on the courtesy light to get a better view.

'What do you think?' she asks. 'It's kind of hard to make out what that actually is.' She points to the image with her pinkie. 'They say the body was on the surface but disturbed by the increased stream of surface water sometime before you came across it.'

'How tall was Gillian Porter?' As I ask, I can imagine Billy's face.

'This girl is taller than Gillian also,' says O'Hare quietly, but at least it shows he has thought of that as well.

I take the picture from him and study it as the rain, caught by the wind, suddenly batters on the windscreen, on the roof, on the door beside me. It interrupts my train of thought. They start to chat amongst themselves, procedural things like who is doing what and who is going where. Grandpa Cop's radio starts to buzz and beep so he turns it off. I turn the photograph through 180 degrees but still cannot identify what the mosaic of light and dark, grey and black actually is. 'You must have some idea who she is?'

The car falls silent, as they recall that I am not one of them.

O'Hare remains quiet; he takes a slow sip of coffee but our eyes meet through the rear-view mirror.

'Or can you speculate?' I prompt, trying to read the situation. 'If anybody has a need to hear your theories then it is me.'

O'Hare shuffles in his seat a little and I hand the Polaroid to Grandpa Cop.

'Billy Hopkirk. Me. Sophie. Gillian.' I then add, 'My brother, my mother, her mother, her husband, her kids – we all need to hear something. A theory?' I add for effect.

'OK.' O'Hare gazes out the front window. 'We need further tests to be sure how long she has been lying there. But she is female, youngish, emaciated, naked, barefoot. All echoes of Lorna.' He stops and rubs the back of his hand against the inside of the front windscreen; it squeaks. A small viewing space appears, another two figures are coming off the hill, one raises an arm. O'Hare flashes his lights in response before taking the picture from Grandpa Cop and turning it round ninety degrees. He holds it in his right hand, his index finger dancing on the surface. 'That is the back of her head. That dark bit is her matted hair, the light bits are her scalp showing through, which is why it's difficult to make out the form of her head on this. And that . . .' he draws his nail along a faint line on the picture, '. . . is her face, buried into her raised elbow, her forehead on her forearm, face down as if she was protecting herself from attack. I couldn't see any obvious injuries but that doesn't mean to say they aren't there.'

'Might have lain down, sheltering from the wind maybe.'

'As you say, she might have collapsed and curled up, waiting to die, in which case someone left her there to do that. Or she might have been hillwalking and got hypothermia. It's not unusual for people with hypothermia to undress. But this is a great dump site for a body; hillwalkers go to the prettier places. There are nearly eight hundred square miles up here with enough nooks and crannies to hide a whole army. Then this torrential rain starts and causes the landslide that trapped Lorna and has helped to expose this lassie.'

'You say that she had no injuries?'

'None that was obvious.'

'So what's that dark patch then, on her leg?' I ask, leaning forward between the front seats to point. 'Right there?'

'You think she had the same cut as Lorna? I can't make it out.'

Costello holds out another picture to O'Hare but I take it. 'Can you see it better in this one? You can see a concavity there – that is interesting. Does it look excised? That could link them, if so.'

'Lorna's cut was clean. I haven't looked at this one yet, have I?'

Costello bites her tongue, she is as desperate for an answer as I am. 'She might be right, though; if that is an excised wound it does link them.'

O'Hare mutters one word and hands the photograph back. 'If.'

I wake up later in the morning in the flat at Ardno. My limbs are aching from the tension of last night and the chemical soup that has been brewing in my blood. I switched off my mobile so that I would wake naturally, fed up with tiredness that is so overwhelming that even sleep is too much effort.

I do not touch the phone, can't be bothered to check the string of messages. I don't feel ready to face anybody. What does this mean for Soph? Is it bringing me closer to her? She might have wanted to run away but the days are passing and there is still no word and the facts remain – she was out running, it was dusk, and she disappeared off the face of the earth.

I go out for a long, slow run in the fresh summer air so I can think things through. There's not a soul about, no tourist buses along the loch side, no seals. Even the Highland cattle, their coats the colour of old rust, are on the far side of the field standing against the drystane dyke, away from the deep mud at the lower end. They're sheltering from a wind that is not here yet, but they are wise in reading the weather, and they know what is coming. At the moment the sky is clear, and it looks as if it is going to be a lovely day. Maybe the land will get the chance to dry out after some of the heaviest rainfall on record.

I jog along by the loch for a couple of miles and then turn back, lack of food making me feel I am running on empty. On the way back I notice that the Shogun is missing, so Charlie is not back.

After a long hot shower, a change of clothes and some toast I sit on the settee and lift my phone. The first voicemail is from DCI Colin Anderson asking me to phone him back or call in to see him at Partickhill station, today if that is convenient for me. But it is said in a way that means I should do it whether it is convenient or not. The second is from a woman who does not identify herself but simply says that, within the bounds of confidentiality of which I have already been informed, she can tell me that the body found last night is not that of Sophie McCulloch or Gillian Porter, and would I keep that news to myself for the moment. I presume she is someone from Jack's office.

There are two calls from Rod, one asking me to phone him back; the other says it's OK now, they've taken Grant to hospital and got him stitched as I hadn't returned their call. They have now made an emergency appointment with a Dr Biggar. Rod sounds unsure about that, so I might phone him back. Might.

Then an email from a Matilda McQueen saying that she got hold of my email address and could I have a look at the attachment. I am not good with the phone screen so I open the laptop and start it up. The internet is buzzing with pictures of the last minutes of Lorna's life as she dives through the night air, caught on the CCTV from the web cam. I close that down, thinking of her dad and his tears. I hope he never sees these pictures.

Once the email has connected I open Matilda's attachment and a picture of a dog appears, a big dog. I look at the name. Ovcharka. I have not heard of them before. Russian guard dogs of some kind? Matilda's question is simple: have I come into contact with a dog like this or one that looks a bit like it?

The answer is no, I don't think I could ever have come across one of them and forgotten about it. The one in the photograph must weigh about ten stone at least. The handler is just visible at the side of the picture and the dog's head is above the height of her waist. It's a friendly-looking creature, half dog, half shag-pile carpet. I type the name into Google and select images. The pictures spread in front of me tell a different story. The sight of an Ovcharka in full attack mode is terrifying. With a powerful head and huge teeth, the weight of that body behind any attack would make it a formidable weapon.

I flick back and go through a few pages of breed charac-teristics. They all say much the same: a good guard dog in the right hands, dangerous in the wrong hands. There is a YouTube clip of the dogs in action, guarding a flock of sheep. A wolf comes too close and pays with its life. The attack of the dogs is short, powerful and deadly, not a fight so much as a mission to kill. The thought does not comfort me. I have a quick look at the websites of the two British breeders who have the kennel names Pasternak and Siberian. There's a bit of intermingling between the two. I save the numbers of both of them in my phone, just in case.

I email Matilda back. No, I have not seen one, don't know anyone who has one. Sorry. I close the laptop, wondering what has led Matilda to that point, doubting that she got that from one dog hair – can they tell the breed by looking at a single hair under a microscope or do they need a root bulb for DNA? Maybe dogs are different to humans in that way. And what is the investigating team thinking? If that hair didn't come from me then it must have been on Lorna. Did it come from the dog that had brought her down? But even as I think that through it does not make sense. Lorna had been clean when she hit the bonnet of that car so the hair must have been caught in her matted hair. But it makes no difference if we can't find the dog. I look at the TV news: a fourteen-year-old boy has admitted killing his classmate, the Rover Probe is doing exciting things on Mars. There is a YouTube clip of a flash mob at Waverley Station in Edinburgh, doing the Time Warp from the *Rocky Horror Show*. It caused some disruption and the commuter slaves were not amused. There is more about the weather; it's going to rain again. Amber warning for floods and high winds, so the cattle are right. The Rest and Be Thankful is going to be closed for a few more hours after another minor landslide. I wondered if that is true or if there's more investigation going on up there and they want the area clear.

Two minutes later Rod phones with yet another non-update and asks if I know Dr Biggar. Grant has cut his knee open to 'let the pain out'. I don't comment about that and tell him another body has been found instead. They've already heard; a neighbour told my mother, who drank a bottle of gin and went to her bed. He then tells me that the Lorna incident has sparked renewed interest in Sophie, more photographs are now coming in from mobiles and all sorts. Everybody who knew Sophie is trying to help, he is almost pleading. I say I'm going to drive down to speak to a DCI today.

'That's great, Elvie, you can move this thing on.'

'So can you put all the pictures we have of Sophie on a disk, all of the ones that people have put on the website, no matter who they're from? Then can you email the file to me? Maybe there's a connection that we're missing.'

'Yes, of course, Elvie.' He is his usual helpful, unflappable self. He tells me his cholesterol level is getting better, he asks how I am doing.

I say I am fine.

He tells me to keep smiling even though he knows I rarely smile.

While it is in my mind I also text Belinda to make sure she forwards me the photographs she has of Sophie, all of them. I want to show Jack O'Hare, Grandpa Cop and Costello that I am making an effort and I want to bring something to the table. Costello appears to be a sheep and easy to handle, but if DCI Anderson has the respect of 'Jack', then I presume that Anderson is sharp. He might be too sharp; I need to prove to them that I am on board. Just in a different boat.

Once I have picked up the Polo I drive to Partickhill and park, watching the exchange in front of me; one life for another. A blond man stands with two children, one a dark-haired girl in her early teens and the other a blond boy. There is not much of a gap in years but they're a world apart in maturity. The girl hurries to the other car before she gets cold while the boy stays close to his dad. The door of the car behind opens and the dad bends to have a few friendly words with the red-haired woman in the driver's seat. They seem hesitant to say goodbye as if there is a lot more to be said. Dad slaps his hands on the roof, steps back and signals that there is a break in the traffic so the redhead can pull out. He waves at them as they go, rubbing the finger where a wedding ring has been until recently. I see the boy in the front seat of the car now devoting all his attention to the small brown dog trying to climb out the gap

at the top of the window. This is a marriage that has gone
wrong, yet nobody knows why.

Billy's Vectra pulls into the gap. He does not move so I
stay in place; Billy wants to play this his way.

The dad then jogs across the street in front of me, his beige
raincoat flapping over his arm. He is wearing a suit but does
not wear it well, in fact he looks like shit, like a man who is
disappointed to find a few more grey hairs among the blond
every morning, a few more wrinkles. I am trying to read his
body language as he approaches the blonde female who is
carrying two cardboard cups. Her hair is neater, she has on a
short nylon coat, but as she turns I see it is Costello the sheep.
Her smile is cursory but she hands him his drink and when
she starts talking, it is a constant stream. He pays attention to
what she says, neither agreeing nor disagreeing with her. This
is merely a transfer of information on a street corner. I notice
she is wearing flat black boots, her black trousers are functional
and sensible. Despite his scruffiness, the man still looks more
polished than her. He still feels the need to make an impression;
she doesn't care.

I look over at Billy's Vectra, thinking that this is getting
farcical. If he wants us to talk to them then why does he not
get out and say what he has to say? I drop my window to listen
just as he gets out of his car and walks past mine to approach
them. I begin to wonder how important they are to us. To have
known they would be here suggests that Billy knows their
routine. As he walks closer I get a better idea of Costello; she
is smaller than me, thinner, a less substantial human being
altogether. In unison they turn to look at Billy; I can see them
both full on. He is pleasant faced but tired. She looks tough,
hard lines on her face as if her recent lack of sleep has not
been recouped.

She catches sight of Billy wandering up looking like a jakey
on the scrounge for extra change. Her recognition is instant,
and wary. Billy continues his slow swagger and Costello sips
from her cup. They stand together in silence as they watch
Billy's approach.

I open my window further to hear the exchange.

'It's DI Colin Anderson, isn't it?'

'DCI,' he says, not friendly. 'So what brings you back from the dead?'

'You. You not doing your job properly.' He is taking lessons from me on the subtle art of making friends, then. 'Uneasy is the head that wears the crown and all that crap.' Billy stands beside them and smiles. They look at him like they have been kissed by a leper.

'Billy the fox Hopkirk,' says Costello, her voice showing some disbelief. Then she adds, with more wonderment, 'Sober!'

'Just for a minute there, I thought the years might have softened you, sweet cheeks. Anyway,' he rubs his hands together, addressing Anderson, 'glad you could both make it, there's someone I want you to meet. Costello has already had that displeasure.'

I get out the car and walk over to join them. Costello tries a weak smile but it fails.

Anderson keeps his eyes on Billy while sipping his coffee. 'Ex-DCI Hopkirk, what are you doing here?'

'I am a concerned citizen. I come with evidence.' Billy has put his hand on his chest and suddenly sounds like an asthmatic Spartacus. 'I bring you the witness who has found two of the bodies.' He points at me, and a look passes between the two cops.

'Elvira McCulloch, the one I was telling you about,' says Costello, smugly.

'Well, you wanted to speak to her. So are you going to keep us standing here until it rains or ask us in?' says Billy, cheerfully.

'Please come in, Miss McCulloch,' says Costello, looking at me like a cat regarding a full litter tray.

'Call her Elvie,' says Billy, as Costello and I wait to see who blinks first.

'I think we all need to have a wee chat,' says Costello, in a low growl with a hint of a threat as she stands aside, suggesting we should follow her into the station. 'I've been reading about you and the coincidences that follow you about.'

Billy smiles at her. 'You always were a smart cookie,

Costello, mouthy but smart. Whenever there's one coincidence too many, chances are it ain't coincidence. More like the link you're looking for. So wake up and smell the toast as they say.'

The cops both ignore him. 'If you have no objection I'd like to go through your statement with you.' Costello's gaze has not wavered. Her eyes are remarkable, a light grey flecked with dark; they are cold, suspicious eyes. I wonder how bad the world is when she looks through them. More wolf than sheep, then.

'Fine,' I say.

'She'll be very co-operative,' says Billy, and slaps me on the back, forgetting his sore wrist. He swears. 'I'll come with her 'cause she doesn't say too much.'

'Probably can't get a word in.' Costello eyes me warily as we enter a small reception area, there are a few nods back and forth. Anderson goes forward to punch in a number on a door keypad. The glass partition flies open.

'DCI Anderson? Parcel for you.'

'Me?'

'Yip. Your name on it. Looks like some computer thing you ordered.'

A small box the size of a shoebox is passed through. Anderson takes it and taps out his number again on the keypad, the inner door buzzes open. Costello follows him and Billy pushes me through before they think better of it. On the other side there is calm, the air scented with fresh emulsion.

'I didn't order anything, did I?' Anderson reads the name on the label. 'East Tech? Who are they?'

'Are they the guys who put the system in? Have you asked for something?' Costello asks, guiding us along a corridor of endless doors.

'Not that I know of. I've been complaining about the whole set-up, though.' Then he stops short. The box balanced in his hand, he turns it. Dull light thud, rattle, dull thud. 'You got any gloves on you?'

'Yeah,' Costello answers, her voice full of suspicion.

'If it starts ticking, RLF.'

'Run like fuck,' explains Billy to me as we watch Costello pull on some purple gloves while still walking. She must keep them in her jacket pocket.

Anderson nods his head towards a door with MI3 on it. 'In here.'

This room also smells of paint, gloss this time with overtones of newly sawn wood. One large table, twelve seats, four computers, empty in trays, empty out trays, one wall is a huge whiteboard. Immaculate.

Anderson places the box on the table and puts out a hand for the gloves, pulling them on with a loud smack, peering at the box closely all the time.

Costello is making non-committal noises as she picks at the brown tape with her fingernails, pulling it off carefully and opening up the flaps to reveal a polythene wrapped cover. Underneath is a sheet of bubble wrap round a small box.

Anderson's face hardens. He sits down. Costello follows suit. So does Billy. I stay standing, watching over her shoulder. 'What is it?'

'Pass me those scissors, will you?'

Anderson cuts through the bubble wrap, opens it up and then breathes out very slowly. 'Interesting,' he says. He pushes the box across for Costello and me to see.

'What is it?' Costello repeats, peering in as she opens up the bubble wrap and lifts out a small black box.

'Is that a gift from your lady friend, Colin? Or is she giving it back?' asks Billy.

Costello ignores him and holds the box out to Anderson. 'Want me to open it?'

'Go on.'

Costello's gloved fingers open the box; a small gold ankh lies on a black velvet cushion. She swivels the box to show him. 'Any ideas?'

'That was Sophie's.'

The words are out of my mouth before I'm aware I have spoken. The pain that goes through me is physical. This does not make sense.

I am already reaching into my back pocket for my wallet when Billy says, 'Are you sure?' It was just conversational, he doesn't doubt me. I pull out the small picture of Sophie from the credit card pocket and place it on the table. Hanging round her neck is the silver locket from our granny and the gold ankh.

Costello gets up and leaves the room, returning with the media photograph of Sophie. Anderson is now fingering the ankh gently.

'It will be engraved, the date of her graduation,' I tell him. 'Eighth of July, 2010. It says round the top, *All lawyers were children once.* Her take on the Charles Lamb quote.'

'It matches.'

'It matches this as well, the unusual style.' Costello compares it to the picture. The two detectives share a few seconds' silence, then she turns to me. 'Are you OK?'

'What does this mean?'

She ignores me. 'We need you to talk us through it. Might take a wee while.'

'So does this make a difference, I mean, will you look for Sophie now? After this, Lorna, the girl on the hill?'

'I have checked, Miss McCulloch, protocol has been followed fully so far.' She looks at Anderson. 'I'm sorry, she was not a priority.'

'Not for you she wasn't.'

'Look, as I am sure Avril explained to you, the evidence pointed to the fact that she had run off with her lover. She is over eighteen. That is not something I can take to my boss and ask to work it as a case. Most people in that situation won't thank you for finding them. And tracking them down is not my job, I have better things to do.'

The most awful thing about her is her honesty.

'You do not have better things to do than this.' My words are chilling.

Costello takes a deep breath. I think I know now how to press her buttons. She concedes. 'But this new evidence might allow us to get it moving, it gives us something to argue the case.' Her eyes lock with mine; the steely grey matches her character.

Billy has a coughing fit and we both turn to make sure he survives it. 'Yeah. But we've got much further than you would ever have got, so put your sensible head on, petal, and think about the evidence we might be able to give you.' He raises his eyebrows, making sure that she gets the point he is making. 'Jesus, Costello, you're getting nowhere with this case. You have two dead bodies now and another two women who might be imprisoned somewhere going through God knows what. Major Case needs to think again, and you need to think a bit smarter.'

Something passes between them, I can't quite identify what. Has he just dangled a carrot for her? A promotion?

'You're too savvy to let this pass, petal.' Again he raises the eyebrows, the sprouting grey caterpillars do a little dance.

She flashes him a little nip of a smile. 'You have no idea how often I have heard that – usually just before I get handed the shitty end of the stick.'

Billy throws her a look, something approaching affection. They have a history. 'At least you know I'm full of shite.'

'I know that more than most.'

'Costello, petal, would I lie to you?'

'Call me petal again, and I'll staple your dick to the table.'

'We'll get this examined. Are you sure she had the ankh on when she went missing?' asks Costello, writing out a series of labels, the same info again and again. She does not look at my face.

'I'm not sure,' I say. But I am sure. My memory is excellent. The ankh was in its box in her bedroom the day after Sophie went missing. It has been there each time I've looked since. Or have I only seen the box and presumed?

'You – not sure about something?' Billy's voice is incredulous. 'You're as sure as death and taxes.'

'She always wore the locket. Sometimes she wore the ankh as well, sometimes not.'

Costello checks the picture again, both the silver locket and the gold ankh are there round her neck, hanging on different chains. She gets up and takes the ankh with her, returning with a pad and a pen.

Billy makes a humming noise, his brain is grinding away. 'It said in the paper on Sunday that Anderson was the senior investigating officer in Lorna's case. Maybe that's why it was sent to him. The question is: why was it sent at all?'

'DCI Anderson is my superior but I am the SIO,' Costello bristles.

'Oh, you haven't been in charge of a murder squad before, this started off a missing person.' Billy's voice is brutal. 'You identified the other body yet? The girl on the hill? Costello, you stand firm because there are too many similarities between them, and if you want me to go and threaten the Chief Constable for you, I will. I've nothing to lose. These girls do. Now is the time to hold your nerve, petal . . . hen.'

Costello's grey eyes flicker over the picture of my sister. 'OK, Elvie, tell me what happened. Right from the start.'

Billy interrupts. 'There are no free tickets, no free ride, Elvie is a bit . . .' He taps the side of his head. 'Why not play her to your advantage? She's an interested member of the public with more than a bit of savvy. She can go places that you can't.'

'True. But that is not the kind of deal we make, you know that, Billy.'

He smiles to himself. 'Well, there is a price for our information.'

'I don't deal.' Costello taps her pen on the pad, annoyed. 'As far as I know, she might be the number one suspect. She does seem to know where the bodies are buried.'

I search her face for a hint of humour and fail to find any. She has the good grace to look away.

'But she could be the link you're looking for. Which is why I'm keeping my eye on her,' adds Billy, rattling out another lungful of phlegm.

'God, I bet she sleeps easier in her bed knowing that,' says Costello with some warmth in her sarcasm.

'She can look after herself,' he whispers.

A smile flits across Costello's face, like sunshine in ice. 'So, Elvie, talk me through it. Right from the start.'

'It was a Thursday night, I was at my flat in Glasgow.'

Costello stops me to confirm the address.

'Rod phoned me at the flat at about half ten that night. I had been reviewing a case study on a patient who had been self-prescribing antibiotics off the internet, a drug called Amoxicillin. I was to present it the following day. He said Sophie hadn't come back from her run.' I recall my thoughts as he told me, *So she's done it, she's gone.* At the time I thought, *Well done you.* 'Then Rod started listing all the folk he had phoned. Olivia, her friend, Belinda at Boadicea . . .'

'This Boadicea – Sophie did their legal work?'

'Yes, Rod spoke to them and was then going through the list of pals that had been at her birthday party.'

'That was the previous Saturday?'

I nod. 'Nobody knew where she was. But why would they – she'd gone out for a run. It was illogical to call them.'

'Was it like her to go away overnight and not tell anybody?' asks Costello. She's thinking about that overnight bag.

I feel Billy watch me as I answer. 'No, not at all. One of the rules of living under Mum's roof – always tell her where you are.' I return Billy's stare, there's a smile playing round his dry, cracked lips. 'The next morning she still wasn't home. Something happened to her.'

'Or she ran off with Mark,' mutters Costello. 'The overnight bag.'

I ignore her. 'I'll show you all the photographs that were taken at her birthday. We've already been through all the ones on the Facebook page and they got us nowhere.'

'OK, but let's get back to you on that night. So you leave the Glasgow flat and drive home to Eaglesham?'

'Yes, Mum's house, Sophie's house.' I explain it all to her, as I had explained to Billy, and he nods along as if it is now his story as well as mine. After a few minutes I pause a little. 'I knew that something had happened.'

'Why did she still stay at home, a successful young woman like her?'

'She wanted to be at home.'

'Why?'

I shrug. 'I found the house claustrophobic since Dad died. But Sophie and Mum were like peas in a pod.'

Costello nodded. 'But then your mum moved her boyfriend in. How did Sophie feel about that?'

I avoid looking at Billy; these cops have minds that think

alike. 'Mum was happy, so Sophie was happy,' I say gingerly. 'Rod was good for Grant, a father figure and all that.'

She is still staring at me; she has not got the answer she wanted.

'You knew Rod before?' prompts Billy.

'Of course – he taught PE at the school where Dad was head. He was a bit like an uncle to us, his wife died years ago. Rod, Grant and Dad all golfed together on a Saturday, they were out together when Dad died, heart attack, seventeenth hole. Dad was lifting Grant's bag when he collapsed. Rod couldn't resus him. I'm not sure who blames who.'

'I'm sorry, Elvie,' says Costello.

'Why?'

'Just losing your dad.'

'You knew him?'

'No, I just . . .'

'Go on, Elvie, about Grant?' Billy prompts again.

'It's complicated, he has a bad knee. Osgood-Schlatter's. Basically he has to be careful with his knee until he's fully grown. But he keeps reinjuring it. Then he blames everybody else. He got knocked back for his dream scholarship, unfit.'

Costello thinks about that. 'So did that lead to any problems between Grant and Rod?'

'No, they're close.'

'So you get to Eaglesham and you go out to look for your sister. Where was Grant?'

'Grant had been out looking for her, he came back as I arrived. He was filthy, he'd been running around. He was washing himself at the sink when I went out in my car.' It takes a few more minutes to tell her the story of me finding the car at the dam. As I recall it in my mind's eye a shiver passes through me.

'So neither you, your brother nor the police found any evidence that she had come to harm?'

'Except Sophie wasn't there. People don't just disappear,' I said.

'They can if they want to,' said Costello, her eyes flinty again. She looks at Billy for back up.

She's not going to get it.

He folds his arms. 'I was a cop for many years, you get that feeling in your bones. As one incident everything that you say makes sense, but if you look at Lorna, at Gillian, the pattern . . .'

For a minute there is a strange feeling in the room, like someone has died and nobody knows where to look.

'So where is Sophie? A high maintenance girl hiding somewhere she doesn't need money? It's not easy to stay hidden, Costello, you know that. So yes, think about Gillian and Lorna, three women who went out running. Think about the remains of the girl you haven't identified yet. Sophie McCulloch was abducted when she was running around that dam. You know that, deep in your bones.'

'I know deep in my bones that we have a young, intelligent woman who was having an affair. Gillian and Lorna had been in the papers, so maybe that gave her the MO for the perfect way out. She engineered her disappearance in a way that would put her family off the scent. She doesn't want to be found.'

She is so close to the truth I can't look at her as she speaks.

'She ran off with Mark. Mark's wife hasn't reported him missing, you know. She's glad to be free of the bugger.'

'That's a bit of a stretch, Costello. Not exactly a hanging offence, is it, running off with a married man? Why go to all that bother?' argues Billy.

'Because Nancy McCulloch needs to live the perfect life. The model who married the headmaster and had three children: the medic, the lawyer, the professional sportsman. Does she want her daughter running off with a wife-battering working-class ned?'

She glances at me to see if I am offended.

'She did not run off with Mark Laidlaw.' I defy them to contradict me.

Half an hour later Billy and I are sitting in the weak sunshine outside Tony Macaroni's on Byres Road, watching the traffic. He's having a latte and a cigarette and I'm warming my hands on an espresso, thinking about that little ankh and what it might mean. No mementos of any of the other girls had been sent back. But Billy still likes his theory that someone has read that Anderson is now heading the enquiry into the two bodies and the abductor now has a name to send the ankh to. The obvious conclusion is that the abductor is saying, *I have Sophie too.* Costello agrees with the theory and I'm now starting to doubt myself about the ankh ever being there. If my memory is right and I did see it there then the only obvious conclusion is that somebody in the house sent it. So I must be wrong.

Billy, however, is following my train of thought a bit too closely. He pulls a face, dropping his head so that I have to look at him. He regards me with a stare that could burn out the sun; I get that feeling again that nobody would have lasted long under his interrogation.

'Elvie, I haven't known you long but I know you well enough to understand that you have a strange kind of brain, you miss every nuance in conversation. You have to look to see if you upset people, you stare people down constantly.'

'No, I don't,' I said, knowing that I do.

'But you have a very good memory. You changed your story in there. I am trained to spot a lie. You did see that ankh in the drawer. She wasn't wearing it when she went missing, was she?'

I stare him down, and he points a finger at me like he has caught me out. 'Did you send it?'

I say nothing.

'So you didn't. If the ankh was still in that house then someone there sent it.'

Billy takes a few long puffs of his cigarette, thinking. He is looking up the street as if he is waiting for a bus. 'People have many reasons to lie, Elvie. I don't doubt that you have the best of intentions, but you should ask yourself if keeping secrets from me is the best thing for Sophie.'

'I'm not keeping secrets from you.' Not only from you.

A young man walks past, dressed in paint splattered denims. He is carrying a bag of chips, a newspaper folded under his arms. The headline reads something about the Night Hunter; The Victim. There was the webcam picture of Lorna falling, captured in free fall, her limbs spiralling, trying to grab the night air.

'Great,' says Billy, and sighs and turns to look at me. 'Look, I am the best detective not on this case,' he smiles softly. I think that his instinct is telling him he is treading on difficult ground here. As an interview technique it is working, he has excellent skills in reading people. I should learn from him. I want to release myself from the burden that Sophie has put me under. This nightmare will not end; Sophie said what she said but that was in a different space and time, and the past is another country. Maybe the best thing I can do for Sophie is tell the truth. If Gillian is where Sophie is then surely I owe it to them. If not, then Sophie is just muddying the water.

Billy lights another cigarette. He appears almost uninterested as he says, 'You do need to trust me.' He slowly puts his arm round me. Anybody watching would think he was straightening my jacket on the back of the chair, but it is the closest to a cuddle that I can remember.

Half an hour later he is following me into the depths of the Goblin Market. On the way over in the car I told him the story of the two sisters in the poem, Lizzie and Laura. I think he gets what I am trying to say. There was one sister who wanted everything out of life, and the other sister who had to stand back and pick up the pieces. There had been promises made and promises broken, but the sisters stayed together.

When we reach the bottom of the garden, we are alone. The lily with its huge plate leaves lying on the pond is still here. Billy is wandering around looking up at the steep walls above us, gazing at the flowers. It is a beautiful day down here, as if the sunshine has been trapped. Dappled daylight plays on tapestry wings of the butterflies, neon flashes shoot across the water to land on the leaves, tracking the iridescent bodies of dragonflies.

For a moment it is deathly quiet. A shiver runs through me; this could be a dangerous place. I am alone with Billy, but there is no danger here. I know I could kill him as easy as I could snap a twig.

'I'm thinking about the brothers Grimm, that story where the wee lassie gets her feet cut off so she can get rid of her shoes. I bet that was written in a place like this. Bloody creepy.'

I sit down now on the bench seat, exactly where I had sat before. I try not to imagine evil little goblin eyes watching me, bony little goblin hands pulling the ferns aside, knowing where Sophie is but not telling me.

Billy sits down on the bench beside me. 'So did Sophie go of her own free will?'

My heart misses a beat but the word trips out of my mouth. 'Yes.'

'Fuck!' He exhales loudly and looks up to the sky.

'But she was going to meet me back here, last Thursday midnight . . .' I can hardly bring myself to say it, but Billy says it for me.

'She never turned up, did she?'

'Soph was adamant that she wanted nobody but me to know. It was our secret.'

'Why? Why would she do that, causing all this pain? If it was because of Mark, she'd just say, *I've met a bloke, he's married, I'm going to shack up with him, like it or lump it.*' He thinks for a minute. 'So she thought about it very carefully and decided she had no option but to get away. So who was she running from?'

I have no answer.

He closes his eyes and rubs them with the palm of his hands, making them redder than ever. He changes tack. 'If you knew Sophie was coming back, why did you need to defer from uni?'

I ignore the question. 'We need to find Sophie.'

'You are very focused, very black and white.'

'That has been said before. Sophie was in glorious Technicolor and I was in black and white. I see things with clarity. We need to find her.'

'You put a lot of trust in each other.'

'You need to understand the debt I owe her; she gave me my life. She noticed that I don't see the world as other people do. She was always three steps in front of me, giving me lessons, showing me the way. She taught me it as a scientific exercise, she was specific.'

'So what's up with you?'

'Do I have a label, you mean? How about Autistic? Asperger's? They have labels for low achievers and high achievers, mediocre achievers. One day it might pop into someone's head that we are a variation of the norm. We are different. We have always walked among you but now we get noticed and labelled and told that we need *help*. It used to make my dad's blood boil.'

'That's the bloody Gettysburg address for someone with communication issues. But you've been like that all your life. Not held you back any, has it? It was something else that made you defer uni for a year.'

I ignore him again. 'We need to find Sophie. And Gillian.'

'And to do that I'll be the judge of what is relevant. The rules of your strange wee life do not apply here.' He stares at me. 'It's not all about you.'

This is a big decision. One I have already made. 'It was March the twenty-first, a Wednesday. She phoned me at the hospital. She sounded frightened. It was the same way she sounded when she told me Dad had died. I thought something might have happened to Mum. But then she said she couldn't go home and had lost her keys to my flat. I was busy, but I told her where I kept the spare.'

Billy nods but says nothing.

'I didn't think anything more about it. I just thought I would go home and she'd be sitting watching the TV, drinking a bottle of wine and dozing on the settee. It was about three in the morning when I got back. A patient with end stage cancer had come in. He died within an hour of being admitted. I watched him die, the physiological process of life was coming to an end. That's all. I had to experience it.'

'The fact that you were there, that's all that matters. And Sophie?'

'As soon as I opened the door of the flat I knew there was something wrong. The flat smelled wrong, it sounded wrong. The only noise was the bath running. She didn't hear me when I came in. The lights were not on, she was sitting in the bath, fully clothed.' I paused for a minute.

'And?' The *fully clothed* meant something to him.

'The bathwater was pink, really nice shades of pink. Like the petals of a flower, red in the middle, fading to pink, and the folds of her skirt were billowing up in the water.'

'Had Sophie been attacked?'

'Yes.'

'Raped?'

'I don't know.'

'Fuck!'

'She was bleeding. She wouldn't talk. Silent. Wanting to be alone. Not wanting to go back home. She wouldn't answer any questions. She just sat in the bath, filling it, emptying it, filling it again. I didn't know what to do.'

'So what did you do?'

'I handed her a pink dressing gown. I went back to the hospital.'

'Christ! And after that, how was she?'

'Haunted.' It strikes me that he does not ask if I know who did it. 'She kept out of my way. Then she asked me to come here. I thought she was going to tell me what it was all about, but instead she told me she needed to get away. But she promised to meet me here on the last day of May, at midnight.'

'She didn't turn up.' Billy is quiet again.

I see the row of weights in my mum's kitchen, Mark Laidlaw raising his hands to me. I'm not easily scared, but I was scared of him.

Billy's chain of thought echoes mine.

'If you think Mark Laidlaw raped her then we need to tell Costello. We have no complaining victim so it's not easy. When these girls were taken, where was he? Has been been . . .?' He pauses, looking at me. 'But you've already thought this through.' Then he says, 'But you're not thinking that Mark has abducted her . . . because . . . because your logical mind is telling you something else. Because you know for a fact that Mark and she are not together, don't you?'

'There was a sighting of Mark, on the eleventh of April, on CCTV.'

Billy rolls his head round until his neck cracks. 'Means nothing, Elvie.'

'I know he doesn't have her because he came looking for

her, and he wouldn't have come looking if he knew where she was, would he? But I didn't tell him anything; she was running to get away from him. I scared him off.'

'I've no doubt you did. But maybe she ran into somebody much worse.'

After stopping to restock Billy with fags we get to the site office of Parnell's Glasgow builders' yard, which is little more than a glorified Portakabin. We are supposed to pick up Charlie and take him up the road to Ardno. It's going on for five and the yard is busy. I'm sitting at a desk near the window with Charlie on my knee, looking across the yard. Charlie's drawing the tractors, the back actors, the fences, the dogs beyond. These are Alsatian guard dogs ready to go out on night patrol at the building sites, sites that are now a treasure trove of all kinds of scrap metal, bricks and unmixed concrete. All valuable on the post-credit crunch black market. Two German Shepherd dogs are pacing the fence; their constant movement is hypnotic. I wonder if there might be a register of guard dog breeders that might know about those Russian dogs.

Mary is looking pale. The ball went on to three in the morning and she hasn't yet recovered. As the wife of one of the main sponsors, she had worn the most expensive dress, and she spent all night being looked at and hating every minute of it.

They had got a last-minute babysitting service to look after Charlie, as my assistance was 'needed in a murder enquiry', as Billy put it. Seemingly Parnell had initially refused but Billy had gone into negotiation mode. Parnell had melted in the spirit of public service once Grandpa Cop had phoned him from Argyll, telling him the same story that Billy had. Except that his was official.

Alex Parnell and Billy are now talking like old friends. They have found some colleagues in common, old cops who now work for Parnell's security company. Once they start on football they are blood brothers. They both support Rangers, they are men in mourning. Mary is sitting on the edge of a table that carries a model of something not yet built. She is not listening but looking out the far window, her mind miles away.

'Are you OK with that, babe?' asks Parnell.

Mary jumps at the sound of his voice.

'I was saying that we need to let Elvie help out as much as she can. You can cancel all your arrangements and take care of Charlie, can't you?'

I wonder what arrangements she could possibly have.

Mary looks terrified for a minute.

I say immediately but as casually as I can, 'We can work it, Mary, don't worry . . .'

'No, she'll be fine,' Parnell snaps.

'Whatever. I'm not happy that there might be some weirdo wandering around Argyll flinging young women out of cars. Anything Elvie can do to help, we have to let her.'

Billy picks up on her discomfort. 'The cops don't need her twenty-four seven, Mr Parnell. And I think you might be happier knowing that Elvie is up at Ardno with Mary. I don't think Mary should be alone in that big house.'

Mary smiles at him; it's a smile of cracked china.

'I don't think she should be left alone, full stop. Buying a dress that shows every bruise she got when she walked into the swing. That whopper on her leg. Every time she stepped forward, instead of flashing a nice bit of thigh she looked like she'd gone five rounds with a kick boxer. Bloody embarrassing.'

Billy glances subtly at me and then Mary; he knows.

Mary ignores her husband and keeps her eyes on some builders tramping the mud in filthy boots and high-vis jackets. They are messing around, joking. One is whistling 'It's Now or Never', very badly. She has that distant wistful look on her face. I think she's in more pain than she is admitting. Then a faint smile, brief and flitting, appears on her face, like a flash of sunshine on an overcast day. She is recalling some happy thought that is at the edge of her memory. Her smile is there and gone in an instant.

'Was that your fault, you monkey?' I jiggle Charlie on my knees, and his pen scribbles on the paper. 'Were you going too high on the swing? I've banged into that pole more than once, when he does that,' I say, adding credence to his story.

'Did you break the swing?' asks Billy.

I flick him two fingers from behind Charlie's head.

Parnell closes the paperwork on his desk. 'And now there's another girl, isn't there? Do they know who she is yet?'

'We'll find out who she is, don't you worry about that,' says Billy. It sounds mildly like a threat.

WEDNESDAY, 6 JUNE

The hands of the clock show it is quarter past six. I look again, thinking that I have slept well, then realize it is half past three and I am wide awake. The bedroom at Ardno is too warm, even with all the windows open. I listen to the noises outside: the odd bark of a fox, the rustle of faraway trees. Rod phoned last night with his usual update of 'sightings' and the useless chit-chat from the Find Sophie Facebook page. He did have a contact for me to 'follow up', as he put it. I told him to tell Avril, but he said that the woman had already been to the police and they had been polite but dismissive about the report of the dog. I went into scan mode when he told me that Mum had a wee fall in the bathroom but had not broken anything, then that Grant had got very drunk in the Eaglesham Arms and the barman had got punched. The police were called and Rod explained they were getting help for the boy. He asked what I thought. I muttered something about we all had our crosses to bear and my brother should man up. Rod said I was a tad unhelpful at times. I asked for more details about the woman on Facebook.

When I wake I'm still thinking about Rod and what Billy had said. Our lives all turned for the worse when Dad died. All the blame going in circles, like Eric's perpetual motion machine. But Rod? Rod had been my dad's best pal, and my dad was no fool. My mum, on the other hand, is an idiot. The one thing that troubles me is that Sophie did not want to come home. It had taken her nearly two weeks to make the decision to run, a long time for a decision but a nanosecond to plan a new life. Soph was very susceptible to Mum's plaintive cries about needing her family around her; she couldn't have stood up to the barrage of emotional blackmail if she'd said she was going. I thought of Sophie, lying in her bath of blood, in pieces – whatever it was, she'd felt she couldn't say anything to anybody.

But 'home' has nothing to do with Mark Laidlaw. And has everything to do with Rod. Deep down I know that ankh was in the drawer. Have I got this wrong? Everything had been black and white. It was all timed and precise, logical. Now I am dancing on quicksand.

I recall the meeting I had on that Wednesday at the uni. The meeting itself had gone as well as I expected. My sister was missing. The uni gave me a deferment for a year due to my excellent academic ability. My tutor said that it was early days yet and I could rejoin in the following October – that gave me about sixteen months. As he said those words we both knew that he was talking about more than Sophie. He was talking about my health and the fact that the medication was not working. Of course it wasn't, I wasn't taking it.

That was the day I left the uni building and walked down to Byres Road, to the car park where I'd left the Polo. I knew there was someone walking behind me; I could smell the sweet, piney aftershave. That was the eleventh, six days after Sophie went out running. Even now, I can recall the conversation word for word. He asked me where Sophie was then immediately said that I was nothing like her. He was that stupid, stating the obvious. I told him I didn't know where she was. Even if I did, he would be the last person I would tell. He then assured me that she would be in touch. He gave me his mobile number, thrust it into my hand. I looked down and noticed that the fingers curled around mine were bruised at the knuckles. He was a powerful man and I guessed that he had probably hit someone recently, and that someone was female.

That conversation was public. He had already been seen on the CCTV standing at the corner of Byres Road and University Avenue. The lights there take ages to change. If Costello or Anderson look at the next camera, the one that covers the car park, they will see me talking to him for a few minutes. I am easy to spot on camera, dressed all in black, looking like a bad tranny.

The foxes are calling to each other outside my window, weird noises like goblins having a party.

When *did* Lizzie become Laura's keeper?

When did Elvie become Sophie's keeper?

It has always been that way. At school, I could sense trouble and I sensed it one day when Soph walked past me to go to the loo. She gave me a funny look, and three other girls followed her. By the time I got in there, they were dragging her across the tiled floor by her hair. One of them, one with stupid make-up, started moving towards me. So I decked her and she hit the tiles. The other one stepped over to have a go at me but thought better of it and knelt down beside her pal, stroking her on the back as blood and snot ran down her face. The third one, the brains of the outfit, stepped back. Sophie, red-eyed, got unsteadily to her feet and I frog-marched her out of the loos.

Now I realize that moment established the pattern of our lives.

I turn in my bed and try to surrender to sleep. It is not easy. I see Sophie in my dreams. She is trying to get out of the bath, but I'm holding her down, holding her under the red, red water.

I wake up. For the first time, I think of her as dead.

The satnav on Billy's phone takes us on a long tour of Bearsden. Once we know we're in the street where Anita Parke lives with her husband and two kids, we get out and walk. This is four-by-four and golf club country, high hedges and very neat lawns. The people who live here could spend all morning reading the broadsheet Sunday papers without getting them in a fankle.

'This is it.' I point at an ivy-clad house. An old but immaculate BMW sits on the drive.

'Hang on a mo . . .' Billy is looking in a skip that is parked in the street.

'Surprised they allow that here.'

'Probably rent it out to some immigrants. I want a look through, you get great stuff in skips in posh places.'

He has a rake through, showing me a Debenham's carrier bag, but I am looking at the old detached villa with ivy veining over the walls. The house next door is a carbon copy, but with less foliage, and the front garden bears scars of works vans, two piles of chips blocking the drive.

He opens the bag and has a good look. 'Two Alistair MacLeans and three Catherine Cooksons!'

'Bit advanced for you, no pictures.'

The Cooksons are discarded to lie back among the bits of broken cistern and soggy wallpaper. He hums as he makes his way up the garden path. 'Great book, *The Satan Bug*. Did you know that MacLean . . .'

I ring the doorbell, cutting him off in mid-sentence.

'Detective Inspector Hopkirk? Please come in.'

Billy corrects the woman so quietly that a bat with a hearing aid would have had trouble hearing him. 'Thank you, Mrs Parke, it's about that message you left on the Find Sophie Facebook page.'

'Yes, do come in. You'll want to speak to Neil.' She shouts up the stairs while pointing us in the direction of the sitting room. I climb over the two bikes that are leaning against the wall in the hall, noticing the tray full of muddy shoes on the carpet. Including Nike running shoes.

A teenage boy with shoulder-length hair enters the room, closely followed by a fit black spaniel. The boy folds himself into a leather easy chair and his mum sits on the arm beside him as the spaniel does a round of tail-wagging and nose-poking.

The boy glances at Billy, rotating his wrist in a gesture of casual nervousness; the rubber band on his wrist shows his support for ending world poverty. Forgetting her son is a teenager, his mother pats his knee subtly. Being a teenager, the boy grunts and recoils.

The woman smiles. They are very alike, both slim, both dark-haired, both with big brown eyes and thick arched brows. Both carry themselves with an inner confidence, strong and straight.

'Mrs Parke, we don't really want to waste your time but we contacted you because we need to have a wee chat with Neil about the night of the twenty-ninth of March. It was a Thursday.'

'You know that we've been down to the station and we've already said . . .'

'Best to get it from the horse's mouth,' says Billy. 'You said that someone had told you to speak to DI Costello?'

'Yes, but I never got to speak to him.'

'Her,' corrects Billy.

'It was someone at the golf club – he's a police officer – and he said that . . . well, my husband said that maybe we should report the incident. Well, it was nothing really, but my son here . . . Would you like a coffee?'

'Thought you'd never ask.'

Five minutes later we are sitting round the table, a gentle thump-thump from underneath as the dog slaps his tail on the carpet. A mug of hot coffee sits in front of Mrs Parke and Hopkirk, Neil and I are each drinking a glass of ice-cold water.

'So – in your own words,' says Billy to the boy.

Mrs Anita Parke looks a little uncomfortable for the first time. 'Go on, Neil, tell them what happened.'

The boy rolls his eyes upwards, bored with the story already. 'I was out running,' he states simply.

'It was nearly dark,' explains the mother.

Billy looks at me as if I really am a cop and should start taking notes. My look back tells him what I think of that idea. But we do get the point. It was dusk.

'And where was this, Neil?'

'In the woods to the back of the house.'

Billy nods, as if he roughly knows where the boy is talking about. 'Do you run on your own?'

'Yeah.' He manages to pull the word out to four syllables.

'And this was . . .?'

'Thursday the twenty-ninth of March. The day after Granny's birthday. Callie ate some bad chicken and couldn't get off the loo,' said Neil with boyish delight.

'His sister,' his mum says.

I point to a photograph on the wall, a face framed with the same thick dark hair, large eyes under arched brows.

'She still lives with us, she's twenty-one.' Mrs Parke answers my next question then moves uncomfortably on her seat. She knows where this is going. She has known all along but didn't want to believe it.

Billy lets the silence lie for a moment then asks, 'So Neil, what happened? Exactly.'

Neil pulls a face. 'Well, I was running through the woods

and I heard a noise. I turn and there's this big dog coming up behind me. It was bloody enormous.' He puts his hand out, indicating how high.

Billy nods. 'Write that down, McCulloch? This might be important.' He hands me his notebook and pen. I start doodling. 'So what happened then?'

'Well, I've stopped, turned round. It was still coming. I was shitting myself . . .'

'Neil!'

'Hey Neil, I've been that scared too,' Billy says to him, inviting confidence. 'So what kind of dog was it?'

'No idea. Much bigger than him.' He points underneath the table. 'I know dogs but I've never seen anything like that. Just as I thought it was going to jump on me the man called it back, and it just turned round and trotted away.'

Billy's voice is very steady as he asks, 'Neil, what was the man like?'

'Nice, apologetic, like he knew he'd given me a fright.'

'So he talked to you?'

'Well, no.'

'So how do you know he was nice?'

Neil thinks for a moment, looking at his mum, confused. 'Well, he kind of waved, he was kind of looking at me once he got the dog on his lead.'

'How close was he?'

Neil looks round. 'Maybe as far as the house over there.'

I don't need to look over my shoulder to know that the distance is too great for a good ID.

'There was nobody else about?'

Neil shakes his head, 'Not that I saw.'

'Can you describe this man?'

'Not really.' Neil shrugs. 'He was just this bloke really.'

Billy looks around as if he's plucking ideas from the air. 'White?'

'Yes.'

'Younger than seventy? Older than seventeen?'

Neil smiles, and the dark downy hair at the side of his mouth creases to a crescent-moon shadow. 'I get it – yeah, he was really old, like forty or something.'

'Ancient really,' agrees Billy, nodding slightly.

'And he had on glasses, sunglasses, he looked like a complete dick with those specs on.'

'Neil!'

'No, really!' The boy is animated for the first time. 'He had this really stupid tracksuit thing on. This skip cap, like he was some wannabe rapper. And he was so old!'

'Did you see his face?' asks Billy.

Neil considers this, his eyes narrowing a little as he thinks. 'I kind of couldn't, with the glasses and the hat and everything.'

Classic.

'And then? Did he turn away and walk back the way he came?'

'Yeah, and he took his big dog with him.'

I am looking at the picture of his sister. 'When you go out running, do you tie your hair back?'

'Aye.'

'She goes running too, doesn't she? Same place that you went, Neil?'

'Yes.'

Billy pauses before asking the next question, following my chain of thought. 'So, Neil, the man called the dog back once you had turned round?'

Neil nods. 'Yeah.' It was another long-drawn teenage effort.

Billy asks, 'Neil, can you do us a favour? Can you stand up and turn around slowly, please?'

Neil looks at his mother for reassurance.

'Go on, pet,' she says.

The boy senses the change in the atmosphere and slowly stands up, flicks his hair back. He turns around slowly, a slim build, five feet five, a wave of sleek back hair curling into his collar.

'Thanks, Neil.'

I say, 'Mrs Parke, we might send a colleague out to have a wee word with your daughter and,' I show Neil my phone. 'What about that dog? Does that look like the one that you saw?'

Neil looks closer, he is concentrating. 'Yes, that's it. It wasn't quite that colour, it was a bit darker.'

Billy and I stand up, moving towards the door. Mrs Parke

leans forward and says in a low voice that cracks with emotion, 'Neil met this Night Hunter man, didn't he?'

'Night Hunter?' asks Billy innocently.

'That's what the papers are calling him. He takes women, and they don't come back alive.'

'Maybe your kids can go running on a treadmill, just for now,' says Billy.

Mrs Parke's mouth forms a perfect O; the corner of her eye waters a little as she realizes what might have been.

THURSDAY, 7 JUNE

I follow Costello up the stairs of Partickhill police station. The smell of paint and freshly cut pine, the unscuffed beige laminate flooring might give it the sense of a show home, but it is camouflage for the bad coffee and stale air. It is still a police station. Costello pushes a few buttons on the wall-mounted keypad, her quick fingers dancing over the numbers.

The door pushes open revealing a central area of desks. There are eight people in the room who all look up as we enter. I see flickers of recognition everywhere; two older guys nod at Billy; another attempts a conversation but Costello kills it with a glare.

'Do you want to look at this and see what you think?' She indicates the whiteboard on the far side wall, entitled 'The Night Hunter'. Down the side a piece of paper is taped, which says 'Operation Beluga'. There is nothing much written about the Night Hunter, so I presume there is very little they know. A few articles scanned from the press are pinned to the wall. They are rather sensationalist – the picture of Lorna falling with the headline, *The Lost Victim of the Night Hunter*. Then, in smaller letters, *Snatched without trace.*

'Do you think she should be reading that?' asks a very good-looking young man with degrees in cheekbones and sarcasm.

'Why not? A child could write this.' I chant out their list. 'Mobile, all-terrain vehicle, familiar with the area, known to the victims, forensically aware, sense of loss, wants to keep the victims, holds on to them. What he has lost he will obtain from others. No shit, Sherlock.' There is a picture of Lorna, another of the unknown woman with the name Katrine written under it. 'You have identified her?'

'No, we named her after Loch Katrine; giving her a name helps keeps the team focused. It's much better than *victim number two*,' says Costello. 'I think we need to focus on the fact that he looks after them; he's not your typical "kill them within forty-eight hours" type of abductor. Lorna had been fed and watered for a fair bit of time. People want what they don't have – they'll desire things they have lost. And he must have his own property – he has property apart from the family home.'

Charlie could deduce most of that. I look unimpressed.

'Geographical profiling shows that he lives in North Glasgow, it's the centre of his activity, where he took the women – well, Lorna, Gillian.'

'But not Sophie. Eaglesham is south of the city.'

Her look tells me to draw my own conclusion from that. 'There's always a distance decay, meaning that people are more likely to commit crimes close to home, in areas they are familiar with.'

'So this guy knows North Glasgow and the Arrochar Alps?'

'A posh hillwalker?' mutters Billy.

'If you can't be helpful . . .' Costello and Billy indulge in some unfriendly fire.

I interrupt. 'The Parke boy was running in that area. He said that the man had a huge dog with him, and that might . . .'

'Who?' asks Costello, sharply.

'We've just been doing your job for you, petal. It'll be in the system somewhere. Anita Parke reported that her son was approached while out running by a dog with a man.'

'A boy wouldn't meet our criteria, so it was not passed on to me,' Costello says and pulls her notebook out and begins scribbling something down with irritable stabs of her ballpoint. Then she looks at me. 'This is the boy you have *just* interviewed?'

'Yes,' says Billy. 'You need to interview him again. It's the break you've been waiting for. I'll bet you ten quid and back my hunch with thirty years on major investigations. Our Night Hunter was expecting the sister, not the brother. The boy has long hair, they're alike enough to be mistaken. She fits the profile of the others. He recognized the dog as an Ovcharka from the picture on Elvie's phone. Matilda from special services found that dog hair in Lorna's hair.'

'And I've never been near a dog like that. I didn't transfer that hair, so it came from the Night Hunter.' I know everyone in the room is staring at me. 'Which means the Night Hunter is technically a dog, you do know that, don't you?'

'What? A dog?' asks Anderson, who's appeared at the door without our noticing. Costello swears under her breath.

'He has a dog,' I say. 'Matilda emailed me about it. The hair comes from an Ovcharka, a Russian shepherd dog. They're bred to kill, big, powerful dogs. They're not fast but they are tireless, and they'll run you down. I've never come across an Ovcharka, so Matilda concluded Lorna was the one in contact with the dog.'

'But she was clean, wasn't she?' Costello's face screws up in frustration.

'But a dog hair entwined with human hair might stay there until combed out at the post mortem,' I argue.

'That is your break, Costello,' said Billy, going into a coughing fit.

'Can this Parke boy ID the man?'

'No, he dresses to hide his face and he doesn't need to get close to his victims, does he? He sends the dog instead.'

'What's the Parke girl's name?'

'Callie,' I answer immediately.

'So the owner of the dog knew that she would be there. He knew her, as he knew the others. Right, I'll interview them now, the mum, the boy, the girl. And who has annoyed me recently? Wyngate. He can do a case review and run them through the computer. I won't let the wee sod home until he comes up with something. We need to find that link.'

'There's no link there, we've checked and checked,' protests Cheekbones.

'Well, there is. So bloody find it,' Anderson whispers and bangs the door behind him. Cheekbones follows him out, ready to argue.

A deafening silence falls on the room; everyone avoids looking at Costello. I look at the media picture of my sister Sophie, on a separate board. She has a case number above her. For some reason that chokes my throat. Is this what my sister has come to? A number and picture? There are photographs and names and dates, including some of myself, then the diagram spreads down over the whiteboard. It reminds me of a family tree, all spread out, all of it laid bare. And there's a photograph of Mark Laidlaw. I stare at it for a long time.

I review the information on Gillian Porter, and then Lorna Lennox. There are more photographs of something that looks like the Piltdown Man, a mass of flesh and dirt: Katrine, the Girl on the Hill. As a display of information it's impressive. As a tool to move the investigation forward, it is proving bloody useless.

Costello starts up again. 'You can't accuse us of not being thorough. See here, we've mapped out Sophie's timeline. Maybe you can fill a gap we have. We don't know what she was doing on the night of Wednesday twenty-first March. Nobody seems to know. Your brother said that she was at home but your mum says that she definitely wasn't, but then she may not be the best witness. Rod agrees that Sophie wasn't home. We don't know where Mark was either. So can you help?' Her voice becomes sarcastic. 'If it helps your excellent memory, that was the night you left the hospital after getting a phone call. The nurse who witnessed you take the call got the impression it was some kind of emergency. We can trace who phoned who. You live about ten minutes away from the hospital.' Her voice drops a little. 'We can talk through here if you want.' She opens the door to a smaller, less formal room with two blue sofas. She has concern in her voice as if I am now a victim.

Has Billy put them up to this? He then answers my question. 'It will be useful for us all to know what was going on in her life at that time, and you're not the best person to judge what we should and shouldn't know, Elvie,' he says, as he indicates I should sit down. 'We need it black and white.'

Costello picks up on Billy's lead and smiles encouragingly. She sits down opposite and places a folder in front of her.

'She was going to my flat but I don't know where she was before that. I was working nights, doing a rotation in A and E, and she asked me – well . . .'

'Well, what . . .?'

I repeat the story. Me going home, Soph in the bath, my suspicion that she had been raped. It doesn't get any easier, telling it again.

The fact that Costello is not writing any of it down means that it is not news to her. 'So you left but she never said what happened to her?'

'No, I don't know what she did, but she definitely stayed for a few hours after I left, judging from the mess.'

'You suspect Mark Laidlaw?'

'I do.'

'Why?

'He's a brute.'

'Any other reason?'

I shake my head. 'It could only have been him.'

'Would you mind if we had a look at the flat forensically?'

'No, of course not.' But this is confusing me. None of this has anything to do with me. It's all to do with the Night Hunter. I put my hand in my pocket to check the keys are there, then I slide them across the table towards her. Billy's hand pats me on the shoulder.

'When does it suit you to go to the flat? You need to be there,' she says, keeping it very professional.

'Anytime.' I get up and walk back through the doors to look at the rest of the women on the wall. They stare back at me for a long time.

'We've exhausted all lines of enquiry on any connection,' says Costello quietly. She is standing right behind me.

'But running takes them outside, alone. Through parks. They're of similar age – does that mean anything? Same stages of life?'

'No. Have you come up with anything in your travels with Billy the Fox that he is not telling us?'

'No,' I answer flatly. I point at Lorna. 'How did she get to the top of the moor?'

'We think she was put out of a car on the road up near Succoth and then she went up the hill making for the Rest. Why she didn't run down the road once the car was gone remains to be seen.'

'Because they sent the dog after her? Maybe that's how he

gets his kicks, letting a girl loose then getting a dog to chase her down, a big, slow dog that never tires, coming after you, relentless.'

'Maybe.' The thought was chilling. We are both quiet for a moment.

'The geographical profiler was trying to get something out of this.' She points at the map of Argyll behind her. It is covered with pins, some large, some small – they are colour coded but I am not told the code.

'That's the house at Ardno.' I point. 'And that – is that Eric's house?' I move my finger to a house at the top of the Succoth road.

'God, no, that's his house, way over there. There are four farms between him and the point where Lorna fell, if that's what you're thinking. And it's much too far to run in any weather. That road on the left is where we think the car stopped and put Lorna out, maybe Katrine too. That's where we dropped you on Monday night.'

'Tuesday morning,' I correct her. 'That might be the last point accessible to a normal road vehicle but that police Land Rover struggled.'

She sighs wistfully. 'I've still got the bruises.'

'So Eric lives way up there on the right, and there's no way you can get between those two points by going across the way?'

'Too mountainous, too rough. We know, we tried. The search team have been all over the place. Nothing.'

I look at the map. The main road winds round the top of Loch Long, a small offshoot goes straight north into the forest park through Succoth and keeps on going into nowhere. Beyond nowhere is Eric's croft, almost up at Ben Vorlich, and that is a long way. I guess it's about twelve miles as the crow flies, but God knows how long on that windy road. Eric's croft is much closer to the hydroelectric scheme at Loch Sloy and the north-west side of Loch Lomond. Costello is right, there's no vehicle access over the top of the hills, so Lorna must have been dumped from the road.

I am still trying to compute that in my mind when Costello says, 'The road to that point at the top of Succoth is less than

single track, it's listed as "a road of limited use". You can get
to Ben Ime here, much easier. We think that's where Lorna
came from, the nearest point of vehicular access, so we centred
our search there. All those farms have been searched and
discounted, all outbuildings, ruins,' she adds. 'So maybe the
holding pen for the women is down here in the city, near where
they're taken. It's easier to hide somebody down here.'

I think about Lorna. Look at her Ali McGraw smile. She
was scared but incredibly fit. I have no idea how we would
work out how far she could actually have run. Would her fear
have kept her going? Knowing that dog was coming through
the darkness behind you . . . 'There's what, nearly eight
hundred square miles.' I look at Lorna's face. Her hair is short,
her face tanned and freckled, with big brown eyes. Trusting.
'If she'd been in a car there would be contact trace, surely,
on her body? Every contact leaves a trace and all that.'

'You've been talking to Billy.' Costello shoots a bitter glance
in his direction.

'We all know how to avoid leaving a forensic trail, that's a
matter of method and patience. Now what about the other
woman, do you know anything about her yet? Forensically?'

'Any further information from that body has not shed any
more light on this,' Costello says carefully, but she's listening
to me.

Billy smiles sweetly as his phone rings. There is something
about his face that makes the room fall silent. His lined red
cheeks make his face look like a pathetic clown; it's obvious
something is wrong. He puts his hand out as he looks around,
asking for quiet. Every keyboard stops tapping. 'Yes, I was
the senior investigation officer at the time.' He listens carefully; the room is listening to him. 'Yes, I know who you are.
We've just been talking about you.'

Costello mouths, 'Matilda?'

Billy nods, his eyes narrowing with incredulity. 'And you're
sure about this? Yes, I know you wouldn't say unless you were
sure . . . Can you send a copy to DI Costello? . . . Yes, here
– Partickhill . . . yes, that's where I am, hen . . . oh, just get
on with it.' He ends the call. 'There's been another match on
that dog hair, just the type of dog, but it's way too rare not

to be connected. Kelvingrove Park, 2005, the murder of Natalie Thom? You remember that?'

'Of course.'

Thoughts start running through my head; I'm glad they're not looking at me.

Billy is talking to Costello. 'If you recall, Natalie was walking through the park on her way to a Halloween Party and had just changed into her fancy dress costume. We found a dog hair on it. It's a familial match to the one that might have come off Lorna.' He breathes out slowly.

'But they're all related in this country. Pasternak and Siberian. Like the House of Hanover. The same DNA will be all over the place.'

'Matilda isolated some saliva. Dogs lick their own hair, the saliva is very sticky so it glues to the hair. If they get any DNA, it will be from the saliva, not the hair itself. Seemingly.' Billy is regurgitating information but his mind is racing ahead.

Costello drums her pen on the top of her desk. 'How big can the DNA pool of these dogs be in this country? We can have them traced, surely?'

Billy purses his lips. 'Do you know who was Natalie's best pal at university, the last person to see her alive?'

Costello looks blankly at Billy.

'Mary Allison.'

'Who?'

It is me who answers. 'Or, as she is now, Mary Parnell.'

'And,' Billy adds, 'at the time of her death, Natalie's boyfriend was none other than Alex Parnell.'

Complete silence falls on the room. Costello and Billy both sit down, leaving me standing next to Sophie's photograph like a teacher with nothing to say.

'So a dog is the connection to all this. Alex Parnell runs a security company. They only use Alsatians as far as I know, but I don't know much about him,' says Costello.

Billy agrees. 'And both the women were running. Police dogs are trained to chase a running target and hold them. These ones could be trained to bring someone down by the calf, hence the injury on the back of Lorna's leg. O'Hare will check if the other woman has the same . . .'

'She did.' Costello opens her file and shows him a black and white A4. 'But both these are cut clean with a knife. No tooth marks.'

'So he cuts out the traceable teeth marks,' I say, not needing to look.

Costello's eyes dart from me to Billy and back again, but there is a flicker of excitement. She knows we're on to something. 'We need to identify that dog.'

'Surely you can do that without clearing it with the boss? Or does it depend on his mood – or his missus? Is she gone then?' Billy snorts.

'Brenda?' A smile flutters on Costello's face, she relishes gossip.

'Yeah, Brenda, redhead, face like a Brillo pad. Where is she? Left him or away on holiday or what?'

'What has it to do with you?'

'I'm an individual concerned for my friend's welfare. Or a nosey wee shite who believes knowledge is power – take your pick.'

'He's out the family home, but they are talking. They're sharing the kids. I think Brenda sees more of him now than she did when they lived together. But she seems happier, she's working again. Accountant. Anything else you need to know?'

Billy says, 'I know Helena McAlpine from way back. Nice piece of arse.'

Costello turns to me. 'How do you put up with him?'

I am looking at the map still. Not interested in this small talk.

'What about DS Mulholland, what's his status?' Billy tilts his head at the desk where Mr Cheekbones was sitting.

'The closest relationship he's ever had is with the mirror.'

Billy is encouraging this chit-chat, it's not like him. He's keen to hang around; his eyes are scanning, taking it all in. 'I'm curious. Do you like it – the new office? Hardly all mod cons, is it?'

Costello's fingers are now on her keyboard and she responds abstractedly, 'Well, it has no fungus, no damp and a lack of

asbestos. Look, do we know the number of the breed society
or anything?'

'Yip,' I read her out the number that is stored in my phone.

'Thanks,' she says, the first time I think she's looked at me
like a human being. She writes the number down, rips the
note off and hands it to a young man in a creased suit.

'Can you action that? Use that phone down there.'

'And what about yourself? You seeing anybody?' Billy slides
on to the side of her desk.

'Is that an offer, Billy?'

'No. When was the last time you were on a date?'

Costello thinks hard. 'Yesterday. Before you ask, it was shit.
Way too many teeth, like having a date with Red Rum. Except
Red Rum had better table manners.'

At that moment Mr Cheekbones comes back in. He could
be a model in the well-groomed but smouldering category. He
glares at Billy intensely.

Costello starts on her keyboard again. 'Mulholland, can you
check this report? It's about DNA from a single dog hair.'

His beautifully structured face looks spectacularly unimpressed. 'A single dog hair?' Mulholland gives me a glance of
distrust as he slides his jacket from his shoulders and looks round
for a chair to hang it on. 'Why don't I have my own desk?'

'You might get your own coat hanger, if you're lucky.' Two
people who do not like each other but work well together. He
is pernickety and gets up her nose. The fact that she is his
boss riles him. He knows that she is the better detective and
that riles him even more.

The door opens, too far this time, and it catches on the
carpet again. The figure behind bangs hard with his shoulder
to get it to open.

'Hi, Wyngate. Glad you could join us.'

'Sorry, the baby was ill.'

'Well, you have a job to do. Go through all the case files
and find a low-actioned report from a Mrs Parke with an e.
It's about a dog. And Wyngate? You smell of baby sick.'

'Oh, sorry.' Wyngate sidesteps to allow the person behind
him through the door. 'She has best practice projectile
vomiting. I did try to clean it off.'

'Well, you didn't succeed.' Costello then turns to me. 'Why are you in the middle of all this, Elvie?' she says, making a swirly pattern with her fingertip then pointing it at me. 'Sophie, Mary, Natalie?'

'Good question,' Billy says out the corner of his mouth.

I am saved from answering by a gentle knock at the door. 'I've . . . Oh, hello, Elvie, how are you?' But her hesitation when she saw me was obvious.

It is Avril, the family liaison officer. Costello invites her to sit down and takes the memo from her. Avril regards me with concern as Costello reads the note then hands it to Mulholland, who reads it then starts scanning my face. He opens his notebook out ready. Everything has changed. We are businesslike now. All these people are higher up the food chain than the normal plod who occasionally accompanies Avril on her visits to my house.

'You've found Sophie?' I see in the corner of my eye that Billy has moved behind me; he has one hand on my shoulder ready for succour if the news is bad.

Avril shakes her head. 'No. But we think we've found Mark Laidlaw.'

'So bring him in, for God's sake,' says Billy.

But Costello is looking straight at me. 'I'll rephrase that. We've found Mark Laidlaw's body.'

We are now back in the quiet investigation room. I have been given a cup of coffee. It is terrible. I need to get out of here.

'Obviously, things have changed a wee bit. We are going to have to reprioritise. So we don't want you to go back to your flat until we say you can. We need to examine it with a different protocol, in the light of the new circumstances.'

'Fine by me. Mark Laidlaw has never been to my flat.'

'As far as you are aware,' she adds succinctly.

Mulholland is now her sidekick. He passes the A4-sized photograph to me. I look at it. I know his eyes are on me as I look. Mark's face is super clean. Death has lent him a dignity he did not have in life. There is a black mark on his left temple.

'That's the man I met in the street. He was looking for Sophie. He called himself Mark Laidlaw.'

'Did you ever actually see him with your sister?'

I shook my head.

'When did you see him?'

'On the eleventh of April. When that picture was taken on CCTV. I think he was on his way to see me. If you follow the cameras you'll see me talking to him. He was asking me where Sophie was.'

'And you were going to tell us that – when?'

'She's telling you now,' said Billy. He sounds disappointed in me. But he doesn't tell them the bigger secret.

'I had nothing to do with his death. But I do know that he had something to do with Sophie's disappearance. That's what you should be concentrating on.'

'Look, young lady, I have had you up to my back teeth. You do not control this investigation. You tell me everything, do you understand? You will tell us everything.'

The scar near Costello's hairline is doing a little dance. I know that each of them is watching my reaction carefully. I ignore her. 'And where was he? Is Sophie there? I think *you* should be telling *me* everything.' I stare her out.

Costello does what most people do, she senses that the aggression is not normal. She calls for reinforcements. 'Avril, can you join us?' She moves along the settee.

'Hi, Elvie, you OK?'

'I'm fine, what have you found?'

'As you know, we've recovered a body and we're sure that it's Mark Laidlaw. It looks like his car rolled into the reservoir; they're searching the rest of the body of water to see if there's anything else there.' She curls and uncurls her fingers, her nails are still perfect.

'What reservoir? Eaglesham? The same one where Sophie parked her car?'

Costello and Avril share a look.

'Yes, it was,' surrenders Costello.

'Was it an accident?' I ask. It seems a natural question.

'Doubt it,' Mulholland says.

'But there's no trace of my sister in the car?'

'There is a six-day gap between him being seen last and your sister being seen last. These could be two separate incidents.'

'That just happened to occur at the same place! Was there any sign of Sophie?' I persist.

'He was on his own when the car went in the water.' Avril plays pass-the-parcel with the photographs to Mulholland, to Costello then to me.

'She never talked about Mark to me.' I take the pictures, place the one of Mark on top of them, and hand them back. 'That looks like a nasty mark on his head.'

'There might have been an earlier bump to the head that bled and he died at the wheel then went into the water. Or he might have lost consciousness and ended up in the water. Or he drove in and bumped his head. His seat belt was still fastened, the key was in the ignition. Further tests at the lab will tell us exactly how he died.' Costello is thinking hard. 'Either way, him and car in reservoir.'

I lift my head up at that. 'Do you think he killed Sophie?'

'He might have been up there looking for her,' says Costello.

'There's no sign that she was there and got out?' I ask.

'No sign that she was in that car, full stop.'

I nod slowly, as if I'm trying to digest this.

'His wife has not seen him since Sophie went missing. She suspected there might have been another woman and thinks that woman was Sophie. Until the full PM results come through we view them as connected but separate incidents. And Sophie might have fallen victim to the Night Hunter, as you've said before. That's the theory that you and Billy Hopkirk have been working on, isn't it?'

I feel the tears sting my eyes. 'Sorry. I need to think about this.' I feel the tingling twitching that I need to release. I am cornered. 'You know, when I saw Lorna lying there, alive, I really hoped that the Night Hunter had Sophie. Then there'd be a chance that she's alive. I know she never ran off with that bloke. You lot were thinking it, but that wasn't Sophie's way. I know that, because I knew her.'

'Just look at the way she actually disappeared; it matches the way the Night Hunter takes them. That's what got me thinking and Gillian Porter's mum thinking. That's what got me involved,' says Billy.

'OK, two heads are better than one. We need to cover all

other lines of enquiry. Elvie, I need to ask you, do you know anything about Mark and Sophie? Anything about their relationship?' Costello asks, playing the team card.

'No, I don't.' That I can say with complete conviction.

It is a typical semi-detached house in Pollok near where they took down the old psych hospital. It's the kind of place that looks posher than it is. Everything is a bit too small, everybody has their driveway at the expense of a front garden. And at the end of the driveway, just across the road, is Helmand Province.

Number thirty-nine is a very neat end-of-terrace. There is no car, of course; that's at the bottom of a reservoir in Eaglesham. The garage floor is so clean it doesn't look as though it was in there much either. The current occupants are a pink bike with stabilisers lying on its side and a baby stroller with a huge hood on it, white fringes dancing in the swirling wind. Billy follows the direction of my glance.

'Why not just stick a hat on the kid? Never did me any harm.'

'You don't know that,' I say as we walk along the path, under the living room window. I hear a call as the woman from next door emerges from her own front door. She looks at me, then Billy.

'Police?' she asks.

Billy does not answer but swings his head around in a way that could be yes, no, or releasing a crick in his neck. 'It's about Mark. Nice wee estate here. I remember the way it was in my youth. I was based in Pollok, back in the day.'

'Aye, it's changed a wee bit since then.' She folds her arms. 'So I heard you've found him then. Stupid bastard.'

Billy has stopped on the path; he's not going as far as the front door. He isn't engaging her in conversation but he isn't moving on either.

'Could I help you in some way?' she says, with ill-disguised nosiness.

'We're here to speak to Rhona Laidlaw. Is she around?'

We know that she is not around. She and her kid have been taken to her mother's house by Avril for comfort, or celebration.

The opinion of both Rhona and her mother is apparently that Mark was a useless tosser.

The woman shrugs her bony shoulders, her hand up to her eyes to shield them from the sun. 'I don't think she's in. I think she left with some of you lot.'

'What were they like as neighbours?'

'Well, you don't like to say, do you?' she says, dying to say.

'Better off without?' I offer, using one of Sophie's stock phrases.

'Well, yes. Don't mean to speak ill of the dead but we all knew about the . . .'

'Violence?'

She snorts, dropping her hand. She is older than I first thought. 'Oh, she gave as good as she got. She's no shrinking violet, that one. Big woman. You wouldn't take her home a short pay packet, ma Bob says. If you look in their hall, you'll see holes in the plasterboard where he punched it before he punched her. Then round the ceiling there's the dents where she flung stuff at him and missed. These walls are paper thin, you know. And he was never at work, he was always . . . well, like I said, I don't want to speak ill of the dead.' She sniffed, her tongue probing the side of her mouth. 'So what happened to him, then?'

'We are not at liberty to say at the moment,' I reply quickly before Billy says too much.

'Well, he was as thick as a Derry dairy farmer.' She folds her arms and looks smug. 'Do you think she'll sell the house now? Oops, talk of the devil.' She mutters and turns away as a Golf pulls up, unmarked. Avril is driving. A big woman with dyed bright red hair, a tight skirt and purple tights hauls herself out of the passenger seat, letting the suspension of the car sigh in relief. Avril opens the back door and the big woman pulls a child out by its arm. There is a constant stream of words that we can't hear; her eyes are reddened and bitter.

Avril stares at us and shakes her head slightly at Billy. The message is clear: *you should know better.*

'And what do you two want?' Rhona yells at us as she strops up the path in leather stiletto ankle boots, the silent child dangling over her arm like a puppet. Billy gets thrown the kid, I get the dirty look. Her oversized fake designer handbag slips down her arm as she rummages for her keys. She is surrounded by a cloud of pungent perfume.

'We were making sure you were OK,' says Billy, jiggling the kid up and down like a Santa having a fit.

'*I* was making sure she was OK,' says Avril, who has just caught up. Now Billy is getting dirty looks as well.

'Shit,' says Rhona, turning the key in the lock, but the door fails to open. She puts her mighty shoulder against it and the door gives way in the face of an irresistible force. She stops to bend down and pick up the mail that has gathered behind it. Her Lycra-clad backside is so wide it fills the width of the doorway, revealing the ladders at the top of her tights. The kid burps quietly and closes her eyes; she has seen all this before. As Rhona spits obscenities, the kid snores gently. Avril and Billy are still arguing in low tones, and all I can hear is *I could get you into so much trouble . . . oh, fill yer boots, why don't you . . .* Then Rhona says *fuck* really loudly.

She thrusts a letter in my face. 'See! See! That's the kind of wanker I was married to! He runs off with that whore and this . . . this . . . I bet it's their fucking wee love nest. And now he's dead, they're after me for the rent . . . me! *Me!* No fucking way.' The letter is in my face again.

'Rhona, Rhona, calm down. Just get some clothes and we'll get to your mother's.' Avril stares at Billy, taking the still-silent child from his arms. 'So you can go now.'

'Yes. We will, thank you, Rhona.'

We walk back up the path, seeing the curtains twitch all down the street as we climb in the car. 'You know, sweet cheeks,' says Billy, pulling his mobile out, 'I'd kiss the Pope's arse to find out where that flat was.'

'The agent is Southside Letting, Battlefield Road. The property reference number is PL007321551. They traced her here through the bank. That might be worth a sniff.'

Billy stares at me, finger poised over his mobile. 'How the hell did you see that?'

'She did stick the letter in my face twice. I'd have to be bloody blind not to see it.'

'Battlefield Road? We need to tell Costello, get some brownie points.' He taps the phone on the top of the steering wheel then decides he would be better having a good scratch at his sore arm. 'The issue is that Sophie has been somewhere for those two months. If she was planning to stay at that flat with Mark, the missing jeans, those boots, will be there. As soon as Costello clocks that, the minute she thinks you have been withholding evidence, your name will be so shit your postcode will be a septic tank – you ready for that?'

'She wasn't with him. But when you're in a hole sometimes you have to start digging.'

Billy hums and haws a wee bit. 'Yeah, you're right.'

We sit in the car as Billy phones Costello. He holds the phone at arm's-length so that his ears don't start bleeding from the pressure of the venom at the other end. 'Never knew ladies knew language like that,' whispers Billy. 'Oh calm down, you tart, listen. Yes, we were at Laidlaw's house but we've got the address of his flat for you, his love nest, shagging pad, call it what you will. And one more thing in your fight against crime – I'd do a hair analysis on the Laidlaw kid. She's drugged up to her wee eyeballs.'

Eric is in the kitchen talking to my mum and Rod, leaning against the worktop, a cup of coffee in his dirty hand. Rod is cleaning his own hands under the tap and the kitchen stinks of Swarfega and curry. Mum is agreeing vehemently with everything Eric is saying as if he is the prophet of all wisdom. He is having a mild-mannered rant about the police who have been asking him about dogs and interrupting his quiet contemplations.

'A big dog? Oh, hi, Elvie, you know about that? The dog thing? Alan McAndrew's getting hell up there; they have him interviewing every farm collie including wee Rosie . . .'

'McAndrew?' Grandpa Cop. 'Oh, they have a lead on a dog.'

'Best place for it,' quips Rod, they smile. I join in, nodding a hello at Mum.

She mutters, 'Lead on a dog, that's funny.'

Rod smiles at me. There's something in the oven that

resembles a biryani. 'You staying for a bite to eat? We've got a takeaway, we can stretch it,' he says.

I nod.

Eric takes up the tale. 'So in the end we drive down to Dunky's place to show him Rosie, incontinent and toothless. Like she's going to do anything to anybody. Anyway, you coming up to see the place tomorrow night, Elvie, now that the cops have tidied it all up? We can have a wee bite to eat at the Oyster Bar. Mary is back up at Ardno.'

'Yes, Elvie, you do that, be nice and go out with Eric for a nice wee dinner.' Mum holds her thumb and forefinger to show how small the dinner will be.

Rod turns towards the window and mutters an apology to Eric.

I stand at the door, realising that they do not know. 'They've found Mark Laidlaw's body.'

Rod turns round slowly. Eric takes a sharp intake of breath as Mum collapses slightly, folding up and catching herself on the worktop. Her wine glass tips and the Merlot begins to drip, leaving red splashes on the white tiled floor.

Rod steadies her. 'Any sign of Soph?'

I shake my head.

'Thank God for that,' he says. He sits Mum down on the kitchen chair and takes the wine glass off her. She picks it up again as he turns to switch the kettle on.

'He was found down at the reservoir.' I watch Rod for a response.

'What – here?' Eric points with his thumb, he is incredulous.

I nod. 'They also . . .'

'Who ish thish bloody Mark, and why . . .' mutters my mum.

'Oh be quiet, Nancy. What, Elvie?'

'They've looked at the flat he was renting. There's no sign that Sophie has ever been there. I thought I'd better let you know. A bossy cop called Costello will probably be out to see you tomorrow. I don't know if this is good news or not.'

'It might be good news, if he is . . . sorry, we might be better having our tea,' says Rod. He flashes me a look that tells me not to talk about this in front of Mum.

'Yip,' says Eric, joining in the usual chit-chat.

'Anybody mind if I use the computer upstairs for a couple of minutes?'

'No, no. Go ahead.' Rod is all concern. His shoulders have fallen; he seems to have shrunk. Eric pats him on the upper arm.

I stand in Mum's cosy kitchen looking at this tableau. The cobweb above my head is still dancing in the draught. The weights are still lined up like Russian dolls. My mum is leaning against the back of the chair, head down. She has a hole in her tights. Eric and Rod share a moment of confidence at the sink that I will not be privy to.

'Where's Grant?' I ask.

Rod smiles his bitter smile. 'Upstairs. I'd just leave him if I was you. He's aiming for a thousand sit-ups.'

'What a wuss.' My turn for the bitter smile.

I have to sit and nibble some burnt pakora before I can get upstairs to look at the computer. Rod and Eric talk about football, the weather, the problems of building new houses in this economy. Rod moans about pensions and house prices. They avoid the subject of Mark. Then they go into the back garden, so they can talk about anything they like. I realize I am looking at Rod differently, observing him. Is he too interested? Not interested enough? Nobody bothers that my mother has wandered off somewhere. I watch Rod get the hedge cutter out from the hut. Eric is holding the door open for him. This is good; it's a big hedge so they will be busy. I will know when he stops by the noise stopping.

I go upstairs where I hear Grant huffing and puffing, counting then resting, huffing and puffing. Every so often I hear him say, *Who's the daddy?*

I am turning the door handle of my room when a cold hand falls on top of mine.

'Not you as well.' Mum sounds remarkably sober.

'Not me as well what?'

'Can't you leave Sophie alone?'

I don't really understand. She seems hurt, her blue eyes flint cold, unreadable. 'I was just looking to see if anything has changed.'

'Nothing changes around here. A change would be some-body coming to this house to talk to me, about me.' She held up one finger. 'Just once.'

'I need something off the hard drive.' I tell her I have crashed my laptop and I need my homework. 'Rod will be OK using Grant's laptop for a couple of days.'

She scowls in her pursed lips way.

'It's for university. I downloaded it here.' Mum doesn't speak computer and accepts my explanation. In my old bedroom I sit at the computer and check the number of photo-graphs on the campaign file on the hard drive. Mum wanders round the room, poking her fingers into places like she's checking for dust.

'You know, I don't think I could cope if anything happened to you.' She's standing behind me now; I can feel her breath in my hair. 'You are all I have left, really, all that is left of the way things were.' She sits beside me looking at me, not the computer screen. Her eyes don't focus that well.

'We'll get her back,' I say as I go through the files, looking for something that is big enough to hold all the photographs. Billy's theory is that Sophie stayed here as long as she did because Mum played her emotional blackmail card then some-thing bad happened. What was Sophie so scared of? What or who was Mum so upset about? Grant? Or Rod? I am looking for things on this computer that I do not want to find. But I do need to know.

The draught of my mum's breathing in my ear becomes heavier, and she slumps against me. She has drifted into sleep.

I know the size of the file that Belinda sent to me. If that holds all the photos taken at the birthday party, then it should match the size of the file that Rod passed on to the police. There are many files. Sophie was popular and everybody wanted a photo of her. Then I find – *sophparty31mar12*. I scroll across to look at the size, then check again that I'm still looking at the right file. It's only three-quarters the size. I had a hundred and sixty-eight in the file Belinda sent me, so there are about forty odd that Rod thought the police wouldn't be bothered about. Or that he did not want the police to see?

Mum sighs; she's wakening up a little.

'Nearly done.'

'So – you thinking about going back, dear?' She sighs the heartfelt sigh of the happily pissed. 'Don't throw away your career, all that educashun.'

'Well, I'll go back at some point. I just need to keep up.' I am rewarded with an unfocused version of the smile she gave me when I got good marks for drawing at school or forming my little letters correctly. She is an intellectual snob.

'You can come back and live here.'

'I need to be near the hospital,' I lie. 'I'm going to take this away and get my stuff off it, OK?'

She goes to look out the window and waves, holding on to the sill for support. 'I'll just ask Rod about the computer,' Mum says in one of her inopportune moments of clarity.

'Mum, he's busy,' I say honestly, then go into lie mode. 'And Rod can keep up with Facebook on Grant's.' All the time I am pulling out flexes and cables as she walks about the bedroom a little unsteadily. The computer is stuck under my arm just as the noise outside stops. I get up and look out. Rod is up a ladder and Eric is pulling his arms into a horizontal line, the way the hedge should be cut. Mum stares out the window at him. Her face becomes unlined, young again; in profile she looks so much like Sophie.

'She's never coming home, is she?'

Angie is a computer genius and like most computer geniuses she looks about twelve. Her mum makes us a cup of tea as Angie plugs in the computer and starts tapping away. She asks us for the exact date the file would have been downloaded. We don't know.

'The original file is here somewhere.' She opens it up. 'One hundred and sixty-eight photos?' she asks.

'There were a hundred and twenty-eight on the disc that Rod gave to the police,' Billy says.

'Maybe he ditched all the ones that were crap?' suggests Angie.

'Why not say so? He said that all he had were there.'

'Here's the file direct from her computer,' I hold out the stick.

'And Belinda didn't delete any?'

'She didn't have time to go through them before Rod asked for them, so she bunged him the whole lot. Rod has been editing these and the police have never seen the ones he kept back. For whatever reason. Can you save them for me? The ones he deleted from the hard drive?

Angie nods like it's child's play.

'Will he know that we've found them?'

'Doubt it. I'll just copy them. Do you want a swatch at them now? You can compare them if you want. I'll run both slideshows side by side. Easy done.' Angie slips in a flash drive, she copies the smaller file and then sticks the USB stick into her laptop. 'I'll leave you to it, I'm going to the fridge for a Coke.'

Billy waits until she has left.

'This could take a long time, but if these are in chronological order then we just skip to the time when Belinda said Sophie looked a bit upset.'

'Eleven-twenty? Eleven-thirty? They would be well pissed by then, so God knows how accurate that is.'

'Go to eleven p.m. Photo one hundred and twelve.'

But all pictures from there to the end are correct, perfectly matched in date and time. So we start working our way backwards. And then we find it; the first non-match was timed just after ten p.m.

Billy turns the laptop round slightly so that we have a good sight of both the images displayed. They are not the same. We go through the photos, clicking back and forth, analysing closely the ones that Rod held back.

Then I notice something. 'They're on a pub crawl up Byre's Road here, making their way to Oran Mor. The photographs indoors are sequential, but there are images missing of those taken out in the street.'

'Do you think someone was watching them from the street and got caught in the odd image? Look at this one, just a drunk girl lifting her skirt up and a bit of the road behind her.'

'Looks like Marilyn Monroe. If Marilyn Monroe had been from Easterhouse.'

'So what or who is it he didn't want us to see?'

I lean forward. 'You think Rod has got something to do with all this, don't you?'

'With rape, violence against women or children, you should never look far from home. He'd better have a good explanation as to why he has been withholding these pictures.'

The slideshow goes on in front of me. I stop it on a photo taken out in the street. Sophie is hanging her arms around some guy. She has on a short bandage dress, her hair is in its usual going-out straight blonde style, framing the sides of her face. Her make-up is still perfect, she had not been crying. She is happy, slightly drunk. Relaxed. There are no signs of the stress of the previous few weeks on her face. It sends a chill through me. Whatever it was, Sophie felt she had sorted it all out. I feel that she had made a decision and had no idea it was the wrong one. There is something we are missing.

We both look but see nothing. Then I stop looking at the pavement and look at the cars coming along from Queen Margaret Drive. It was late, dark, but the junction at the end of Byres Road and Queen Margaret Drive is chaotic, no matter what time of day it is.

I point at the screen. 'There.'

'Where?' Billy leans in close, giving me a lungful of nicotine air. 'What?'

'That Ford Focus. Silver.'

'And?'

'A Silver Ford Focus with a dent in the wheel arch. Grant did that. Mum went crazy.' A thought is forming in my head, a thought I don't want to think.

'So Grant was there at his sister's birthday, so what?' Billy sniffs a little.

'He wasn't invited. What time is this, about ten-thirty?'

'Who do you think is driving? Grant or Rod? I can't tell from this angle, it's a shadow. Anderson can get the image blown up and clarified.'

'It's Rod.' I know it. 'Grant is taller, more powerfully built. That's his car. He tried to stop us from seeing this. He has lied about where he was that night. Mum was drunk, he sneaked out the house. I'm going to hand this over to Costello and get it enhanced.'

'She'll rip him apart.'

'But if I'm wrong?' I am finding this hard to accept. 'There's no going back from this.'

'Elvie, think about it. Sophie ran away from something. From the minute you said that only you knew what her plans were, I knew that she was running away from someone in your house. Your mother seems like many women, can't live without a man in her life. A man is what makes her complete. It's also what makes her vulnerable. Sophie would have been torn between love for your mum, and her suspicions about Rod. She knew that your mum might just not listen.'

'You don't know my sister . . .'

'I'm not sure you do, sweet cheeks. I can see the evidence with my own eyes. You have such clarity that you see it but kind of miss the point of what you see. You record but don't interpret. Your mum is living in a bottle, hiding from something. Sophie runs. Grant has demons that are driving him to self-harm. But Rod copes with everything, sails through it all. He has happily been at the helm of the investigation on behalf of the family from day one and neither you nor your mum have questioned it. He can direct the campaign or misdirect it. Your poor mum. Sophie's gone, Grant is psychotic, you've never been normal, and now we're about to question the validity of her other relationship.' He bites his lip. 'But you must ask yourself: what exactly was the relationship between your sister and your mum's boyfriend?'

FRIDAY, 8 JUNE

The back of the French Café is crowded. Billy has ordered us coffee and a tea for Costello but it's taking its time in coming. There is a babble of waitresses at the machine, lots of talking but not much movement.

Costello is wearing a plain navy blue suit with a mandarin collar; she must be due in court later today. She glances at her watch and swears at Billy. 'So I should thank you for bringing me this!'

'Calm down petal, be nice,' says Billy.

Her sarcasm is well honed. 'Sorry, yes, you're right, of course. I *should* thank you for bringing me this. I seem to spend all my time in there playing office politics when you two are out doing the job I thought was mine.' But she smiles, and it knocks about ten years off her. 'Elvie, have you actually witnessed anything untoward between your sister and Rod Banks?'

'Would she know?' mutters Billy.

'Not at all. She would have punched him if he'd tried something.'

'Family trait,' says Billy. 'But you're not the best judge of character, Elvie.'

'What do you mean?' I ask.

'Sometimes it can be difficult to see your own family as others see them. One person's "outgoing personality" can be another's "outrageous flirt".'

Costello puts her hand up to stop Billy. 'I'm more interested in why Rod stays in that house. Your mum is an alcoholic, Grant is a nutter, so what's in it for him? And you're never there so you really have no good idea what goes on.'

The image of Sophie in the garden, in her bikini, teasing Eric, quiet, kind teddy bear Eric, flits through my mind. 'Sophie was a lawyer for women's rights, she worked for the refuge, she was not a victim so . . .' They are saved by my phone going. It's Mary, wishing me a good time that night.

'It's not a date, it's only Eric!' I reply, confused. Mary never phones me for things like this.

'Well, you must tell me all about it one day. Thanks for all you've done, Elvie. OK? Better go, bye. Just . . . thanks.' And she rings off.

I stare at the phone. 'Odd! Very odd for Mary.'

'Mary is odd,' says Billy. 'Anyway!'

'Yeah,' Costello says. 'It's a line of enquiry that we must follow. And these,' she puts her hands flat on the disk we have just given her, 'will be a great help. We will tread very carefully.'

'There was no sign of Sophie ever having been at that flat with Mark Laidlaw?'

'None at all. And no sign that she was in that car. Elvie, ninety-five percent of people who disappear do so of their own free will. Sophie was a bright girl; maybe she went because she didn't want to break up your mum and Rod, maybe something happened between them, maybe something did not. We still haven't found the clothes that she took that night.'

'Someone sent you that ankh.'

'And the Night Hunter has never sent back trophies. The ankh might have been sent by someone in the house, you know that much, Elvie. We have no evidence one way or the other whether she took it with her or left it. It doesn't move the situation on.' Costello's bitten fingernails are drumming the table top.

'Elvie, if I lived in that house I'd run like fuck and never stop,' says Billy. 'You got out but Sophie stayed – why?'

'Keep your friends close and your enemies closer,' suggests Costello.

'Any news on the hair?' Billy asks. 'Dog hair. Russian Bonzo.'

'It got us nowhere. We checked out the two breeders that are registered in this country and all their dogs are accounted for, and are no exact match. The dogs are so rare over here that each dog's DNA is kept on their own database so that closely related dogs don't breed. They have the distant relatives of the dog the DNA came from, a Pasternak dog, but have no knowledge of the dog itself.'

'And a hair of a dog of that family was found on Natalie's body in October 2005?'

'Yes. But that could be four generations ago. Somebody is freelance breeding these dogs so they are not on the register. It will be corroborating evidence once we find the Night Hunter, but it doesn't . . .'

'Move the situation on.' I'm getting a bit tired of hearing that phrase.

'I spent all night reading the Natalie Thom file . . . you recall it?' asks Costello.

'Of course I do. The hair was found on her after she had changed into the Snow White costume, not on any of the clothes she was wearing before,' Billy adds quickly. 'The costume was straight out of a posh hire shop, just dry cleaned. Conclusion was the killer left the hair. Natalie and Mary parted company in the pub, Natalie went to her flat, got changed and cut across the park to go to the party. She never made it.' He chews on his lip, dragging up unpleasant memories. 'Oh, I had plenty of sleepless nights thinking about it and burn marks on my arse where I was pulled over hot coals for it, but that's a damn sight better than having marks on your arse from sitting on the fence, Costello.'

She ignores him.

'Maybe the same killer has refined his style a little. Instead of hanging around in the park, he sends the dog after them?' I am thinking out loud.

'Do you think I can take any of this to Anderson?' Costello counters. 'He's being so cautious. Budget-wise, I mean.'

'Well, if he doesn't want to take it any further, tell him that I'm applying for access to that evidence so that I can have it tested at my own expense,' says Billy. 'I can pull strings. Certified lab, of course, all kosher and above board.' Both Costello and I turn to look at him. 'I'm serious. I'm working for Gilly's mum – I can apply to have evidence examined.'

'You really believe that there is something in pursuing that as a line of enquiry?'

'I really do. I've twice your experience, petal. There's something in Natalie's case that is an echo of this. Tell Anderson you need to get that dog hair retested. And if you stick with it, we'll level with you.' And he told her everything, about Sophie disappearing, planning to come back, about Goblin

Market. Then the fact that she did not come back. Taking us all back to square one. I watch his mouth open and close, not believing the words that are coming out, all my secrets, all Sophie's confidences.

Costello listens, I can hear her teeth grinding.

'Now you know all there is to know.'

'Like I said originally, Sophie needed to get out that house: they're a bunch of nutters in there. That is a mile away from women being attacked by dogs and left to die on remote hillsides.' She shakes her head slowly from side to side. 'There is no Sophie case, is there? She's just decided not to come back. I'll tell you what, I'll work on the real victims: Lorna, Gillian, Katrine. Sophie is of no interest. No interest to me at all.' Costello starts waving her finger around again. 'Or she might be, but as suspect not victim. Suspect in the death of Mark Laidlaw.'

'Way out of line, Costello.'

'Mark Laidlaw is dead, drowned with a bump on his head.'

'That rhymed.'

'Oh, fuck off,' she hisses quietly, picking up the disk and flicking her hair from her forehead. The little scar appears like an angry smile. 'And one more thing – if you have anything else, do you mind telling me about it, Miss McCulloch? Anything that you think might be relevant, share it with me. Or I will be back with DCI Anderson and have you charged with withholding information or perverting the course of justice or wasting police time or anything else that I can think of. The fiscal will throw the friggin' book at you.' She leaves, the door closing behind her with a resounding thump.

'Not a happy bunny is she?' I say.

'She didn't mean any of it.' Billy seems thoughtful. 'If she'd meant it, there would have been two of them. When she's on her own she's safe, we can deny everything. You're good at that.'

'So we're OK, then.'

'Unless she comes back with Anderson, of course. Then we are in the shit.' Billy sips his coffee. 'She took the disk though.'

*   *   *

The meal at the oyster bar at the top of Loch Fyne starts awkwardly but Eric is well known and there's a fair amount of chat with a senior waiter about rainfall and salmon as if the two are connected in some way. Eric is caught between being my friend and staying loyal to his mate Rod. The cops have been to see Rod about the pictures, so Eric knows I've been sneaking about behind his back.

'Rod says he's fine with it. He knows he was daft not giving the cops all the photographs, but he was going through them and put all the dully lit ones to the side, just that most of them were exterior. He never put them back. You know that he's turning over every stone. He knows you're doing the same thing.'

'He didn't help, not handing over all the pictures.'

'Different stones. Well, he's told his story and the police are following it up. He was in Partickhill nick for three hours. He wants you to know that he'll move out the house until this is sorted.'

'Mum won't let him. I don't care if he stays.'

'He knew there was something wrong with Sophie. He was concerned, that's why he followed her. Once they walked through the front door of Oran Mor, he judged she was safe and came home. The CCTV will follow the Focus. It will put him in the clear. If he was her real dad, his actions wouldn't be questioned, would they?'

But he's not her dad. 'OK.'

'You know him, Elvie. You know he's OK. He's smoothed it all out with the police.' Eric changes the subject; he's not one of the world's natural conversationalists. How am I finding working with Mary and isn't wee Charlie great? 'Mary is like your sister in many ways, always a kind smile and a kind word for everybody. She's good for Alex, better than any of his other women were.'

'You've known him a long time.'

'Back to our days at uni . . . Oh, here's my sea bass. Just look at that.' He pokes his fork at the poached egg, watching the yolk swell and burst.

I turn over my bream with my knife. I think what Costello said about Soph, 'Is that how you really see her? Soph and Mary?'

Eric thinks for a minute. 'Yes. OK, maybe a bit higher octane than Mary. More of a Ferrari than a Focus.' He smiles, pleased with the metaphor. 'Magda was pure bred Ferrari.'

'My memories of her are vague.'

Eric's face falls. 'Your mum was so kind when Magda left. I feel I should have helped more, over this. All this Sophie stuff.'

I try to think what he means. I take a mouthful and let the fish flake in my mouth, waiting.

'I do feel for you. It's very painful, but time passes . . .'

'And you don't want to revisit the past?'

Eric nods. 'I'm aware of the pain of Not Knowing. That's a phrase that's bandied about a lot, but few have felt that pain. I was upset when Magda left but then the police showed me proof that one of her credit cards was being used – she'd bought a pair of shoes, expensive ones in London. That was very "her". It was upsetting, finding that out, but . . . I thought, well, I suppose the same things that cross your mind every time you think about Sophie. How could she do that? Why did she not say? I couldn't sleep for thinking that I had done something wrong or let her down. I had to know. I was talking to Alex and he offered to look for her. I now know what it means to own a security company. Not just security guards; it means that he can find anybody anywhere. Within two weeks he found her living in Stoke Newington with one of the jobbing brickies who'd been up landscaping the garden for me. I should have known, in my garden all day but nothing ever got done. But once we found her, she stopped using the credit card, she moved, she went under the radar. She drew a line under it.' He smiles at me. 'But it was a relief in a way. I knew she was well and it wasn't what was important to me that mattered, it was what was important to her. She left me, the house, the croft behind.' He shrugged.

I wonder how much Rod has been confiding in him. 'So what is the croft like up here?'

Forty minutes later the Land Rover pulls to a halt outside a small two-storey stone construction built into the lee side of a hill. Further down the hill, about a hundred yards away, are

the ruins of old sheep steadings, little more than heaps of
rubble. As I climb out, the road beneath my feet is little more
than a dirt track.

As he walks me round the outside, showing me the thick-
ness of the walls, he tells me that it hasn't been a working
croft for years.

'At the moment I think it's the local coffee stop for cops
trying to figure out what happened to Lorna. It's been extended
over the years, of course. These close outbuildings were
absorbed by the main building then an attic was added. A
kitchen was put on in 1910.'

I see the porch looks barely weatherproof, the front door is
panelled wood with flaking veined paint, but the area in front
of the croft is landscaped immaculately, just like his house in
Eaglesham. There is a round pond and, set in the middle of
it, a wheel of small buckets.

'Perpetual motion?' I ask.

'Fascinating, isn't it?' He pads around, still talking, followed
by Rosie, the little fat collie with no teeth. All this is his land.
He offers to show me the nearby hydroelectric scheme one
day, and proceeds to wax lyrical about the POWs who worked
on it, the engineering feat involved. I know the four huge pipes
that run down the hillside to Loch Lomond; it's always looked
a bit Dr Who to me, never mind hydroelectric.

I can't help but look over to Ben Lomond lying to the right.
The Rest is well hidden by the hills. There's no way across,
it's too far, too rough. The only way is down on to the road
and drive the long way round. Costello was right about Lorna
coming out from a car. The sun is setting, the night is warm,
summery, and the clouds are gathering over the hill tops.

The lack of light makes me look at Eric; he seems his usual
slightly potty self. He is mesmerised, watching the buckets
fill and empty as they go round.

'That's impossible,' I say.

'The trick is the water that's pumped up the central column.'

'So you cheat.'

Eric laughs and says that he has something interesting to
show me. Inside the house smells like Eric, of Land Rover
and damp dog. I follow him under a frame of scaffolding that

seems to be holding up the ceiling in the hall, to get to the door of the living room. It has a sofa of worn cracked leather, and carpets so dirty the pattern is long gone. A large barometer has pride of place on the wall opposite the wood-burning stove, and there are books stacked high in the corner. Only Rosie's basket seems to be devoid of dog hair, her water bowl is pristine. There are drawings and files everywhere. Two drawing boards, both of them broken, are lying against the wall. I stop and look at something on top of an old wooden sideboard, a construction of glass tubes, like the one Mary has in the hall at Ardno. He sees me look. I run my finger along the topmost pipe. It's so narrow you can't see the inner cavity or the walls; there's merely a hint of moving water. At first it looks like a huge hotchpotch of glass tubes, but on closer inspection there is a precise symmetry to it all. It's so dense it's impossible to follow one pipe to another. It's like a transparent three-dimensional maze.

'Do you like it? It's something I've been working on.'

'What is it?'

Eric smiles. 'It's a water clock.'

'Oh, Mary has one in the house. Do they work?'

'Alex's is one of mine. Yes, they're the oldest form of time-keeping in the world. Incredibly accurate, engineering at its finest and purest. They're called clepsydra, the thieves of time. I've been working on this one for some time and it's nearly right but not quite.'

I am fascinated by this. 'How does it work?'

'Would you be interested?' He smiles. 'I thought you would think it was a waste of time.'

'Anything that you have a passion for is never a waste of time.'

'I'll get it going.' He opens a drawer on the sideboard, takes out a syringe and places it on the sideboard. Then he smooths out the felt that the water clock stands on and lays a spirit level on it. He picks up three bottles of coloured ink – red, blue and yellow – then lines them up with a precision that I would be proud of. He draws a tiny amount of blue up into the syringe and injects it into the tap at the end of the bundle of three neatly bound glass tubes. He repeats it with the yellow bottle and then the red, injecting each into a different place. He stands back, checks his watch. He waits. I sense I am to watch this and not comment. Once his wrist-watch has reached some pertinent time, he opens the tiny tap at the top of the maze and waits. And waits. And watches. With all the expectancy of a young lover awaiting the first sight of his sweetheart, he holds his breath as the first drop of clear water winds its way down the narrow glass pipe where it meets a bubble of black dye. They float towards each other, embrace, and an azure cloud forms. A slow blue comet rolls it way to the end where it forms a perfect sphere. It steals yellow, and turns deep emerald, hinting at lime round the edges. The colour is not constant, it swirls to the colour of olives, then weakens to buttercup. The water halts at the edge of the tub, pauses before taking the final plunge on to the aluminium gutter below.

Eric leans in and peers at the water drop as it forms a red teardrop; the surface tension builds, then it lets go. The receiving cup takes charge of the red drop with a quiet 'bip', a rather pleasing sound like an honest raindrop. Eric holds his breath, watching again, waiting again; that fascination will never leave him. Another drop runs down the channel, hesitates, then also slips on to the cup below. For a moment nothing happens but then the cup begins to register the extra weight, recognizes its own tipping point, and begins, infinitesimally at first, degree by degree, to sink down on the end of its off-centre spindle. Just as slowly, the next cup lowers to take its place. Eric looks at his watch and frowns a little.

'That has turned the wheel exactly one sixteenth of its circumference, twenty-two point five degrees. One sixteenth of a minute, one cup every three point seven-five seconds. One minute per rotation. It has to be perfect, it has to be right. But it isn't. Yet.' Eric sits back on his old velvet chair. 'There is more to life than simply increasing its speed.'

'Gandhi?'

'Correct. But all time is an illusion.'

'Einstein. It is beautiful, isn't it?' I sit down on the other chair, a battered old brown leather thing. As the cups fill with water, a small glass slide is being counterweighted and it slowly lifts like a portcullis. The dark blue water scuttles under yellow, they mix in wave form but stay separate.

'Now that is clever,' I say, impressed. 'So when that little bucket fills it lifts the door slightly.'

'And as the level of the water rises it escapes into the bucket, which becomes heavier and lifts the barrier so the water gets through, reducing the pressure. When the weight drops the barrier falls back. Its own little perpetual motion system, if such a thing could ever exist.' He leans forward and closes the small glass tap on the pipe. The dripping stops, the wheel slowly stops turning. Eric Mason can stop time.

I then notice that the sofa and the chairs in the room are all pointed towards the water clock, the way my parents' chairs used to point towards the telly.

'You spend a lot of time looking at it?' I ask. He looks at me to see if I'm taking the mickey. 'I can see it being therapeutic, watching time pass like that. This is a work of art, but do you see a practical use for it?'

'Do you?' He regards me with sludgy brown eyes. 'I mean, they are effective timepieces but you have to have a very small electric pump in there and that kind of spoils it. If it were outside, though, all I have to do is regulate the rainfall. That's the experiment out there, but it's broken with all this rain pissing down all the time.' He turns a tap again, the water starts moving, almost imperceptibly.

'Is there a pump in the one in Mary's hall?'

'At Alex's house.' He corrects me automatically. 'Just listen.'

Then I hear it, the sound of water and time passing in perfect harmony. A metronome of life.

'Has that always fascinated you, the dance of water and time?'

'Time and tide wait for no man,' he says. 'They both go quickly on their way. No matter what happens to water or minutes, sooner or later, they both . . . I can never find the right word . . . escape, retreat? Water can be diverted, dammed, blocked or stored. Time can be ignored or delayed, but they will both pass. The end result is always the same, water goes to ground to join the great cycle of life. Everything goes to ground.'

He closes his eyes again, his head back, fingertips meeting, tapping one on the other in time with the drops of the water clock.

I lean back in the seat and do the same. The water drops tune into my heartbeat, and for a while they are one.

Complete peace falls on the room.

We both jump as a playful tinny tune sounds out in the room. He looks at me in horror.

'Sorry,' he says. 'Mobile.' He gets up and digs about in various pockets of the jacket he left hanging over the door handle. He looks at the number ID with some surprise.

'It's Mary,' he says to me.

'Is there a problem?' I ask, reaching into my own pocket for my mobile. There are no missed calls on it.

Eric takes the call. 'Mary?' he says.

There is silence, and he pulls a face at me. He is about to repeat himself when a quiet voice says, 'Hello.'

Not Mary.

'Hello?' Eric tries again.

Silence.

'Mary, is that you?'

'It's me.'

I am now on my feet; both of us know that something is wrong. Eric holds the phone so that we can both hear the childish whisper, the rasping breath.

I say, 'Charlie?'

'Yes.'

'It's Elvie here, and your Uncle Eric.'

The reply is automatic and polite. 'Hello, Elvie. Hello, Eric.'

'Hi, is your mum there?' Eric asks, keeping his voice light.

'No.'

I take the phone from him and watch as Eric puts his shoes back on muttering, 'Bloody kids, what's he playing at?' under his breath.

'Does your mum know you're on the phone?'

'No.'

'Can you go and get Mum for me?'

'She's not here.'

I roll my eyes heavenward. 'OK, Charlie, where did you get the phone?'

'On the floor.'

'And where is Mum?'

'Not here.'

Eric says, 'Alex is in Glasgow, she must be there.' Just as Charlie is whispering in my ear, 'Nobody here.'

'You say there's nobody there?' I repeat for Eric's benefit.

Eric looks round; Charlie is not a stupid boy. 'And where are you?'

'Kitchen.'

Eric puts out his hand for the mobile.

'OK, look, Charlie. It's Uncle Eric here, and this is what I want you to do. You end this call and I'll phone you back and you answer, OK? Do you know how to do that? Don't turn the phone off now.' Eric presses End Call and waits for the number to go red to show that Charlie has hung up. He then calls Alex's landline. 'Mary will be about somewhere.'

'Unless she's had an accident,' I say.

Eric looks at me, one eyebrow raised. All kinds of things are running through my mind. Has she fallen down the stairs, had some kind of fit?

'There's no answer.' He holds the phone out for me to hear it ring, then go on to answerphone. Still nobody picks up. Eric ends the call and scrolls back up to Mary's mobile number and presses Call. It is answered immediately by scratching and bumping. I imagine the clumsy little fingers over the touch screen.

'Uncle Eric?'

'Hello, Charlie, did your mum give you your tea?'

'Yes.'

'And where is she now?'

'Dunno.' There is a faint sniffle. 'Mum's not here.'

Eric picks up his jacket and swings it over one arm, knocking some papers to the floor. I bend down to pick them up, handfuls of drawings of extensions and chimneys, water clocks and swimming pools, reinforced floors for indoor pools and a drawing I recognize as his own back garden. I put them back in the file, in roughly the right order, when he taps me on the shoulder and mouths *jacket on*. I get up and slip the fleece back on, check my own phone, and we duck under the scaffolding to get to the front door. I jump at a deep grinding under the floor, then a whirring sound surrounds us.

'Generator,' explains Eric. 'Come on, we need to get going.'

I look out the hall window across the barren moor. The clouds have closed in, the heather is waving around in the gale and rain spikes down. Eric still has the phone clasped to his ear. I follow him as he walks to the front door, keeping his voice calm, teasing. 'So she's not being a lazy big sleepyhead and still in her bed?' He steps over the dog's bowls, still talking down the phone.

'She's not here.'

Eric slips his arms into his jacket, then picks up the keys to the Land Rover, and I follow him across the grass. 'Where are you, Charlie?' He opens the door to the vehicle.

'Kitchen. I'm cold.' He is nearly crying.

'Cold?'

'Yes, Eric.'

'Why are you cold?'

'The door's open.'

'What door?'

'The back door. I'm hiding in the kitchen.'

'Hiding?' Eric starts the engine, he raises his voice. 'Why are you hiding, Charlie?'

'In case they come back.'

It is three minutes past midnight when Eric punches in the numbers on the keypad. The Land Rover grinds to a halt on the monoblock near where Charlie has his swings.

I jump out of the Land Rover and run across the paving, up the steps to the shattered glass of the patio doors. Even in the darkness I can see the blood. Eric is saying to Charlie, 'I'm just outside, son, but you stay where you are.'

The patio door swings open at the push of my fingertip.

'Charlie? Are you still here?' Eric goes up the steps to the kitchen; I grab his arm and pull him back. There appears to be blood smeared everywhere. He reels slightly, both hands to his mouth, silencing the horror. There is one set of shoe prints, tramlines of drag marks. I hear Eric mutter, *Oh, Mary*.

'Don't stand in that,' I say. Something awful happened here.

I carefully step round the kitchen that Eric designed. White units, black and white marble tiles. Mary keeps it pristine. Her handbag lies on the floor, open, contents scattered as if she had dropped it. That's how Charlie had got the phone. Fruit has spilled from the basket on the worktop and an apple has rolled as far as the toe of my shoes, leaving its own little bloody track. We are both silent. I lift a large knife from the rack. Eric looks at me, shocked, but I am not taking any chances.

He turns the phone off and we stand still, listening. I move round the central island warily. I can deal with anything if I have surprise on my side.

'Elvie?' Eric is still at the door, pointing. I see smears on the white tiles then notice they have been made by a foot too small to be Mary's. It is the perfect outline of a little boy's shoe, dragging the blood towards the kitchen cupboard next to the Belfast sink.

'Charlie?' I say, with as much authority as I can muster. 'It's Elvie. Do you want to come out?'

'No.'

SATURDAY, 9 JUNE

Alex Parnell looks like any other successful businessman who's just got out of the car after a long drive; the only sign of his stress is the play of the fingers of his right hand on the cuff of his left sleeve. He wears a well-cut lightweight suit, a brittle blue that matches the colour of his jumpy eyes. His silk tie lies loose at his neck, his polished handmade shoes click on the marble floor as he paces. He has an iPhone clasped to his ear.

DCI Anderson retreats into the living room with the gold table and the Chinese rugs. He wasn't at work when he got the call and is dressed in a sweatshirt and jeans. He watches Alex Parnell unobtrusively then glances at the original Howson above the door, a pastel of a bare knuckle fighter in grey and black, as if making the connection, the hard man connection. The water clock is still in its glass case, ticking away with a *drop, drop, drop*. It seems to be mocking me.

Parnell was on the phone when he first walked through the door, and has remained so ever since. Even when Charlie ran from me into his daddy's arms, the wings of his Batman pyjamas crumpled and flapping, Parnell only interrupted his conversation briefly to bounce Charlie on the arc of his hip. I heard him whisper into his son's ear about him being a brave boy and to be a wee bit braver for a wee bit longer. Mummy would come back. Anderson has followed me into the living room, to give the man some privacy in his own home. Only Costello, a nosey wee tyke at the best of times, remains to watch. I presume that's part of her job. The stairway down to the kitchen is taped off; in the absence of any other explanation, it is a crime scene.

Parnell is no sooner off the phone than it rings again, and he holds up his hand in apology. Charlie is burrowing his face in Parnell's trouser leg, gripping on to the silk with small sticky fingers. Anderson nods in acknowledgment while Costello pulls a face of ill-concealed impatience.

Parnell is saying, 'Thanks, I'll let you know . . . yes, as soon as I do . . . I might take you up on that . . . but I really have to go now . . .' and on it goes. The voice at the other end rattles on. He walks up to one of the four marble statues, a Greek goddess holding a lamb, before he turns round and paces back. Costello stalks him, walking up to the same statue, bending down as if to see if there's a price on it. She glances at the white staircase, then to the Howson, the double-opening front door, the security locks. She is clearly thinking one thing. Money. Money. Money. If Mary has been taken by the Night Hunter, Parnell might go down the *I have the money, the expertise, the contacts. I'll flush the bastard out myself* route. The same thought went through my mind. But Mary was taken indoors, she was snatched. The others had been taken while out running. Was that a different MO or a progression of the same?

Costello wanders into the sitting room. 'Did you ever meet Natalie Thom?' she whispers to me as she goes past.

'No.'

She floats away.

Parnell hangs up the phone and sticks it in his pocket. 'Go to Elvie now,' he tells the wee boy, and Charlie rushes over and climbs up my trousers. I see Costello's eyes narrow. She stands like a soldier at the gates of Stalingrad. She gives Parnell no privacy. I've been through it, Eric has been through it. It strikes me how strange that is. Parnell, for all his wealth and power, is about to come face to face with the Not Knowing.

'Maybe it would be better if Elvie stayed,' says Costello. 'Eric can take Charlie to his room, read him a story.'

Anderson nods his agreement, he is keen to get on. Parnell kisses Charlie, and Eric takes the boy away. There is a quiet, hurried conversation between Eric and Parnell that Costello cannot overhear, no matter how hard she tries.

Now all four of us are in the living room, standing on a Chinese rug that smells of money. Four white sofas sit round the large glass and gold coffee table.

'Sorry about all that,' says Parnell, sitting down. 'I spent the journey here from Glasgow talking hands-free to some female detective.'

'That was me,' says Costello, bristling at the 'some'.

'I'm DCI Colin Anderson. I've been put in charge.'

So Costello *has* been bumped from the top of the tree.

'Can I confirm that you have found nothing missing, no signs of robbery?'

'Any burglar would have taken credit cards, money, artwork, but there's nothing missing. Apart from my wife.'

'Mary,' says Costello, still bristling.

Anderson sits down opposite Parnell, smiling an understanding *all men in it together* smile.

'And a housebreaker wouldn't take my wife, I would presume. She's been kidnapped, hasn't she?'

'It must be the obvious conclusion.' Costello sits down beside Anderson. Her smile is more: *If you have anything to do with this I'll have you.* She sinks deep in the big white leather sofa, one leg crossed over the other like she owns the place. Or wants to.

Anderson is listening to Parnell. I hear them going through Mary's daily routine, her contacts. I've already done my bit. I wonder who has been on the phone telling them to pull out all the stops for Alex Parnell and his missing wife. Alex Parnell is one of the richest men in Glasgow. They will all have to be on their best behaviour. I am calculating how soon I can get away and speak to Billy.

'Mary has a chip,' says Parnell.

'Pardon?' asks Anderson.

'Here in her arm, she has a location chip, GPS. You should know from the get-go that her actual location is not a problem. I know that it might not be appropriate just to go and get her but . . . we will know where she is. That must put us ahead of the game.'

'And can you do that now?' asks Anderson.

'Soon.' He glances at his watch. 'Hence the phone calls. I'm sure after Madeleine McCann disappeared every parent thought *if only that wee girl had been chipped she'd be traceable*. If only. Well, I'm rich enough to make the "if only" a fact. I know I might be a target for certain types of crime, so I liked the chip idea. Location chipping can track kids anywhere. Thank God I made sure that Charlie had one. He was nervous having it done, so Mary sat beside him and got one as well. And I'm so glad she did.' Parnell wipes a tear from the corner of his eye. 'Thank God.'

'So why are you sitting here?' asks Anderson, carefully. 'If it was me I'd be out there, all guns blazing.'

'Because it needs to be activated first. And because it won't help if they have a gun to her head, will it?' Parnell smiles weakly.

'Activated?'

'The GPS needs to be activated.' He looks at the door, but it remains closed.

'So, just to be clear, you have your wife tagged?' asks Costello.

'Chipped. In here.' He taps the top of his arm. 'It looks like a vaccination mark.' He jumps as the front door opens and a tall man comes into the room, laptop under arm and a page torn from a notepad in his hand.

Parnell is on his feet. 'Gary, is that it?'

'Yes. I've not tried it yet, sir.'

Parnell sits down further along the settee to let Gary sit down. I notice the beads of sweat on his forehead, the way the fingers of his right hand are coiling and uncoiling; his self-control is slipping. I almost feel sorry for him. Almost.

Anderson's voice is gentle as he asks, 'So this device can trace Mary wherever she goes?'

'Yes and no. An activation request has to be made by someone who knows a code and can offer further security information. I phoned from the car and they're getting it up and running now. It had better bloody work. This is Gary Irvine, my IT guy.'

Gary shrugs off a leather jacket and sits down beside Parnell, placing the laptop on the coffee table. 'I've already typed in the activation codes they gave me, now you put in your PIN number.' His voice is trembling. 'I've never done this before.'

'I was hoping you would never have to.' Parnell types four numbers into the laptop with two fingertips and watches intently. 'Mary knows that she has the tag on her, she knows that we will come to get her. She'll be OK.'

Anderson and Costello glance at each other, then at me. I

think I know what they're thinking: if these cases are linked
– and that's a big if – then all we have to do is track Mary
and she'll lead us to the other women. Including Sophie.
Costello's distrustful eyes are boring into me.

'All we have to do is press Enter, and he said it should just
. . .' Gary's finger clicks and he sits back, eyes on the screen.

Anderson cannot resist getting up and walking round the
back of the sofa and Parnell moves slightly to allow him a
better view, and Costello slots in behind. Only I remain in
position, watching their faces.

Gary bites on his own thumb. 'Oh my God, it's loading.'

Anderson leans forward looking at the screen; a map of the
UK disappears to be replaced by a map of Scotland, then Glasgow.
A tiny blue dot appears, consistently pulsing, then it starts
to spawn ever-growing circles. The dot floats north from
Glasgow, then stops over Argyll. The blue turns red. The pulsing
stops.

Parnell puts his finger on the screen, a gentle pressure like
a kiss, and says quietly, 'Mary.'

Three hours later the red dot has not moved. It remains on a
green part of the map, above the treeline of Glen Lyon, very
near the Rest and Be Thankful, too near to be a coincidence.
Less than an hour from the Parnells' house by road, much less
by a powerful car at this time of night. But there is no car in
the lay-by at the bottom of the hill, so why is the red dot
coming from up a mountain? Anderson looks down over the
loch, at the surface of the water, grey and pockmarked with
the speckles of warm summer rain. There are more clouds
ready to close in. The grass verges of the old road are full of
cars, two Land Rovers, the dog unit and the small minibus
with the armed response team. Anderson hopes they will not
be needed. He looks again at the small dot sending out the
ever-expanding circles; it is not moving, so Mary is either not
moving or is not being moved.

Parnell had insisted that I should be here. I am the fittest,
Mary knows me and I am medically trained.

Arty Simon, the search team leader, just noted the number
on my high-visibility vest and nodded. Now he holds his arm

up, signalling that we're ready to go. The group gathers. Simon takes charge of the palm-held device and its flashing signal.

'The dog goes first. Then those with torches. If the first contact is in any way problematic then we fall back. The target has not moved, not a good sign. We need to keep Parnell at the back of the group.'

'I'll be down here. Costello will keep Parnell with her, don't worry,' said Anderson.

'And you had better keep your head, stay calm – no matter what.' As Simon checks the medical pack on my back he says quietly, 'I have no idea what we might be walking into.' He looks round at the line of dark grey mountains. 'We have to go. Has Parnell got the scent source? Tarka is better than any electronic device, so if Mary is up there, the dog will find her.'

'The locator will take us to within two metres,' says a gravel voice behind us. Alex Parnell stands on the broken tarmac of the single track road. 'I have the pyjama top she slept in.' He holds out a slightly bulky plastic evidence bag, sterile so the scent would not be contaminated.

Anderson and I watch them walk away, Simon introducing Parnell to the dog handler. Simon then comes back, moving into tactical command mode. He checks the palm-held device; the signal is strong, and the battery has plenty of charge left. He then lifts his arm and the rest of the team fall in line. Eight men in all. And Costello and me.

Tarka and her handler move to the front of the line. The Alsatian bitch pulls gently on her lead, her tongue panting, the rain making crystal baubles on the black diamond hair of her back. She sets off up the path, nose sniffing the air.

Parnell speaks to Anderson. 'But the locator is telling us that Mary is over there. Why are we following the dog in the wrong direction?'

Anderson pats him on the arm. 'Just let the dog do her job, she'll take us the way Mary was taken. We'll end up in the same place, don't worry. If the dog goes quickly then Elvie can keep up.' He gestures to me to get going and I go past. Costello's grey eyes narrow as she puts up her hood; she is suspicious of me even being here.

Parnell shakes his head. 'Oh no, I have to be there.'

'You will stay at the back with me,' says Costello, no argument.

Suddenly we are moving. Tarka sets off up the narrow path through the trees, pulling on ahead, her nose twitching as she works. She keeps her head steady as she follows the airborne scent. I wonder how the dog can smell anything in the heavy, damp air that is already thick with the smell of pine cones, but Tarka appears to have no trouble at all. The handler follows her confidently. There is no path that I can see but the SOCO on the search keeps flashing his camera at broken twigs and disturbed pine needles on the ground. I notice that the handler is walking slightly to the side of the marks of Mary's path, leaving any evidence uncontaminated by his feet.

The dog handler holds up his hand, stopping us. I am surprised at how spread out we are already; the lead group is moving much quicker than the rest. He says to me, 'They were moving in single file, running from the look of it.'

'Running?' The thought of Lorna being chased by a dog crosses my mind.

We quicken our pace. We walk through the constant pitter-pat of rain against the trees accompanied by the brush of nylon sleeves against tunics, feet through undergrowth. The dog pulls us along through a dense part of the forest and out the other side, older trees, wider spread, then she stops and sits. The handler raises his arm . . . I stop. While we wait for the others to catch us up I hear Costello mutter from somewhere in the darkness that she is bloody knackered.

The handler points, asks for someone to shine a torch. He crouches down. 'There's something here.'

I see it in the beam of the torch, covered by grass and a fine scattering of pine needles, some of which had been exposed longer than others. It is a flat black shoe, like a trainer but with a Velcro fastener.

I move aside to let Parnell stand in front of me; he palms his mouth with his hand and nods slowly. 'That's Mary's.'

'OK, we go on.' Simon points to the ground next to the shoe and the SOCO moves forward with his camera. Ten flashes in quick succession, then he places a yellow triangle down and waves that he is ready. Simon gestures that they should be careful to walk round. There is another signal to Costello to keep Parnell back; he is worried about what we might stumble across. Our column moves on, quicker now, walking with more purpose. Simon checks the palm-held. The dog is still walking away from the signal but she is moving confidently, pulling to get into a thicket of younger pine trees. She sits again.

'Here!'

Simon points and says quietly, 'There's another shoe there, and a pile of black material over there.'

He points to the dark rags, soaked through in the rain. He reaches forward and lifts it carefully with a gloved hand, not enough for it to clear the ground, but enough to make out the zip and two legs . . . black jeans. Simon turns slowly, making sure that Parnell is not within earshot.

I nod. 'Mary's.'

Simon says to me, his voice low, 'Abducted, driven to a remote spot, chased, stripped. This is only going to have one outcome.' He backhands the rain from his brow. 'Parnell shouldn't be here.' He lifts his radio and I don't quite catch what he says but I do hear: 'Don't care, but use all your personal charm to get him out of there, and keep him away.'

We are moving again now. The dog moves on to find a black zipped sweatshirt then a light blue T-shirt, darkened with the rain. I register the rips in the fabric. Simon points ahead; a white bra is strewn on the grass in a clearing, its white lace stained black.

Or red.

The SOCO leans forward to photograph it.

Simon raises himself from his crouching position and lifts his radio. The whole team is silent, only broken by the steady pant of the dog.

The group has barely moved five metres when the dog stops again, and sits down.

There is nothing to be seen. The torch beam sweeps back and forth. Nothing.

Simon looks at the palm-held. 'She's brought us round in a circle. Mary should be here.'

'The dog has found her mark,' says the handler, looking around him.

'OK, we need to get a grid up here,' says Simon. 'Check all this area out; she must be round here somewhere. According to this, we should be right on top of her.' Absurdly he looks at his feet.

I stare, looking down, moving the grass with the toe of my shoe, looking for anything, but there is nothing. 'How close can she be?'

'Can I let the dog go?' asks the handler.

'Yip,' says Simon, standing back slightly.

The dog pulls her head free and takes a few steps forward into the longer grass, towards my feet, and snorts hard. Then she sits down again, staring at the grass, ears pricked as if she is listening to something that the rest of us cannot hear.

The dog handler sweeps his gloved hand through the grass and withdraws it. Veins of blood.

I am closest so I kneel down and carefully part the grass, noting the drips of blood, the larger stains.

'If you find anything don't touch it.'

I know there will be only one thing to find. I part the grass again, seeing the way the dog reacts, her ears pricked eagerly. The source of the scent is here. Then something catches my eye, a small disc on a blade of grass. One centimetre in diameter, glistening, the edge of it more visible. The underlying colour is flesh beige.

The chip.

SUNDAY, 10 JUNE

I am sitting on my big red velvet settee back in my Glasgow flat, watching the clock, trying to calm my mind. It's gone ten a.m, and I can't sleep. I stare high into the ceiling cornices, following the patterns. Simple stuff but it allows the thoughts and images in my head to bend and collide, letting them twist and reform into something else, something better. I feel as if my body has given up on me but my mind refuses to surrender.

The police did not find Mary. They took us off the hill. Costello leaned against the car talking to me. She asked me if I knew that Mary had a chip. I didn't, so I doubted that many people did. She wanted to know if I knew anybody that Parnell owed a lot of money to. I had no idea but we agreed that it did not make sense: taking her away in a car then walking her across country, when the car could have been in Glasgow in an hour. And why her? Why not the kid? He'd be the soft target.

I am intrigued by where the chip was found, up in the hills, like Lorna had been, or the Katrine girl. Mary had been running. Like Sophie.

Is there something I am missing? Something I am so familiar with that it does not register? The last time I saw Sophie in this flat was the twenty-first of March. It was a Wednesday. That was fifteen days before she went, of her own free will. I do not know when she really went missing. I was lying on this settee as I am now while she was in the bath, bleeding. I left her alone. I try to think of anything that she said but all I can see is Charlie hiding in that cupboard.

Sophie, too, went into hiding.

Alex Parnell had broken down once we were back at Ardno and even I found it difficult to watch. The serial number on the chip was a match to the one that had been inserted in Mary's arm. He was to stay at Ardno with two officers for

company. They had instructions not to leave him on his own.
I was taken down to Partickhill station to discuss what I knew.
I'm not sure who Anderson is more suspicious of. I am sure
if I was pretty, he would suspect me and Parnell of having an
affair. Costello had more than suspicions once we got to the
matter of Mary's bruises; she was ready to hang Parnell by his
gonads until he sung soprano and told us what he had really
done with his wife. She had a minor rant to Anderson, pointing
out one obvious fact: only Parnell knew that the chip was there.
Whoever took her knew the security code of the gate.

'Or they could have taken her over the back wall, there's a
gap in it.'

'It was noted,' said Anderson coolly.

'Have you found a connection between Parnell and Sophie?'
I asked.

'Yes. You.'

That conversation was at eight o'clock this morning.

My phone rings. It's Parnell's number. I pick it up. His
voice is rushed. 'I can't speak long but you and that guy,
ex-cop . . .?'

'Yeah.'

'You're looking for your sister, aren't you?' He did not
pause to hear the answer. 'Well, I want you to find Mary. You
can go where the law can't. I have a security company, you
can have anything you need. I want my wife back. Understand?
Tell him he can name his price.'

'I'll mention it to him,' I say and cut the call. Is Parnell
playing with me? I can't tell.

Now the phone beeps again, a text message. *'U busy?'*

I recognize the number. Billy.

It bleeps again before I can answer. *'I'm outside. Can we
chat?'*

At this moment, even Billy is slightly more appealing than
the mess that is rolling in my head. I text back.

The reply is immediate. *'Put the kettle on.'*

The downstairs entry buzzes before I get to the kitchen.
Minutes later Billy comes in, red in the face and wheezing
after climbing the stairs. He half collapses against the worktop,
dropping a Morrisons carrier bag on the floor.

'What the fuck! Do you need oxygen to get up here? You get a good view down on to Everest from your window?'

'Shut it. Coffee?'

'Yeah, you got a dining table?'

'In the living room.' I point the way through.

'Nice flat. Any chance of a bit of toast?'

'No. I've heard from Parnell. He wants us to find Mary.'

Billy makes the disgusting slurping noise that I now know is a sign he is thinking. 'Really.' He seems unimpressed. 'Yeah, he lost Natalie Thom, now he's lost his wife. Bit careless.'

'When you met me, did you come to that meeting to see me because of Sophie? Or because you knew that Parnell was my employer?'

'Can I be enigmatic and say both? You just count your fingers after you shake hands with him. You ever seen him hit Mary?'

'Never saw it. So does he know you – Parnell? He doesn't recognize you.'

'He's too arrogant, and I was deskbound in those days, but I know him all right.' Billy shakes his head. 'You know he married her within months of Natalie being killed? Natalie and Mary were best pals at uni.' He tuts a little, happy with his implication. He then echoes my thoughts. 'He had a hand in the design of Ardno. But why have a security gate logging you in and out the front gate then not be bothered fixing a gap in the back wall?'

'They kept coming out to fix it, but never did.'

'Who?'

'Builders from his company, I presume. A fat one with a limp and a wee guy who whistles badly.'

'So you would know them again?'

'Of course. Has this got anything to do with Sophie?'

'Well, when you started looking for her, he got you under his wing sharpish. Right where he could keep an eye on you. Neat.' He shrugs. 'Toast would be good.'

'So would a lottery win,' I reply. Before I have left the room Billy has removed his jacket and dropped it on the floor; he then kicks off his shoes. By the time I come back through with the tea, toast and Marmite he is massaging his foot with

both hands. He has two holes in his left sock. The stink of
stale cheese is horrendous. 'My mother always says that sore
feet show in your face.'

'I knew your face must be like that for a reason. Nature is
not that cruel.' I pick up my Snoopy mug of tea from the floor
beside the settee and take it over to the small pine dining table.
I notice that Billy has emptied the Morrisons bag; a pile of
buff files lies on the table top.

'What's that?'

'Stuff about Mary. I've been having a chat with a few folk.'

I look at my watch: less than twelve hours have passed
since the call at Eric's house. It seems a lifetime away. Billy
has been busy.

'Just remember that Costello is a smart cookie; she's keeping
you close so that she can keep an eye on you too.'

'Yes, I know. I've nothing to hide.'

'So where were you when Mark Laidlaw went into the
water?'

At times my lack of emotion serves me well. Deadpan, I
reply, 'Nobody knows when Mark Laidlaw went into the water.'
I take four photographs out of a folder and point at the numbers
on them. 'Should you have these?'

'Copies. Elvie, I'm devious, not friggin' stupid.'

'Either you've had these all along or you got hold of them
very quickly.' I shuffle through the rest of the pictures.

'Never ask a question you don't want to know the answer
to. Three women, maybe four. Mary could be five.'

'So it could be kidnap? You don't think Parnell has just
paid someone to throw her in the Clyde?'

'No, with his money, he'd have taken his private yacht out
to sea and dumped her where the tide is stronger. But for the
moment, go with me. Tell me if I'm right or wrong.'

'Why me?'

'Because DCI Anderson is straight as a die. But Costello
needs a break on this case. If we hand this to her she'll go
easy on us. Anderson will play it by the book but Costello we
can bargain with.'

Billy is right. I look through the photos and hand them back.
He places them down and then swaps two of them over. 'This

first one is Lorna Lennox, then Gilly Porter, then Sophie McCulloch; we might add Mary to the end. And Katrine, the unknown girl on the hill. We need to look at Lorna.'

'Why?' I pull my face slightly.

'Because we know her end point. That might lead us to the others.'

I look at the photos again.

'With Parnell's connections, Anderson will get a big budget to investigate the Mary Parnell case. I'd like to piggyback that case with these three women, Operation Beluga. I think Costello has similar thoughts. But you and I don't really think they're all connected, do we? Not all.'

'It's too different, the way she was taken.'

'Yes, but Mary was never allowed out on her own. There was violence there, control. The stalking and watching element is there, but the execution – for want of a better word – is not there. And those three were all their own people.'

'Mary wasn't.'

'As far as you know.'

'Runners can be observed, they have a uniform, a routine. The Night Hunter has no need to speak to them, he just needs to observe. Mary didn't run, so maybe another approach was needed.'

Lorna, Sophie and Gillian were smilers, Mary less so. Perhaps she is the most striking of them, but not the prettiest. There is no photograph of Katrine. Billy's phone rings; its weird plinky-plink ringtone gets on my nerves.

It's Costello – she is blunt and to the point. 'Tell Elvie we're coming to search her flat. We know you're both there.'

'I think she heard that.' His eyes look at the files, willing them to disappear.

'Has Parnell been in touch with you?'

Billy raises an eyebrow. 'Yes.'

'Asking you to find Mary?'

'Yes.'

'I bloody knew it! Look, I want you to do what he asks but keep us informed every step of the way.'

'We're always willing to help.'

'And if you don't I'll have you both done for con—'

'Yeah, heard it,' he says and cuts the call. 'I presume you caught that.' He looks at his phone. 'That's interesting. Her back is right against the wall and she knows it. It's my investigative genius she is after really, of course. I'm going to need a fresh cup of coffee.' His eyes wander round the room, over the old fireplace and the pictures on the mantelpiece. 'Is that Sophie?'

'Yes.'

'Nice picture. Who's the raven-haired wee sweetie with her?'

'That's me,' I say.

'Bloody hell, hen, what happened to you?'

'Long story.'

It has not been a good way to spend a Sunday. The whole world seems to have gone mad. Billy lifted the files and left just before Costello appeared with a whole search team. They are going through the flat here, and then Parnell's in Glasgow. Later they're going up to search the property at Ardno. She advised me that I could object.

I don't give a shit, and said so.

In the end, though, they are polite and quick. They move through the flat, two going into each room. They ask which room Sophie used when she slept here and which room was mine. Where was I when Sophie was in the bath, what did I see? I sit down on the red settee and again tell Costello what happened that night. When did I last do the washing? she asks. Sophie has been missing for sixty-seven days. Of course I've washed the towels.

Costello is particularly annoyed about that and her expression reaches a new height of sourness. 'We could have had blood or DNA or all sorts on that. I suppose you've changed the bed sheets as well?'

'Mine, yes. Don't know about hers.'

She breathes out, her fingers playing with her hair, thinking hard.

'Would the bath be any good?' I ask. 'I never have a bath. I use the shower and I'm rarely here. The shower is not over the bath. I'm thinking . . . plughole?'

She smiles at me. 'Fuck! What else am I missing? I'm just so tired.' She goes through and talks to some white suits who promptly trot out of the bedroom and into the bathroom.

'Two bathrobes on the back of the door, Elvie?'

'The black one is mine.'

'And this one?' She holds up the pink one at arm's-length in gloved fingers. 'Sophie's? Bag and tag. We can take you up to Ardno as soon as we've finished here, if that's all right? You need to be present when we search your flat there. Does Parnell have a key to it?'

'Probably,' I say.

'Elvie, did you ever see Mary talk to anybody else? She hasn't spoken more than a few words to her parents since she married Parnell. She only seems to see you or him, or both of you.'

I search my mind. 'No, just the book group. I ran her there, went off with Charlie and came back to get her, then ran her home. Otherwise she was never out of my sight. That's why I was employed, and she knew that.'

'As a bodyguard rather than a nanny?'

'As a spy rather than a bodyguard. Parnell is not thick; I think he was keeping tabs on her even when I wasn't there.'

'Maybe that's the real reason for the chip. Chipped, beaten and spied on. Poor kid. Her phone just has calls to you, Eric Mason and Alex on it. She lived in a bubble.'

I remember a day when Charlie and I had been down at the lochside. Mary had stayed up on the road. I heard Mary laugh, not something I heard often. She was on the phone. I replay it in my mind. Not her touch pad phone? There was no sweeping of the finger . . . In my memory she was tapping buttons, using an older phone. Did she have two phones?

'Did Charlie say anything?'

'He saw nothing. He's being interviewed by a play therapist but Parnell insists on sitting in, so it's not ideal. The boy doesn't want to speak until his dad approves. Is he like that with his mother?'

'No, he jabbers away like a wee monkey.'

'Her parents get a card from Charlie every now and again but they don't speak.' She pulls out her phone and checks it.

'Funny, I don't see Mary as the type of person that would cause an estrangement. She seems a bit weak-willed, a follower.' She closes her phone; something has displeased her. She gets called from the bathroom. I hear her say, *That's great* and *Get it back to the lab.*

She reappears, her mind back on the job. 'We need to get moving now, you have five minutes to get your stuff together.'

By half past four they have already gone through the apartment above the dining room with all kinds of forensic stuff. The flat is tiny so I couldn't be shuffled about and kept out of the way as they look under cushions, look at my books, examine Charlie's drawings on the fridge door. It took a tenth of the time it took them at the Glasgow flat.

The forensic presence has been at the big house all night. I've gleaned that Mary was attacked when she was alone in the kitchen. She cut herself on the broken glass as she was dragged through the patio doors, then she was taken across the lawn and over the field to the damaged wall. They avoided the electronic lock on the front gate. Any car waiting there would have a good run to Glasgow but they stopped halfway and chased her up a hill.

It doesn't make sense unless Mary got out in some way and tried to escape. Was she then chased down like Lorna?

I'm back down on the patio with Charlie; he wants a go on the swing. It's a good place to watch the comings and goings of the team while Charlie asks me a thousand times, in a hundred different ways, when his mother is coming back. I recognize one of the team as Matilda, the wee forensic girl who found the dog DNA.

My phone goes again, it's Billy. Pushing Charlie on the swing with one hand, I listen as he tells me to 'follow any leads'. Then specifically he tells me to trace the other women at Mary's book group or find if there's another mobile phone somewhere, with numbers that might tell us about some other life. I tell him I am way in front of him; he does not seem surprised.

I hang up and give Charlie an extra push. The good thing about a small community like this is that everybody knows everybody's business.

Or they think they do.

I organize a game of hide and seek with Charlie. While I can see him hiding behind the police car I make a few calls. It takes me exactly three minutes to get the phone number I need.

'Come out, come out wherever you are.'

MONDAY, 11 JUNE

Rachel sweeps her long hair behind one ear. 'So it looks as though she was kidnapped. Alex is loaded.' She moves some library books from the top shelf to the trolley. This takes up a lot of her available brain power.

'I haven't known Mary for a long time but you're the only person whose name I've ever heard her mention, as a friend.' That's a bit of a stretch. Rachel is the only person I ever actually heard Mary mention.

Rachel looks up. 'Really?'

'So can you tell me anything that might help us find out where she might be?' It sounds a very stupid request, not one that would stand up to any scrutiny, but Rachel mulls it over.

'Not really. Haven't seen her for a while, but she wasn't happy, was she?' The books move from the trolley back on to the shelf. 'I think, wee things . . . like the group would stay on at the coffee shop to have a gossip and a cuppa, but she would never come. Never on the nights out. Like she was scared of him. She was always checking her watch so that she wouldn't be late back.'

She looks out the window. Dunoon is hiding behind some light summer rain. 'Funny, when she joined the group, we all thought Mary had everything. Posh taste in reading, Austen and Thomas Hardy. No *Fifty Shades* for her. We didn't really take to her. Incomer, married to the rich man, building her own house up here . . . But she was so not like that. She was quiet, timid. A bit boring really.'

I can't help but notice that we are talking about Mary in the past tense.

'For someone who had everything, she had nothing.'

'It's often the way,' I say. Sophie taught me to leave such statements open, so you get more.

'Well, a wee thing. Kim had this really battered laptop, up for grabs. Mary looked at it as if she'd won the pools. Kim phoned me afterwards, you know, thinking – God! All that money yet she wants something like that! That's how they get rich, isn't it, these people? Just don't spend it.' Rachel looks at me, remembering why I'm here. 'Still, hope she gets back OK.'

'You said you hadn't seen her for some time?'

Rachel has a good think. 'Oh, not since a while.'

'A while?'

'Well, before Kirsty had her baby.'

That's supposed to mean something to me. 'And how old is the baby?'

Rachel smiles. 'Oh, about twelve weeks, Sienna-Faye, a real wee poppet, she . . .'

'So you've not seen Mary for three months?'

Rachel shakes her head. 'Not hide nor hair of her. Took that bloody laptop and we never saw her again.'

'Do you recall the make of the laptop?'

'Nah. And to think she could afford a state of the art tablet. Nothing as queer as folk, eh?'

So each time I dropped Mary at the door of the library, she went elsewhere. Two hours on her own. It gives me a wee kick of hope. She had a life we did not know about. There was the day she took the four-by-four somewhere and Parnell wanted to know the mileage. And a phone and a laptop.

What was she doing while Charlie and I went to the beach or to the pier to watch the ferries come and go? And with who?

The blood did not lie; the chip had been cut out of her. That she carried it was something she didn't confide in me. But would she tell a lover? Or someone she thought was a lover? What kind of trouble had she got herself in?

Had she run away from Parnell just to run into somebody much worse like Sophie had?

Billy is interested in my theory. 'So what do you think about that?'

'Well, people run to type. Mary had studied English, she loved the written word. Everything she did was monitored by him, but then she gets a chance of a laptop, to write. Imagine the freedom of mind that would give her.'

'A diary? A misery memoir?'

'Same thing in her case. The problem is, I've never seen a laptop like that in the house. Everything is the latest high-spec stuff that Parnell likes. So where do you think she might have hidden it?'

'Where are you now?'

'Standing among the trees in Hell's Glen, there's nobody here for miles around. I need to think.'

'No you don't, you need to get back to the house, act casual. Act like you're worried about Mary. Then search the house right under his nose.'

'Just like that?'

'There's a whole search team there but they're not looking for what you're looking for. Oh, and don't get killed.'

Back at the house I think about Mary as I put the orange juice in the fridge, in date order just as Parnell likes it. I put the kettle on for the ever-growing army of cops and SOCOs drifting around, and I think about her life and her love of literature which has been denied her since she married and moved here. The old laptop makes sense but I've no idea where she has hidden it. I get up and move round the house, putting away clothes, cleaning a little, trying to think like Mary. She would certainly think of somewhere Parnell did not go. And Mary would be clever about it.

The last of the forensic team are packing up, chatting after a hard day. I go into her bathroom, the en suite one; not the best place to keep a laptop. She likes long baths and gets the place all steamed up. Beside her bed are her books: *The World of Emily Dickinson* and *Complete Poems of Christina Rossetti*. A cookery book about baking for kids. And that is that. The Rossetti book is a shabby second-hand copy of an old edition; its jacket is missing. The sum of three pounds fifty is scribbled in pencil on the flyleaf. Probably from a charity shop. I never knew she had it; she had never mentioned it, not even in our *Goblin Market* conversations.

I sit on the bed for a long time. Someone downstairs is shouting for car keys. The place already seems emptier without Mary.

I go to the kitchen and find Parnell and Charlie drawing. Parnell is guiding Charlie's hand, his other hand is on his mobile.

'Do you want some juice, Charlie? Fruit Shoot?'

'No, thank you,' he says politely. He is drawing a woman being pulled out the door with blood shooting from her arm.

'Maybe you should show that to the nice policeman,' I say. Parnell suddenly notices what his son has drawn and nods. Even he seems more tense than usual.

'Well, I'll leave you to it.' I pick up a duster and nip to the big library, running the cloth over the bookshelves. The collector's edition of Rossetti is still there on its stand, still in its cover. I dust down the leather-bound volumes that have never been read. Then I go to the lower shelf where Mary keeps her own precious collection: Jane Austen and the Brontës, Enid Blyton and J.K. Rowling, the books that she is keeping for Charlie. And then, wedged between them, *The Complete Poems of Christina Rossetti*. Three copies? But it's just the old cover, wrapped around something about ten inches high, slotted upright between the books. Something laptop-shaped.

Parnell is about and he is sharp. It might be something, it might be nothing. If it's nothing, then Parnell need not concern himself. If it's anything to do with her kidnap then I will tell Costello. Either way, Mary did not want her husband knowing and I will not tell him. She had her reasons, as did Sophie. *Goblin Market*. It's about the mistakes women make for men. One sister has to look out for the other. I need to find Mary. If I find Mary, I might find Sophie.

'You find what you were looking for?' The gruff voice of Parnell speaks behind me, very close to my shoulder. If I turn round, he will be eyeballing me.

I do not turn. 'I was thinking about Mary and Sophie, wondering if they are together.' At that point I turn round. We eyeball each other, I know that he cannot read me.

He looks annoyed. 'I have to go to Glasgow. I'll be back tonight. I want you to take Charlie upstairs to the flat, and don't let anybody in. I'll phone when I get back, do you understand?'

'Of course.'

He turns, his shoes clicking on the marble floor. He pauses, looking round as he walks out the library. He knows I was searching for something.

By eight, Charlie is lying on the settee eating some of a Cornetto and rubbing the rest on his face. We have modelled with Play-Doh and we have watched *Bob the Builder*. He thinks it is about his father. So far, Parnell has not called. Once he had driven off, I told Charlie that he had five minutes to find his Play-Doh and his DVD and meet me at the front door. The back door is out of bounds. I heard him running around being as noisy as possible as I went into the library and opened the laptop. No battery. I go back and find the flex coiled up behind the books. It took ages to power up, even longer to let me open the document. Charlie shouted something; *Bob the Builder* had gone AWOL. I said he could have another ten minutes. I pulled the flash drive from my pocket and inserted it. There was only one Word document. I didn't care what it was, I just copied it. It took forever.

Once it was finished I turned the laptop off, closed it and returned it to its hiding place. When I came back Charlie was staring through the banister, watching my every move.

'What are you doing, monkey woman?' he asked.

'Monkey things,' I said.

Now he has his DVD and his Cornetto, he will lie like that for ages. All I have to do is pay attention when he tells me there is a funny bit. And laugh.

The start of the narrative is simple. And awful.

Today he told me that I was having another keeper.

So that is how she thought of me? A keeper?

This will be another pretty girl, young enough to be impressed by Alex. I wonder what kind of regime he will have in store for this one. He will have told her that I am bored, or that I fantasise and need to be kept an eye on because I might harm Charlie. She will look at him doe-eyed.

I was glad to read that she changed her mind a few pages later once she met me. *I kind of like Elvie, she's weird but nice* . . . Eric had already told her about Sophie, she writes

that it gave her a creepy feeling. Then a name jumps out
at me . . .

Natalie.

She writes about Magda and Natalie, she writes about the
Not Knowing. The style is elaborate and flowery. I scan on
looking for their names – *murdered on her way across the
park – I have not cried yet, it rams home all that Mum and
that Dad have been saying. I might not stay at uni after all.*

There is a gap, then something written at a different time.
Growing up in East Kilbride. She sounded trapped even then.

*Our house was at 37 Cloverview Brae, it looked on to a
field and I always had a view of something else going on,
another life . . .*

My phone interrupts. I close my laptop, deep in thought.
Some of that diary is obviously typed up from some other
notes Mary had. Notes about Natalie. Natalie who had introduced Mary and Alex. Natalie, who was only eighteen when
she was murdered. And Billy was in charge of that case and
did not solve it.

I answer the phone. It is Parnell.

'How's Charlie?'

'Fine.'

'Can you put him to bed in the big house and meet me
there in twenty minutes? Hopkirk will be joining us.'

TUESDAY, 12 JUNE

I walk up behind DI Costello as she waits to cross the road outside Partickhill, and tap her lightly on the arm.

She gasps. 'God, you made me jump. Has Anderson called *you* in?'

'Well, yes, but you wanted to be told if anything happened with Mary. A ransom demand arrived yesterday. It was sent to the Glasgow address, plain brown envelope, posted in Glasgow. Half a million. Parnell is going to pay it. He doesn't know where or when yet. And he doesn't want you to know.'

We are at the bottom of the steps of the station. Costello does not miss a beat. 'You will keep me informed?'

'You'll find out anyway. Does Matilda work at the forensics lab in the university?' I lower my voice as we go in the door.

'She does.'

'I think Parnell is going to get his private security company to commission Forensic Services to test the paper, the envelope, the glue. You can keep track on it. You can get the results.'

'You're very public spirited all of a sudden.'

'I don't want him doing anything that you don't know about. If there's anything in those tests that relates to my sister, I want to know.'

'Not that public spirited then.' But she smiles.

'Thank you for coming in,' says DCI Anderson.

I give him my shrug. I do notice that the kindness has gone out of his eyes, as though he's joining Costello at the steely-eyed school. He has a file and a large plastic envelope in his hand; he puts them on the table as he slides on to the seat opposite me. Costello does the same. Her hair is fluffier today, and the scar at the top of her forehead is clearly visible. It is very red, angry. Every trace of the friendliness of the wee chat in the street outside has gone.

'We need to talk.'

'So talk.'

'We are bit concerned that all this is following you around.'

'I had noticed.'

'The flat at Ardno had white goods, a sofa, a bed. All the rest is yours?'

'Yes.'

'So can you tell me where this came from?'

It's the copy of *Catch-22* Mary gave me, wrapped in a plastic envelope. I explain this to Anderson. 'She was thinking about suggesting it for the book group.' But I now know this is not true, she was not going to her book group.

He nods.

'It was on the coffee table.'

'We found a few of your fingerprints on it.'

'As you should.'

'And Mary's.'

'It was her book.'

'And a few others.'

I nod. 'People touch books,' I say, not following where he was going.

'One was a match for someone on our database.'

A small flame of hope begins to burn. 'You mean the person who took Mary?'

'No.' He is talking slowly as if I am retarded. 'We lifted a few epithelial cells. The fact that we could means that the book must have been touched recently, as the cells had not degenerated in any way. Can you explain how somebody missing since 2006 has their fingerprints on a book that was not printed until 2011?'

For some reason this makes me look at my hands, at my own fingertips. 'Missing since 2006? Who?'

'Magdalena Freeman.'

That name means something to me.

'Magda Mason,' Anderson goes on. 'Eric Mason's wife.'

In my bed I am thinking through everything that has happened. A woman that had lived next door to us, who went missing six years ago, is still alive. Then Gilly went missing, then Sophie, and now Mary. Lorna was taken six months ago and escaped. The unknown girl, Katrine, might have died as she too was dumped and ran. None of it makes any sense. But it is real, as real as the book that I pushed across the desk with my finger, sliding easily in its plastic bag. Anderson told me that he had fed all the information into the major incident computer. My name started flashing like a Christmas tree.

I am sure Alex Parnell's did as well.

So I have to go back to where it started for me.

I open the drawer and look at the photographs. In my mind I am asking Sophie what the hell is going on here, why she has dragged me into this nightmare. Billy is sleeping downstairs; Charlie now has a bronchitic minder. I'll be going back to Ardo tomorrow.

Rod has moved in with a sister and I don't know where that is exactly. Mark's wallet had an ATM slip dated fourteenth of April and Costello is slowly forming a timeline of his movements to that point. The post-mortem has concluded that his death was caused by a slow bleed from his middle meningeal artery after a blow to his head sometime earlier.

I know I did not react. But Anderson asked me politely if I would mind handing over my passport.

I recall the pressure of his hands on my arms, the desperation in his eyes. I nod and tell Anderson I am not going anywhere.

The big question in my mind is how Magda's prints got on that book. Eric has been questioned, he is as confused as anybody. Magda has been around here somewhere, she touched that book. Mary and Magda had met.

Maybe she's come back to the Glen, where she was born. But it's a sparsely populated place, she would be noticed. So how has she stayed under the radar? Did Mary track her down? Why would she? For Eric? Maybe there is no mystery, except that Magda Mason, née Freeman, was last heard of in Stoke Newington six years ago and hasn't been seen since.

I snuggle up underneath the duvet and fire up my laptop. Mary knew something, I'm sure of it. I just hope she wrote it down. Mary was a precious child, to older parents; a previous child had been stillborn.

My parents had a great life mapped out for me. I learned to ignore and dismiss my own will as if it was of no importance whatsoever. They were determined I would not spend my life mopping the floors in the Italian café like Mum or spending my winters under cars getting covered in engine oil like my dad. As a child my week was carefully planned, scheduled to the nth degree, and on a Saturday I was allowed a packet of sweeties, but no chocolate.

I did well at school, very well. I studied really hard, taking a break every hour so I could look out the window over the green field of Cloverview Brae where next door's kids played on the grass. I wanted to lie down and roll down the slight hill with the other kids, join in the nips and dumps. I wanted to join in.

Then I got into Glasgow uni, and decided that I could reinvent myself. Or so I thought. My parents were talking about selling the house and moving back to the West End as I was going to the university there.

That was the first night that I can recall crying myself to sleep.

Crying herself to sleep?

I don't see why she didn't just tell them all to piss off. However, she got a lucky break when her parents realized how high house prices in the West End had spiralled. Then her dad came up with Plan B. He would drive to the bus stop and pick her up. Every day. She wrote, *The world had just slammed shut in my face.*

I get up and refill my coffee, padding lightly across the floor in my bare feet. Then I go back to reading, realising the degree of control Mary lived her life under. When she studied, her mum brought her food on a tray so that she wasn't interrupted. Then she met Natalie, a fellow student who was impressed by Mary's insight into the world of the demented and the bored in the novels of the Romantics. I guess Mary would have been good at that. Natalie tried to take Mary out for a drink. It was her first taste of friendship, I think.

It reads as though Natalie was outgoing and fun-loving and took her awkward new friend under her wing. I can relate to that. Natalie then suggested Mary as an interviewer for the uni newspaper, interviewing her boyfriend at Alex Parnell's Glasgow office.

Mary recalls that meeting with humour then writes about the next day when Natalie did not appear at the lecture, leaving the seat beside her empty. She was in the library when she heard the body of a young woman had been found amongst the trees in Kelvingrove Park, and deep down, Mary knew.

Natalie had been strangled.

They never got the man who did it.

She had noticed at the funeral how Natalie's parents, supposedly Alex's good friends, avoided him, leaving him to be comforted by his friend, Eric. Mary had noted how upset Eric was – she'd thought he had no time for Natalie.

> *Did he marry me on the rebound? Or because he lost her and he was not in control of that? George Bernard Shaw once said, 'To be in hell is to drift, to be in heaven is to steer.' That sums Alex up.*
>
> *Deep inside I know it is my fault Natalie was killed. She wanted me to stay on in the pub then go up to her flat to change into some costume she had for me. Then we'd go across the park to the party together. I declined, I left her in the pub. If I hadn't, she would still be alive.*
>
> *Alex and I bonded over our loss and I was flattered by his attention, if I'm honest. After one interview the police phoned my father to take me home and he told Alex I wouldn't be coming back to university.*
>
> *Alex had other ideas.*
>
> *Three months later we got married in Gretna Green. His friend Eric and a woman we met in the cake shop were witnesses. I thought it was very romantic.*

So Eric and Alex had been friends for a long time, and close friends.

> *But once Charlie was born I overheard his secretary say that it was odd Alex's two kids were both called Charlie. He had been married before, had been a father before. I asked him about his other family. That was the first time he hit me.*

WEDNESDAY, 13 JUNE

In the end Vera Haddow was easy to find – Mary had left enough clues – six stories up in a block of flats in Broomhill. It was getting away from Parnell and Charlie that proved difficult. Her flat is only a mile from my own flat in Glasgow, and I have a million and one reasons to drive down to Glasgow early on Wednesday morning. By half past ten I am standing on the concourse of the tower block, looking up, thinking what hell it must be to live here with a child. The residents seem happy, though, cheery folk who meet on the stairs and chat to each other.

In the lift I ask two of them what number Vera Haddow lives at, and they look at me with some suspicion. I say the paperwork I've been given refers to the wrong tower block, that I'm here about young Charlie.

'Charles,' I am corrected. But they accept my knowledge as some kind of proof that I'm legit.

One minute later I am outside her door.

She is a thin woman, of a similar type to Mary and Natalie, small boned and dark, her hair in a very modern spiky cut but her face much older, more weary. Her short nails constantly rake the white skin of her forearm as she holds the door open a crack.

'Hello, I'm looking for Vera Haddow,' I say.

'Who's looking for her?'

'My name is Elvie McCulloch, I'm a friend of Mary.' My name is not a surprise to her. 'She came to see you? I'm worried about her.'

'Mary? Is she OK?' The door opens a little.

I can tell by the way she said it she knows something bad has happened, and she is not surprised.

'I'm not sure. I'm trying to find her,' I answer truthfully. 'She mentioned you in a diary.' I'm out of ideas now. 'Why did she come to see you?'

She leans her head on the side of the door. 'It was about Charles.'

'Your son?'

The lips purse into something like a smile. 'My Charles, yes.' She explains. 'My son is Charles Alexander Parnell but my ex-husband thinks my son is not good enough to inherit the name. Hence Mary's son is also called Charles. I hope he fares better, for his sake.' She holds open the door so I can see into the living room, where a chubby boy of about ten is staring at a huge computer monitor. Letters appear on the screen in a grid, he clicks on the mouse. Makes a word from the letters and moves on. He gets 'hose', then 'stern'. His focus is total. He does not look up as we cross the narrow hall to peer into the living room. My mum used to give me a row for ignoring people like that.

'That's Charles. He doesn't speak much, he has something like autism.' Vera stands at the door, leaning against the frame.

'That makes him a wee bit special,' I say quietly, recalling my dad's words to me. Charles finds the word 'tins' and moves on.

She looks at me and smiles, properly this time. 'Well, the minute Alex noticed that there were issues, he didn't want the boy around. My ex-husband is a perfectionist. I was acceptable but our disabled son was not. Alex wanted him to go into care. So I left and I took Charles with me. It was the only time I ever defied him.' Her eyes flick along the narrow hall as if to say, *and this is what I got.*

'But why do you live here? Alex is a millionaire, he should support you.' The boy finds the word 'tern'.

'I don't want his money. I don't want him tracking us down.' She rubs her cheekbone at some memory that is still too close for comfort. 'He doesn't know you're here, does he?'

'No.'

'Good. Mary just wanted to see Charles, to see what had become of us, to see how far Alex Parnell will go to get his own way. Take your pick.' Her voice warms a little as she regards her child. 'She knew the rot was setting in with Alex, another woman will be waiting in the wings somewhere. Mary realized she was expendable.'

Past tense. I watch Charles find 'nest'.

'Do you think he would do anything that would bring harm to Mary?'

'Apart from the odd beating, a punch, a slap,' she pauses, lost for a moment, then shrugs. She looks me straight in the eye. 'Please don't come back here again,' she says politely. 'We are happy as we are.'

The boy tries 'tini'.

'Of course,' I say, then I turn to the kid. 'You can get "shine" and "shiniest", and if you look carefully, "itchier".'

'OK,' says Vera. 'Maybe you can come back after all.'

But she closes the door in my face just the same. I know that Alex Parnell can find anybody anywhere, Eric told me that. A closed door won't stop him.

By ten o'clock Charlie is fast asleep in his bed, dreaming whatever troubled four-year-olds dream about. I've promised him that I will stay the night in his bedroom, on the big Mickey Mouse bean bag in the corner. Since Mary has gone, Charlie is becoming more distant from his dad and more clingy with me.

He shocked me at teatime, dipping his soldiers into his egg and telling me that his mum is with Sophie and that's a good thing. If he hangs around with me while I look for my sister, he will find his mum. This logic seems to make him happy.

Once he's safely asleep, I go out and sit in the garden with a strong coffee. I must have been out there for nearly half an hour when I hear Parnell's car. He drives right to the rear of the house, gets out and waves at me. I wave back, welcoming him back to his own house.

'Hi, how is the wee man?' He walks across the patio towards me, places his briefcase on the wrought-iron chair opposite, followed by his phone and his car keys.

'Charlie's fine. Well, he's asleep. I said that I'd stay with him tonight, in case he wakes up.' I am telling him, not asking him.

He lifts his case slightly then places it back down with some unspoken change of mind.

'He was getting grouchy so I thought it better he went to

his bed rather than wait up for you. But he wants you to give him toast soldiers for breakfast tomorrow.'

His shoulders fall in some kind of resignation. 'Yes, I suppose that's best. Do you want anything?' He gestures into the kitchen. 'I'm going to get a drink. You mind if I join you out here?'

'Not at all.'

He purses his lips. I can't read what is going through his mind. Is this a powerful man rendered impotent or a guilty one trying not to get caught? He walks away across the patio to the house.

When he returns a few minutes later he has loosened his tie, his top shirt buttons are undone. His fingers are tight round a crystal tumbler of malt. He sits opposite me and the silence between us is restful and reflective. He closes his eyes, absorbing the quiet and dying heat of the day.

'It's only now that I can appreciate what you have been going through for the last four months. This is worse than when my mum died, just the worst thing.' He takes a heavy mouthful of malt. 'It's an old cliché but it's true: there's nothing worse than not knowing – we have no idea where Mary is and we have no idea when we will get her back, *if* we will get her back.'

'I know exactly how bad it is. That's why I can't sit and do nothing. I need to find Sophie.'

He places the tumbler on the table, glass against iron. The ice tinkles against crystal, the noise sharp and cold.

'You shouldn't drink much more of that, in case you get a call and have to drive.'

He smiles at me. 'It's good that you care. Not many people do.'

'I'm sure that's not true.'

He throws me a look of disbelief.

'OK, maybe not for you, but they care for Mary. For Charlie.'

That gets a shrug of resignation. 'Walk a mile in my shoes before you judge me, Elvie. I bet you're sitting there thinking what a bastard I am. She told you about Vera, didn't she?'

It crosses my mind that he has had me followed. So what? He doesn't know about the diary. 'I went to see her today; she doesn't know any more than we do.'

'Vera is a good girl. Not the brightest. You see me as a man who takes a young wife and hides her away in the middle of nowhere, who doesn't let her mix or have any friends. A man with a big house, all the money in the world and a lovely son. A man who threw out his first wife when our son was born less than perfect.'

So he knows what was said. 'That was running through my mind,' I say glibly. 'But like you say, I'd need to walk a mile in your shoes.'

'Vera should change the record.'

'It was a legitimate part of the investigation, as Billy would say.'

'Leave nae stane unturned,' he quotes, mimicking Billy's broad accent.

'No matter what crawls out.' I meet his eyes. He knows he doesn't intimidate me. His gaze floats out to the middle distance.

'Do you know what the problem is with women like you?'

'Enlighten me.'

'Sorry, that came out wrong. I'm tired.' He rubs his face with his sleeve, looks round the garden as if he will find better words in the shadows. 'You're . . . nice; you've grown up in a nice world. Nice detached house in Eaglesham with your mum and dad, your sister, your brother, the family Volvo, the university. This little piggy went to law school, this little piggy went into medicine. Mary was cosseted, protected from the evils of the world. She sees it as a nice place and she's wrong. The security, the anonymity you take for granted I have to buy. Charlie is my son, Mary is my wife. They are not normal by that definition alone. They are something of value. And I will do all I can to keep them safe. I get bloody angry when Mary doesn't see that. You think I am controlling, but I'm just concerned for their welfare.' He looks down into his glass. 'Do you understand that I need to keep my family safe? I don't know if I ever recovered from Natalie's murder. Life can be gone in an instant. Now Mary is gone. Do you see why I would have done anything to avoid that?'

'I do see it. But lack of freedom is not easy to live with.'

Alex talks on, like he has not heard. 'Vera refused to see

it. But I loved her and I loved Charles. There is absolutely no truth in what she told you – that I turned my back on them both because of the way he is. My marriage to Vera was perfect until he was born. And then he became the entire focus of her existence, she began acting more and more strangely and pulling Charles with her. He was a difficult child. We went to the best specialists to find out what the issue was. By the age of two he was starting to lose all the skills he had gained – the kid was going backwards. Toilet training wasn't happening; he became clumsy, he had no expression. No more smiles for Daddy. We were told that all he needed was a bit of help, some extra attention and social exposure. And that putting him in care in those early years would be the best for him, so his stimulation was twenty-four seven. A therapeutic environment. But Vera was having none of it, she was his mother and she knew better. So she went to more and more specialists until we had diagnoses up to our armpits. It was a fucking joke. The more symptoms they mentioned the more of them Vera saw in Charles.'

'Maybe she was just worried about him.'

'Really? When he cried I wasn't even allowed to pick him up. I wasn't allowed to feed him or change him. I wasn't allowed to put him to bed because I didn't do it right. I wasn't allowed to look in at him after work in case I woke him up. She even slept with him; her whole life was focused on the kid. I tried to get help for her but she said only she understood what wee Charles was like. And I was only doing it all to try and take Charles off her.'

I recall Vera's account of the same story, seeing the common ground, but I could see each parent believing their own version.

Parnell takes a gulp of whisky, more than is good for him. 'It's bloody impossible to live a life like that, living in the same house as your family but never invited to be part of it.'

He looks over the glass, back to the middle distance. 'It was not the way I wanted my life to go. Do you know, it was a bloody relief when she left. I could just come home and put the TV on, have a takeaway and a pint.'

'I visited them, Alex. Your son is growing up without a garden.'

'And that's your idea of the breadline, is it?' He is laughing at me now. 'She chooses to live that way. There's money in an account waiting for them; all she has to do is visit the hole in the wall and take it out. But she thinks that will give me control over her. Or that it will allow me to find out where she lives, as if I don't know. I have money in a trust fund for him, for his future, yet he will never learn to eat properly because Vera prefers to spoon-feed him. It's her that has the problem, not him.'

I say nothing, but my mind is turning. Those fingers over the keyboard, competent. Then Vera the first wife meeting Mary the second wife, and talking about Parnell the control freak – how did that meeting really pan out?

'As it is now, I know where he is and that he's safe, and when the time is right I will intervene. I know what he does every day. He's in a new day care facility at the school and Vera goes with him as a classroom helper. I have contact with the woman who runs the place, we speak often.'

'So in effect you're looking over her shoulder all the time?'

'You would think less of me if I didn't.'

'Fair point,' I concede.

He takes another sip. 'I do what I can. I will be there whenever they need me, and that's the best I can do. Are you sure you don't want to join me in a drink?'

'No, one of us should stay sober at least.'

'Are you and Hopkirk busy on Friday?'

'Why?'

'Because you are now. I want you to go and get Mary back.'

FRIDAY, 15 JUNE

Queen Street station on Friday afternoon is noisy, busy, sweaty and chaotic. From my seat at Costa, I watch Parnell walk over to a central bin and place the large holdall on the ground next to it. His instructions are to stay there for ten minutes as if he's waiting for a travel announcement. The station is getting crowded now, so I walk around to keep the bin in view. There is that familiar prickle in my legs, usually a sign that I'm stressed about something. My watch says three-thirty, way too early for rush hour, but the station is filling up with groups of young people, student types. There is standing room only on the concourse now. I see Billy leaning against the wall at the toilet dressed like a jakey. A man is taking an outrageously long time in the queue at the coffee kiosk; every so often he scratches his ear then I see him talk up his sleeve. He has a mike on his wrist. Billy notices and gives me a shrug. Something odd is going on, there is expectation in the air. The station is too busy. I see a man wearing a blue top, his hat hiding a microphone and a radio. I'm looking around as if for a poster, or a notice of a special bus service, a sign to queue here for a concert or something, when a loud clang shatters the air.

Everything stops.

The first two chords of Michael Jackson's *Thriller* ring out.

There are whoops of delight. People either look round or stand up. Then everyone in sight is on their feet, moving, dancing.

I lose sight of the bin. I look left and right and can't see the guy at the coffee kiosk or the one in the blue sweatshirt. All I can see is a heaving mass of bodies moving to left and right, dancing like zombies. They are out of sync, and the music is too loud and distorted. I get up on a rail, trying to gain a viewpoint. Billy has had the same idea, but a young girl with auburn ringlets pulls him down, forcing him to join the dance. I see the guy with the blue shirt now, standing on a bench, screaming to be heard down his mouthpiece. I see him point to the North Hannover Street exit. I climb down and push my way through the crowd and out the door to see a man cycle off down the steep hill to George Square, a holdall strapped to his back. A holdall that was the same style, but not big enough to hold the money. There is no point in giving chase. I go back in. The zombie walk moves towards the far end of the station as one living mass, revealing the bin. The bag and the money are gone.

I run out the door down on to George Square but there is nothing to be seen. A motorbike goes past. At first it looks like there's a pillion rider, but it is a large holdall strapped to his back. A big-enough holdall. The bike turns down a pedestrian lane behind some hoardings and is out of sight, moving north towards the motorway. The scream of the bike engine fades to nothing.

He is well away.

And so is the money.

'Did you get anything?' I'm sitting in the seat next to Costello; Billy sits opposite us. The café is busy, there's a queue out the door and the air stinks of sausage rolls. Costello is biting the corner of her lips.

Billy is moaning; he has injured himself climbing on the rails at the station. 'I feel like I have a wasp up my arse. I should be on danger money for this.'

'Have you ever had a wasp—?'

'Oh, shut up, you two.' Costello calls the waitress over and orders. 'And can you be quick? We only have five minutes.'

'We close in four,' says the girl without a trace of humour.

'Make it very quick then.'

'Just give me any bun you have left,' says Billy.

The girl looks at him blankly, then heads slowly back to the counter.

'So what did you get? We got nothing.'

'A load of students walking about as if they'd shat their pants?'

Costello ignores him. 'CCTV got three holdalls, all in the same brown and red pattern as the one that Parnell was asked to put the money in. The big one with the money was passed hand to hand to a bike outside, which went uphill through some roadworks, through the barrier, out the opposite way towards Springburn then away.'

'That was all I saw. You probably got ten seconds more than we did.'

'They knew the flashmob was going to go off – they took advantage. It worked very well. The three students we got hold of say they were asked to do it as an experiment to "quantify the reliability of eye witness statements". We haven't yet traced the root of that, all social media. Load of crap, of course, but they knew the flashmob was going live at some point so it seemed a legit experiment.'

'The drop was well planned, though; they thought that through well.'

'I'll make sure they get a gold star,' says Costello bitterly.

'What is the point of those flashmob things?' asks Billy. He's trying to sit down properly, testing the weight-bearing capacity of his backside.

I shrug.

'There is no point, that is the point,' Costello tells him. 'It's called enjoying yourself. Not a concept I'm familiar with myself, I have to confess. Well, not lately.'

'Not going well with Red Rum then?'

'Piss off.'

Billy says, 'I thought they were spontaneous. Flashmobs.'

Costello replies with ill-concealed contempt. 'Within a few hours – yes, but all they need is the internet link. They'd told Parnell to be ready with the money. As soon as they knew when the flashmob was going live they told Parnell to be there pronto. There have been flashmob incidents all over the place. Summer madness. Last week it was Waverley station.'

Billy slurps his tea from an old-fashioned mug, rips some

jam doughnut with his teeth then palms a Tramadol. 'Are you tracking the chip in the money?'

'Are we hell! I wouldn't have the budget to track my granny round Marks and Spencer, never mind stolen money across Glasgow.'

'Parnell's team are tracking it,' I say. 'When it gets to its final destination, they'll get in touch with us.'

'And you will get in touch with me.'

'Of course.'

'No heroics.'

'No.'

'So now we sit and wait.'

Plinky-plinky-plink.

'Billy, I will kill you if you don't change that ring tone.' Costello is getting stressed as his clumsy thumbs struggle to answer the phone before it goes to voicemail.

He answers it, listens. 'The chip in the money has stopped moving. It's in a bin in Milngavie Country Park. The money's gone.' Billy then listens intently to Parnell. 'Yes . . . we'll meet you there, sure. Yes, she's here. Yeah, we know.' Billy puts the phone down.

'Well, they knew about the chip and took it out.'

'Sounds familiar. What's going on here? I suppose it's not beyond the realms of possibility that the modern kidnapper has a device for checking tracking devices.'

'So how do we find Mary?'

'Parnell will have something up his sleeve. We've to go round to Park Circus for a meeting right now.'

'Well, you'd better go then. Keep me posted, won't you? If anything happens, I need to know. Shame we don't have the budget to chase this.'

'You mean you don't have a pot to piss in now you have a nice shiny office, hen?' says Billy, backhanding jam from his lips and smearing it on his face. Even Charlie has got the hang of that one.

'Well, I'll stand you the tea and doughnut.' Costello gets up to leave, and her phone goes. 'Hello, Matilda, what can I do for you?' She sits down again, her face growing paler; her lips smile but her eyes crease. Conflict, a bittersweet memory.

'Oh, that is interesting. Yes, you did the right thing to ask me. OK, I'll sanction it. I do know that name, Sean McTiernan is a blast from the past. Thanks, Matilda. Don't tell Parnell that we've spoken. Act like you're doing him a big favour. I'll deal with the dynamic duo at this end.'

SATURDAY, 16 JUNE

I t takes us over an hour to drive to the coast. Once we
leave the Glasgow city boundary the rain stops. As we pass
Irvine the clouds begin to break up. By the time we reach
the seaside town of Ayr, the sun has broken through. Billy
opens the window of the Vectra, letting the warm breeze swirl
round his face. He spent last night going through the files of
Sean McTiernan's culpable homicide conviction and had
decided I needed to know all the details. Especially the fact
McTiernan had a temper and had stamped on his victim's face
then kicked him so hard in the stomach that his liver had
exploded.

Matilda had found his DNA on the envelope the ransom
demand came in.

It concentrated my mind.

Suddenly Billy pulls the car to a halt in a lay-by on the main
coast road, unwilling to turn down the single track lane that leads
to the beach. We are looking for a hamlet of remote cottages.

The view is breath-taking. On a day like this it is paradise.
I know all about the trouble that can hide in paradise.

'Can it be as easy as this?' I ask him.

'No,' says Billy. 'Costello is a twisted cow but in many
ways she is a dinosaur, an old-fashioned instinctive cop. She
was taught the hard way. She got to know this McTiernan
through a case, like I said. She doesn't think McTiernan is
right for this. I trust her judgement. And McTiernan has been
squeaky clean since, living down here with his lady.' He does
his slurping lips trick again. 'But the lab found his DNA on
that envelope so it flagged up.'

'He is dangerous.'

'Well, you don't serve time for culp hom because you played
pat-a-cake with somebody. But a kidnapper should know better
than to handle the envelope after varnishing something. It was
a forensic gold mine, a bit too much of a gold mine: traces

of pine dust, red stain and radioactive *fucus vesiculosus*, to be precise.'

'What's that?'

'Bladder wrack seaweed. The radioactivity means west coast, Hunterston. The entire nuclear arsenal of the United Kingdom is just a few miles up the road from here. All that in a red stain that Matilda got from the back of the envelope.'

'Strange combination.'

'Handy, leads us straight to a joiner who lives on a beach, as McTiernan does. Strong, intelligent, a runner – what more do we want?'

'A big Russian dog?'

'That would be nice.'

'Yet, with all that, Costello's instinct was to not bite.'

Billy nods and shuffles in his seat a little. 'Just taking the weight off my brains. Any other cop would say, "Great! Got the bastard!" But she didn't.'

'Maybe because she doesn't have the evidence,' I suggest. 'Technically that belongs to Parnell. She doesn't know about the link with McTiernan officially. We're following a lead that doesn't exist for the investigating team. She's trying to follow the book.'

'Oh, she wouldn't let that get in her way if she thought McTiernan was the Night Hunter. It's more than that: her instinct is that he's not right for it. Anyway, we tread carefully. He might be very dangerous. Do not take him on even if you think he has Sophie tucked away in his back pocket. Promise?'

I murmur something. The sun is in my eyes, so I lean down to my rucksack to get my sunglasses. Alistair MacLean is still there, lying tattered, a ripped cigarette packet marking his place. The book from the skip. 'He's a joiner?'

'Yip.'

'The Parkes' next-door neighbour was having work done.'

Billy is deathly quiet. 'Christine has had an extension done.'

'And Lorna's dad said they had a training pool put in. Builders all over the place. Joiners.'

Billy turns to look at me; it's a slow *Exorcist* head turn. 'You are good, Elvie. So, we go carefully. This could be dangerous. We do have one thing in our favour. If any of us looks like a serial killer, it's you.'

'You OK to go ahead with this?' asks Billy, once the Vectra reaches the beach car park. He pats the back of my hand for comfort. His comfort, not mine.

'There might be a perfectly simple explanation for it all. If there is we won't find out sitting here, will we?'

'Nope.' He leans over my lap and takes some binoculars from the glove compartment. 'Bring these. We can pretend we're looking at birds.'

The lane down to the beach is pitted with deep potholes, overgrown hedgerows on either side. It twists and turns as it makes its way down to the sea. Every time we look up, the view is different, sometimes a beautiful sight of the sea, sometimes a green wall of thorn.

In tacit agreement we both quicken our pace, past the one-in-ten gradient warning sign, the Use Low Gear warning sign, the No Passing Places Until Beach warning sign, then we round a corner and see Ailsa Craig, a little dumpling of an island sitting in its own faint blue mist, the waves around the steep cliffs twinkling in the sunlight.

Once on the beach itself Billy stops and looks along the sand to Culzean Castle high on the cliff top, then he lets his eyes rest on the shoreline. He points up above the high-tide line to the soft folds of sand, some scrub, a path and a fence where hardy bushes clump and grow together, hiding something. There's a barely visible roof.

Sean McTiernan's house.

Billy instinctively steps sideways, back into the cover of the dunes.

'Hand me the binos, will you?'

I hand them over, and stand on a mound of rough grass to gain a better view myself.

'Well, there's life about,' he says, almost reluctantly.

'What were you expecting?'

'No idea.'

'We're here for Mary.'

'Here for all of them, sweet cheeks.' He hands me back the

binoculars and we move down on to the beach, our feet slipping on the pillows of soft sand as we make our way to the water's edge. We take our time. I close my eyes, tasting the salt on my face and relishing the kiss of the sea breeze on my skin.

Even with my sunglasses on, the glare of the sun on the water irritates my eyes. It's firing up the acne on my cheeks; I'm trying not to scratch. I can just see the sails of a yacht on the horizon. I turn and slam right into Billy, who has stopped dead in his tracks.

'Look,' he says.

I shield my eyes with my hand and look along the beach. There are four figures, two larger in front and two smaller ones behind, milling around the sand right at the water's edge. Something dashes into the sea, is caught by a wave, disappears and then re-emerges. I hold up the binoculars and look, adjusting the range until the figures in the distance come into clear focus. The tallest figure is a slim blond man, long-legged with a youthful walk. His jeans are cut off at the shins, and his baggy T-shirt billows around his chest as he bends over into the waves that chase around his feet. I note his shoes. He is grabbing a dark fur ball and pulling it from the waves.

'Well, he has the puppy version of the big dog.'

Billy is sweating, not only with the heat.

The man picks up the puppy and holds it high, bringing it down to his face to kiss its nose. Then for an instant he looks right at me. But his eyes crease, and he laughs as he says something over his right shoulder, still holding the soaked puppy.

'See?' I let Billy have a look.

'It's him all right. I suppose flinging sticks into the sea for a puppy would get some radioactive seaweed on your hands.'

I take the binoculars back and pan the beach, searching for the other two of the group. I am too quick on the first pass, the figures just flash across my field of vision. I pan back slowly, my heart pounding, and there, framed in my sights, is a small, thin woman with long blonde hair that tumbles free in the wind. She walks with a limp, as if she is frail. Her face is angled slightly down, she is walking with one shoulder dropped, her arm out. Her skirt billows out in the wind, then drops like a falling curtain. It reveals a small blonde child, chubby-legged and barefoot, tramping unsteadily along the sand. As she turns I focus on the child. The puppy bobs into view, tongue lolling, having a grand time.

'Is that the Night Hunter? Remote house. Fit. He has on Brooks Glycerins. Running shoes, not trainers. His job could take him all over the place. Dog. In paradise.'

'Do you want him to look like a monster?'

'Right, come on, let's get it over with.' I take a purposeful stride then I feel Billy's hand on my upper arm.

'No heroics, hen, just let them come to us.'

They hover around the waterline, dancing back and forth with the rhythm of the waves, the perfect family having a walk on the beach on a lovely summer's day. Billy and I stand on the dunes and watch as they approach. We pretend to look out to sea, pointing to things we know nothing about.

I do an occasional sweep with the binoculars, noting how close they are getting.

I see McTiernan point at us, a casual lift of the hand.

'He's spotted us,' I say quietly. Billy is staring out to Ailsa Craig and does not turn to look.

'Has he stopped walking?'

'No. She's picked the kid up, though.'

'Wait here until they're close.'

'Do you have a plan?' I ask out the corner of my mouth.

'No.'

The puppy solves the problem, running happily towards Billy. It stops to shake itself, and I see that its fur is not so dark after all, just wet. It comes over to us, tail wagging, like a dog that has all the friends in the world.

Billy takes his cue and bends over to pat the puppy on the head, and the puppy immediately rolls over and exposes a pink, hairy tummy to be rubbed. As McTiernan approaches, I back off, ready. McTiernan is tall, with that lithe build that belies power. Billy is playing a blinder in the body language stakes, putting McTiernan in control by making himself appear vulnerable and weak, doddery and old. Maybe not a lot of acting there.

'Great puppy!'

Sean nods.

'He's going to be a big dog.'

'Husky.'

'I thought he was one of those big Russian things. Same colour coat.' Billy smiles engagingly.

McTiernan smiles back but does not seem to react. He is simply indulging an old guy on the beach who likes dogs.

I stand behind Billy, looking at her, the small, fine-boned woman. She looks about twelve, dressed in a long skirt soaked by waves at the bottom, holding her son on her hip. There is something of the Cinderella about her, incredibly beautiful in a fragile way. Her skin is almost translucent, her blue eyes large and innocent. Her expression is unreadable.

She moves slightly behind her husband, as Mary usually moves behind Parnell, but that is the only echo. This woman is happy to be here with this man. Her hand twines into his, tender and loving.

McTiernan lifts the puppy up. 'Come on, you.'

'Do you know Alex Parnell?' asks Billy.

No plan then.

McTiernan misses a beat, looks at Billy then at me. He does not lie. 'Yes, of course I do.'

'How?'

'What's it to you?'

I hear the aggression in his tone but Billy is all sugar sweetness.

'He's employed us to find his wife.'

'Oh, right.' He has reverted to a casual easy acceptance. The puppy wriggles to lick his chin. 'I heard about that, I thought it was just rumours.'

'When did you last see Parnell?'

'I haven't seen the boss since, since . . .' A long exhalation. 'Last week sometime, we were having trouble with a roof, rotten right through it was.'

So he works for Parnell's building division.

'Well, we have a wee problem. Your DNA is on file and it was picked out as a direct match to some on the envelope, of interest to us.'

The look of confusion seems genuine. The woman looks from my face to her husband's and back again.

'We're aware of your past . . .'

'I've nothing to do with this, nothing.'

'Exactly. Mr Parnell says that you have an excellent character so he wants us to try and sort it out before the police get hold of it.'

'You know what they can be like, small-minded, a bit thick?' I add.

'So who are you?'

'Parnell's security,' I say.

'Have you seen this before?' Billy holds out a photograph.

'It's a photograph. Of an envelope,' says McTiernan, shrugging.

Billy holds out the picture further, forcing McTiernan to put down the puppy and take it for a closer look.

'So it's a brown envelope. The address on the label means nothing to me.' He holds it out to give it back.

Billy does not take it. For a moment they stare at each other, the silence broken by the noise of the waves tickling the sand.

I am the one that breaks the tension.

'Come on, Sean, help us out here. Mary has been kidnapped, and God knows what she's going through. You know Charlie is four years old. He's frantic. So think on, eh? The forensic report was clear – on the flap of that envelope is red stain, freshly sawn pine, from down this coast.'

It has the desired effect. McTiernan looks back at the envelope; even the woman steps forward to peer at it.

I start talking again, playing my role as the brains of the outfit. Billy plays with the puppy. 'And no, we don't think for a minute that you have anything to do with her disappearance. But kidnappers by their nature tend to recycle, cutting up newspapers for letters, reusing envelopes, you know all that. So at some point in time you have touched that envelope, and if you can tell us when, or where, it might give us a lead to who sent it.'

McTiernan smiles slightly. He is trying to appear helpful. He turns the photo over in his hands, strong, long-fingered hands. I feel a shiver go through me. He shakes his head. 'Sorry.' He shows it to the woman, who looks at it but doesn't respond. 'We don't get mail at the house so I don't know where I might have touched it.'

'What about work?' I ask. 'Where have you been using red stain?'

'I work all over the place.' He frowns slightly, turns the photo over again and shrugs. 'Red stain?'

'There was some red stain on the flap of the envelope, and dust that seems to be pine. You been in any houses where you might have picked the mail up?'

'Most of the work I do is indoors, rebuilds and major refurbs; the places are empty. But red-stained pine – that's a combination for outdoors, a chalet maybe. Eddie's place? Maybe you should ask him.' McTiernan turns to look north, up the coastline.

'Eddie?' I ask.

'Eddie Underhay, he works for Parnell as well. He'll be on your list, I'm sure. He's been at the house at Ardno, doing a wall repair, lives in Glasgow but has a chalet about forty miles up the coast near Portencross. Ailsa View, I think it's called. He was putting in some extra insulation and I gave him a hand. A bit of work, a few beers, a curry.'

Billy and I exchange glances.

'And does Eddie have a wife?'

'Somewhere, but she's not . . . on the scene, as you might say.' McTiernan hands the envelope back firmly. 'Nice bloke.'

'So you might have been working there and touched this envelope, then Eddie might have put it in the bin and someone took it out again?' I suggest.

'I've no idea. But that's the only time I recall using red stain on pine. It's not my thing. Wood is beautiful as it is, don't you think? Some things are better left as they are.'

We drive in silence up the coast, a sign that Billy is thinking about something. It is bitter cold in the shade, deceptively warm in the sun. The car stinks of fags. I open the window, which gets stuck halfway down. Eventually we arrive at Portencross Castle.

'I think we've come too far. Do you not think we should tell Costello?'

'We'll make sure of our facts first. Has this Eddie guy ever seen you at Ardno? One look at your face and he won't have forgotten it.'

'Cheers. Do you do a lot of this confidence-building work?'

'It's all part of my charm offensive.'

'Minus the charm. Just the offensive. Stop and ask this guy for directions to Ailsa View.'

A weather-beaten man is texting from his tractor seat with a bright-eyed collie beside him. He points us back down the road. 'The chalet park is about two miles down there, on the other side of the road,' he says. 'What is it with that place? You're the second lot this week.'

Billy feigns a lack of interest. 'So who was that then?'

'Why, who are you two? They were better dressed.'

'We're working for Partickhill CID.'

I notice the slight nod at the truth but the farmer shrugs as if it is nothing to do with him. 'They were cops as well. They had a better car.'

'A car? Not a four-by-four?' I ask.

The farmer looks at me, so does the collie. 'No, it was a car. Noisy exhaust. Two men, middle-aged. What can I say?' He turns his attention back to his phone as it buzzes in his hand.

Billy executes a very bad three-point turn in the narrow road and nearly gets stuck in the ditch. I get the feeling tractor man is enjoying Billy's bad driving.

The only indication of the holiday park entrance is a wooden archway among the trees. We drive in over speed bumps made of logs. The chalets need a good coat of varnish but it looks pleasant enough if you like spending your summers as a midges' buffet. A few cars are parked, three dogs are tethered to stakes in the tiny front gardens, an old woman is weeding. I can hear Radio 2 from somewhere, there's a smell of fried bacon. It's nothing flash, just comfortable.

As the car drives along the dirt track Billy whistles the theme from *The Good, The Bad and The Ugly*.

He stops the car in a space marked 'visitors', and we get

out. Each chalet has space to park one vehicle. Billy indicates that we should go round the back of the chalets.

'Are you James Bond Secret Squirrel after all? Walking down the main drag will look a damn sight less conspicuous than you coughing and spluttering your way through the under-growth like some kind of asthmatic pervert.'

'OK.' But he is rattled.

'Look, you're an old git out for a wee donner – a quiet stroll in an old gits' paradise. Look as if you're thinking about buying a chalet. Keep in plain sight. I'm going to skulk about the way us fit young things can.'

And I do.

It takes me forty-five minutes, moving high on the hill, stopping every now and again to look through the trees at who's about. There aren't any people here of working age. They're all older. It's nearly four pm on a Saturday. I might recognize Eddie from the time he's been up at Ardno.

The site straddles a small river, and there's a rather shaky wooden bridge. None of the mobile homes can come across here, so there must be another way in. I look back up the main drag to see Billy chatting away to someone with a similarly well-nourished beer belly. A cigarette is offered from one to the other. Billy seems to be asking about the site, the man is waving his hands about. I move on down to the road to cross the bridge. Then I see the last chalet; the lie of the road means that it is much closer to the sea than the rest. Its front window is almost on the road, making it very difficult for anybody to see in.

Easy for them to see out.

The door is on the far side. It has the same little veranda arrangement the others have. Then I notice the patchwork of wood, due to recent restaining. I walk past the chalet into the field beyond where there is a wall where I can sit. From here I can see any movement from the corner of my eye.

My phone bleeps. It is Billy texting me. *I see you, I'll keep going down to beach to look in front window.*

I stay put for ten minutes. Then I see him, a daft fat figure on the beach skimming stones in the water, old enough to know better.

My phone bleeps again. *2 people, 1 sitting, 1 moving about.*

I wait for another few minutes, looking around as if I'm waiting for somebody. I see a man put his head out cautiously. A small dark-haired man. He starts whistling something badly –'It's Now or Never'. I've heard that before. At Ardno, while he was fixing the wall. His fat mate has the limp. This is the wee skinny one. And that wall never got fixed. He knew the house was vulnerable; he had his way in and out.

His back is to me, I can take him easily. I climb off the wall, stretch my quads, my eyes fixed on him. I give him a slow count of ten. He looks up and down, and leans back in to open the door a bit wider. A slim female steps out, dressed in black, dark hair, her hand bandaged.

Mary.

I work out the line of attack. The eyes, the balls, the knees. But I don't. I retreat, trying to make sense of it. She looks well, even though she's walking with a slight limp. He grips her elbow, but I'm too far away to see how tight that grip is. He brings her down the steps with his arm locked on hers, keeping her close. A holiday park, this is a good place to have her. No one would think of looking here.

My phone beeps. *Is it her?*

Yes.

Is she OK?

Think so.

I'll call Costello.

I turn away, keeping my eyes on the sea, the bright, bright sea, and away from the road above me. I am confused. I think I could get her right now, but what would that mean for the others? This could lead us to them. I take a deep breath and wait. We have Mary. I know there's another caravan park at the bottom of the Rest and Be Thankful. Is that where they are? Or are they around here? Does he move them about? Or has he moved them since Lorna nearly got away? Then I do turn round, some instinct telling me that what I am seeing is not what I want to see. Mary has big dark glasses on, to protect those blue eyes so sensitive to the sun. Then I realize that it is not what I see, but what I hear.

She is laughing.

She sounds happy.

*   *   *

Two hours later Eddie Underhay is in the back of a police car. One team of police are interviewing the residents while the other is searching for any sign of the other women. Mary has been taken away by two female police officers. I tried to read the look she gave me from the back of the car. Betrayal? Pity?

I am still sitting on the wall, Billy is beside me. Costello doesn't know what to do with us so we are stuck here like two naughty gnomes.

'Why was she being so nice to him? She was laughing with him.'

'Stockholm syndrome?' suggests Billy.

'Or have we have misjudged this from the start?'

'They've found the ransom money in that wee hut that houses the electric meter, so the guy was half a million up on this. That's all the evidence you need. Remember Mary's diary – you said yourself. She has an A-level in compliance, that woman. She'll do anything that makes other people happy,' Billy argues. It all adds up to him.

'And never try to get back to Charlie?'

'Do you buy the fact that she left her kid to run off with her fancy man? I buy that one even less.'

'But the way she was laughing . . .'

'Stockholm syndrome, I tell you. Oh shit, here's the main man.'

Anderson is walking over, carrying a plastic envelope containing a big Jiffy envelope. He raised it as he approaches us.

'Before you start, there was a farmer down in the field in a blue tractor. He said two guys in a loud car were asking for directions to this place last week. Might be something or nothing, but don't accuse us of not telling you everything. Those guys were nothing to do with us.'

'Have you found any trace of anyone else? Of Sophie?'

'We're going through the place forensically, inch by inch. If there is something there, Elvie, we'll find it.'

I catch his look up into the hills. 'They could be anywhere up there and nobody would ever find them.'

'Who is he? This Eddie person?' asks Billy.

'Eddie Underhay. He's worked for Parnell Engineering for

two years, no previous that we can find. But he's had access to Parnell's building sites, to Mary, and I'm sure if we look close enough we'll find that he had access to the other women as well.'

'Gillian Porter's mum had an extension put in,' I say. 'It has Eric's signature porthole window. The Parkes' neighbours . . .'

'Who?'

'Neil Parke. The boy with the hair? Their neighbours were having work done in the house, you recall the skip? Well, he might have been working there and seen the Parke girl coming and going.'

'Oh.'

'And Lorna had had a training pool installed.'

'You should check if one of Parnell's building companies did that,' Billy adds. 'Or sub-contracted it.'

'Fuck,' said Anderson quietly. He pulls out his mobile and starts chattering down it.

'Right,' he ends the call, 'Mary is in hospital. Can you come round to Partickhill for a statement this evening? Any more of this and you two will get your own parking space.'

'Is Edward Underhay the Night Hunter?'

'Who knows?' says Costello. 'He's saying nothing, absolutely nothing. Lips as tight as a cat's arse.'

We are sitting in the nice interview room at Partickhill. It has comfy foam seats that are so low and deep that Billy has to sit forward or his feet don't touch the ground. It makes him feel slightly vulnerable.

'Parnell has gone on record as saying that he gave the original ransom demand to the lab,' Anderson tells us. 'The DNA result flagged up on our system. He also paid the ransom money. So you are with us up to that point. He claims he knows nothing about the two guys in the loud car. The theory is that Eddie or a friend of his picked the money up and then brought it down to the chalet, where we found it in the wooden shed that houses the electricity meter. Bloody stupid place to leave it. It was locked at the front but there was an unsecured panel underneath. He obviously thought that nobody would look there.'

'So that's all it was? The kidnap of a rich woman for ransom?'

'Yes, and he nearly got away with it.'

I notice that they are all looking at me.

'What they're saying, Elvie,' Billy says softly, 'is that this has nothing to do with the abductions of any of the other women.'

'But he must have known them. Maybe that's why he's saying nothing, he doesn't want to incriminate himself.'

'No ransom was asked for any of them,' Anderson points out. 'You said yourself that the MO was totally different. The timing, the way she was taken from the house. He wasn't stalking her the way the Night Hunter stalked the others. He simply took his chance when he knew the wall was down. He chatted to Mary, he had it all set up.'

'Half a million's not a lot of money. And what was he going to do once he set her free? She knew him!'

'Maybe he was going to kill her?'

'Big step for a brickie.'

'Agreed, and he wasn't that bright. Parnell thinks that Underhay was disgruntled at being passed over for promotion and the credit crunch wage cut he suffered, so he took the law into his own hands. He maybe sensed Mary might see his point, and she is certainly not reading the riot at him.'

'Could be a case of Lima syndrome, where the kidnapper falls for the victim, or Stockholm syndrome which is the other way round,' Costello chips in. 'They were stuck in that wee log cabin for long periods of time together. Mary is a clever woman and she would have talked to him, agreed with him, tried to keep herself safe. But she's saying nothing to us. Traumatised. PTSD. Must have been a picnic after living with Parnell.'

'So Underhay is saying nothing and she's saying nothing?'

'That's right.'

'So how do you know what was going on? Has she seen Parnell?'

Costello gives me a hard, flinty look. She is trying to tell me something she cannot voice.

'She hasn't seen him yet, and she says she doesn't want to.'

I sit there, less than convinced. Costello's theory does not fit well with me, but then how well do I know Mary? The way she was laughing with her kidnapper, the way she shuts up whenever Parnell raises his voice. Maybe I don't know her at all. Where did she go when she was supposed to be at book group? The compliant Mary would not have kept that diary; she had already grown into someone else.

'And Mr Parnell for his part has taken Charlie to the hospital but has agreed not to see his wife. She will stay at the private hospital until she is better. She's been offered counselling, but so far she is refusing it. We have done everything we can.'

'Does she have an injury to the back of her leg?'

'No, she does not. Elvie, stop it. This has nothing to do with Sophie.'

Billy touches my arm on the way out.

'You can't just do nothing, not now.'

I look at Billy and his look tells me that nothing is exactly what he is going to do.

SUNDAY, 17 JUNE

S unday is a day of rest, which is very easy when there is no real work to do. Ardno looks empty and insulted, robbed of its grace by police searches and memories. Areas of the house are still taped off but the phone calls have ceased. To use police parlance, the situation is not being advanced. Charlie is away with his dad. Alex Parnell has paid Billy and me handsomely.

Mary is in the private hospital, still saying nothing. I chinned Costello about what happens now. Paperwork, was all she said. She promised me she hasn't forgotten about Sophie, my sister has not been sidelined. The investigation is regrouping and refocusing.

'Is that bullshit?' I ask.

'Yes.'

At least she was being honest.

'All is as it was before.'

But that is not true. The team are having a rest, they are taking a breather. Costello and Anderson are being called in to explain themselves to someone high in authority. Costello said having afternoon tea with the Spanish Inquisition would be preferable.

I go for a run, I need to clear my head of all the confusion and rid myself of the feeling that I have not done right by Mary.

My days here are numbered. Parnell hasn't told me to pack my bags yet but it can't be far away. I can't go back to Mum's house. She blames me for Rod moving out; I took the computer, I questioned the photographs. My mum has always shot the messenger. Grant has locked himself in his room. He wants Sophie back and has now decided that lying in his bed all day crying will achieve this. Rod has been a gentleman; he phoned me earlier today to say that he thinks Grant will refuse to go to the psychiatrist. Can I do anything? The boy is suffering.

I hung up. I am fed up being my family's keeper.

So I will go back to the flat in Glasgow, which is tainted with memories of Sophie in the bath, bleeding. They have not started running the tests at the lab yet. She *is* being sidelined, and that is making me angry.

I head up Cruach nam Mult, running swiftly and steadily through the bracken and the fern, taking a path that does not exist. It's still raining, it has been all day. It's slippy and marshy underfoot. The wee burns that scar the hillside are full of water; I have to run through those I usually jump easily.

That single sad footprint of Lorna. The rain has got me thinking.

It's got me thinking about that dog again. It must be huge. Not like Eric's wee collie Rosie. Her food bowls? No, not that. I am trying to think about something before the food bowls. When Charlie rang us on Mary's phone. Rain, rain and more rain filling Eric's basement. Grandpa Cop had said something about him needing to get it pumped out. But Eric lives right on top of a hill. Water drains away. Up here it is running down the slope in sheets. I reset my mind. After the water clock, after the call, putting my jacket on . . . I feel my arteries start to tingle, it's coming through. I quicken my stride. Concentrating. Eric knocked a file to the floor, papers spread out on the dirty carpet. I picked them up. Drawings, estimates, columns of figures, a plan for an indoor swimming pool, a training pool. Lorna had a training pool. My mind flicks back to Eric looking out the window of his Land Rover and telling me that people do disappear up here. His farm had been searched, he had told me that, he had been making coffee for the cops.

I turn round and head back down the hill. I need to ask Billy if he really wants to earn his money.

'It's a Sunday. He's never here on a Sunday, is he?' I slide out of the car, leaving Billy behind. At times like this I feel invincible. I can face anything that Eric Mason can throw at me. Sophie could be here somewhere.

I scan the horizon and the old croft. I feel another spit of rain on my face. The great wheels of the garden clock are

moving slowly. I take that movement as a good omen: we are
setting something in motion here. A deep grinding sound like
a drawbridge being hoisted slowly over a moat rumbles through
the ground, coming from somewhere under my feet.

Billy rolls down the window of his Vectra and listens. 'You
feeling the earth move?'

I look down at my trainers, thinking. The generator, Eric
had said.

'That was a joke, hen,' says Billy, lighting up.

I ignore him. Something makes me look down the hill to
the old part of the wood that belongs to the croft. There is
a collection of ramshackle old buildings, and wire fences
full of gaps. I wonder how far the police took their search.
I hear Billy peep the horn. He puts his finger in the curled
fingers of his other hand and jerks them apart. *Get the finger
out.*

I look out across the moor; the wind is getting up. There
is a smell in the air, something feral and dangerous. I follow
the worn strip of grass up to the front door and knock. No
answer. I put my hands in my jacket pockets and smile
inanely as I look around. Anybody looking would think I'm
doing exactly what I appear to be doing – waiting for
someone to answer the door. But nobody comes and there's
no sound of anybody moving around inside. I knock again
and wait a little longer. The rain is starting to come down
hard now and the wind is catching at my breath. I tug at
the handle on the weather-beaten front door, but it's locked.
There are cobwebs over the panes of glass that cover the
top half. I cannot see through them. I go back down the
path and signal to Billy that I am going to have a look round
the back. I walk round the perimeter of the outhouse ruins
and the old sheep steadings crumbled to rubble a long time
ago, then look across at the buildings in the cover of the
trees; they are even more decrepit. I check the remains of
a window, smashed, brutally sharp jagged edges. This is a
hundred yards away from the main house, deep in the cover
of long grass and bracken.

Looking back, the rear of the main croft has had a lot of
work done to it. A row of conifers has been planted to provide

some shelter from the wind. A new wicker fence breaks up the land at the back; someone is trying to domesticate this.

A scent drifts towards me. A smell of animal life, like a fox lair. I walk back into the open land, point at Billy and then to the ruins. He responds with a nod and points at his watch. I trot back over, my trainers making a comforting thud as they hit the pillow of damp conifer needles on the floor of the wood. It is immediately warmer in here, protected from the wind. I stand still for a minute, not sure if I'm hearing something or not. The hairs on the back of my neck start to prickle. The trees are close, oppressive. Or is it more than that? I hear another noise, a gentle rustling, like the sound of a light chain being dragged. The noise is more definite this time, but there's nothing to see apart from piles of wood, and an old hut with half a roof and only three walls. I feel that there is someone standing behind me, hidden in the trees. I turn round. Nobody there, just the shadows of the trees and the wind whistling in the high branches. My heart stops. I stay stock-still. I know I am being watched. And whoever is watching me is invisible.

I look along the ground. It is uneven, as if it has been hit by minor earthquakes here and there, clods of earth sticking up like the crust of an over-cooked cake. Roots of trees trying to hold on before they were cut down. The walls of the old hut that are still standing block the view. The feral smell is stronger now, fox urine and rotten meat. I flex my fingers, stretch out my legs a little. I need to be ready. I walk up to the wooden sections of the old hut; the mosaic of pine needles show some recent disturbance. I grip the upright of the wooden partition, pull it forward slightly, and look behind it. There is a break in the surface here, creating a mini-cliff about two feet high. The smell fills the air. I can make out an old metal grille on the gap, to keep something out or to keep something in? I lean forward as far as I can, staring into the dark. I see a couple of amber eyes stare back out at me.

They are not human.

I don't even know if I say it out loud.

Hello, Night Hunter.

*   *   *

The sensible thing to do now is turn round and walk away. I should go back to Billy. I should phone Costello. But I know Sophie is here.

To fetch one if one goes astray.

I make my way back across open ground to the cover of the conifers and I raise a thumb at Billy, telling him I have found something. I am on a mission and I do not want a fat old git and his respiratory issues getting in my way.

I have found what the women were running from. Two dogs, ten stone each. Powerful. Cuddly and furry. Deadly.

To strengthen whilst one stands.

As I jog I think of them running after me, grabbing my calf, pulling me down . . . then what? Does Eric stand and watch, ready to call them off? Does he 'rescue' the frightened women, take them to the Land Rover, offering them a run home . . .

My neighbour, teddy-bear Eric.

I find a window at the back of the croft. Something that looks like old rolls of carpet is piled up against glass patterned with mould and cobwebs. No one has disturbed this for years, but at the top a narrow hopper is rusted, and open. I put a finger behind it and it lifts with a loud rasp, so easily it must have been broken from its hinge.

I feel in my pocket and check my mobile. I have charge, and a weak signal. I have Billy outside and adrenaline in my veins. I climb up on to the stone window ledge and gauge the best way to get in. I put my head through, then my shoulders, and brace my hands on the cross frame. Holding tight and punching with my legs, I kick against the ledge and let the weight of my upper half cantilever me over. I slide head first down the other side, open arms above my head steering my face away from the mouldy damp carpets, and let my legs follow until I am sitting on a filthy worktop watching the silverfish scurry. Then my feet are on the flagstone floor, behind some old two by four planks of wood. The place is freezing and deathly quiet.

I pull up the sleeves of my fleece. I think I am alone but you can never be too careful. There is a noise that might be the wind, so faint I can hardly hear it. But it is more than noise, I can feel it through my feet.

I leave the kitchen and walk into the old hall. At the front is the sitting room, the room with the water clock in it. I cross under the scaffolding that holds the ceiling up to the bottom of the stairs. The noise is getting louder. I backtrack a little and open a door next to the front door, opposite the room with the water clocks. This is a more modern kitchen, modern as in 1970s and not 1870s. There is a series of mugs, upside down as if they have just been washed. And in the corner is a boiler, working. I can see the blue light of the gas burner. I look round, feel the old radiator. It is stone cold. The boiler looks brand new. I wonder where the heat is going. Is he keeping someone alive in here? That was something that the Prof guy had said about Lorna: she had been kept out of the sun. Underground? I have found the dogs. Have I now found the place where he keeps the women, alive? Sophie? Well, Lizzie went to save Laura.

Then Lizzie weigh'd no more
Better and worse;
But put a silver penny in her purse,
Kiss'd Laura, cross'd the heath with clumps of furze
At twilight, halted by the brook:
And for the first time in her life
Began to listen and look.

Well, it worked out for them; they grew old, they lived to tell their daughters the tale.

I check the hall at the bottom of the stairs. The pipes go down there. Back to the kitchen? No, it's way too cold in there. Underfloor heating in a flagstone floor that's over a hundred years old? I don't think so.

I feel bile rise in my throat. A basement.

I feel movement under my feet again.

No sunlight. Underground. I go back out to the hall and look under the scaffolding to the rear of the house. There is a small door, and beyond it a small staircase heading downward. I try to keep my breathing steady as I go down, my hand trailing on the stone wall, but it only leads to a small room, like a basement cupboard. It is stacked with shelves on either side. This doesn't feel right; it is not logical to shelve walls on left and right while the wall opposite the door is free, with just a few pieces of MDF leaning against it. I am twitching; I know that there is something here for me. When I lean my cheek against the gritty plaster of the wall, I sense something different; not warm exactly. Just less cold. What about the MDF? It's more recent than the mouldy stuff upstairs. Eric has been doing work down here. I feel the wall carefully. There's a definite gap at the top and down the sides, but if it's a door there are no hinges. No marks of it scraping on the floor as it opens. I try to push it – nothing. I stand back and think. Eric is clever – he is an architect, an engineer. He likes puzzles, things of beauty and symmetry. There's not a lot of room, so does it slide? I place my palms against it, getting a slight purchase on the rough plaster. I try to push it to the right, it does not budge. And then to the left. Nothing. Knees bent, I try to lift it.

It gives, there is a deep rumble from the other side. The door settles back down. The rumble ceases. I had nearly set something in motion. I think of the little gate on his water clock, a single flat piece of glass that can rise and fall counterweighted by the water at the other side. Is this the practical version? A water door?

I sit on the floor and stick my fingers into the space at the bottom. It should be full of dust and bugs but it is clean. Clean means it's been used, frequently and recently. I curl my fingertips under the concrete slab. Again a slight lift and then it settles back. I think of the water clock with the little portcullis and the counterweight tub of water. It needed the weight of the water to pull up the portcullis. It has been raining steadily all day. It had been raining hard before Lorna fell out of the sky. My heart almost stops when I realize that Gilly and Sophie had waited until the rain went off before they went out. Now I know a connection.

I put my fingers under the door again, it feels slightly lighter. But I still can't lift it. Nor can I walk away. Sophie could be in there. I am not going to leave her there. Or anyone else.

I go back up the stairs and into the hall. I pull out my mobile phone and press Call.

Billy answers immediately. 'Hi, how are you doing?'

'Think I might have found something.'

'Found what?'

'Everything, the dogs, a basement. Billy, I think . . .' My voice cracks.

'Get out of there.' His voice is strong.

'I need to . . .'

'You need to get out of there, sweet cheeks.'

'Sophie.' My voice is a sob.

'Look, hen, get out. We'll get Anderson.'

'I need proof.'

There was silence on the other end.

'I don't want the proof of your dead body. You can't stop one of those dogs, can you?'

'No. But I know where the dogs are. I need you to do me a favour. Walk to the front garden, watch the tub fill with water, then when it tips into the ornamental pond. Tell me if the earth trembles when it stops, as if something underground is moving.'

'OK, not the kind of thing that usually turns me on, hen, but I'll give it a go.'

I hear him open his car door. I can hear the rain. As he shuts his phone I hear him mutter, *fucking pissing down.*

I go back down the stairs, watching the signal on the phone fade. And I stand again at the lower door. I kneel, I try to lift it again. It definitely shunts up a little higher before it falls back down again. I'm sure I am right.

I go back up to the top of the stairs and look at the phone signal – one bar. It's not much but it's enough. The phone goes, I answer it immediately. There's nobody at the other end, just a noise as if the phone's in someone's trouser pocket.

Instinct tells me to say nothing.

Then I hear a muffled *hello*. It's not Billy.

I push the phone hard into my ear, looking round me, looking for a way out. I can't ignore the feeling of unease that is rising in me. I hear Billy's voice say, 'Hello, Eric, how are you doing?'

'Can I help you with something?' The clang of a heavy door, the Land Rover.

'Elvie? I was thinking you might know where she is.'

'Why would I?'

I recognize Eric's voice, but it doesn't sound like him. It is harder somehow.

'Just wondered. Parnell said she was up at Ardno but she seems to have gone walkabout – or runabout in her case. I thought she might come to you, you being an old pal. Have you seen her?'

'I don't know what she would be doing here.'

'I don't think she's been thinking all that clearly with all that's going on. You know her family. I'm worried about her.' I hear the rhythmic rustle of his trousers as he walks. They must be standing out in the yard in the pouring rain. 'She told me about this clock thing.' Billy's voice sounds full of admiration.

Eric starts talking about the water clock, his voice more normal now, louder. He has obviously moved towards Billy. Billy explains why he is concerned about me. I have been out running in the middle of the night, not the actions of a sane woman. Does Eric know of anywhere else I might go?

There's a pause, as if Eric has shaken his head. 'I'll be in most of the night, I'll let you know if she turns up. But Mary would be your best bet. Elvie might have gone to the hospital to try to speak to her.'

'Well, if she phones you, tell her to call me. I'll be fucking furious once I stop being worried.'

'She's always been odd,' says Eric.

'Well, here's my number.' I hear the phone cut off.

And that's me stuck. I hear Eric at the door. I hear his voice say 'Hi', and for a moment I think he's talking to me. But he keeps talking. 'So she hasn't been there?'

Has he phoned Parnell? I creep closer to the bottom of the stairs to listen, keeping my eye on a length of scaffolding pipe. I can get to it before he gets to me.

'Just that Billy guy said that she was up at your house earlier.'

Silence.

'So you've been in Glasgow all day? I must have misunderstood him.'

I hear him close the phone.

'But I don't think I did,' I hear him say. Then there is a slow, soft footfall, like a teddy bear.

Now I am trapped in the house. And he has a heads-up that I am here. I listen to him moving about, and tuck back in behind the door as far as I can, trying not to breathe.

I track his movements. His car keys going down on a hard surface, soft sounds of a coat or jacket being taken off. He is muttering to himself. Then I hear his footsteps on the floorboards in the hall. Only inches separate us; we are back to back with only a thin wall between.

I hear the drag of metal on wood, then the front door shuts.

I let out a slow breath but stay in my place for a while, making sure that he has gone. Then I nip out back through to the dirty kitchen window where I see him walking across the moor to the trees and the older part of the croft. He is going to let the dogs out. And even I cannot outrun them.

I go to the front of the house. It's still raining heavily. There's no sign of Billy or the car. I try him on the mobile; he has switched his off. He will be going for help and I just have to hide until it gets here.

Or I can try to find Sophie.

I go back to the basement stairwell and hide, glad that that filthy carpets camouflage my muddy shoeprints. I bet Eric thinks he's so clever that nobody would ever find their way in there. I take that as a challenge and think back. Have I left any signs that I have been here? I don't think so, nothing but a scent. As soon as those dogs run free he will have his answer.

In the basement I slide down against the wall, thinking of a way out. Or a way in. Or I can hide and strike him over the head with that piece of scaffolding as soon as he appears. I look for it but it has gone. He took it with him, of course.

Which means he feels the needs to defend himself. He knows me too well.

I turn my mobile off and sit for a while, thinking. He must be out there somewhere, running the dogs up on the hill. Is that where he thinks I am? I am still thinking this through

when I hear the noise again, that deep grinding noise from
under my feet, but it is closer now, right behind the wall.

I look around the cupboard and see a rubber torch on the
shelf, near the door. If I make a move I have to make it soon.
This is not going to be quiet, so I need to do it while he's out
with the dogs. I place my two hands under the plaster slab
and lift; it moves easily now. I hear a noise like a cistern
running. Then it stops and the plaster slab stops. It moves up
about twelve inches before it falls back, but the downward
movement is slow. I stick my hand underneath it, feeling its
depth. A couple of inches or so. I wait until it is down fully
then stick the torch between my teeth. This time I am ready.
I put my fingertips underneath it and pull up hard. The door
rises and I roll quickly underneath, letting it fall to a close
behind me with a surprisingly gentle *snick.*

I am through.

No matter what is in here, there is now that slab between
me and those dogs. I am sitting on another flagstone floor. It
is dark, but warmer. This smells like a house with life.

I sit for a minute as my eyes adjust, not wanting to put the
torch on until I know how far the light might be seen. And
by whom.

Nothing happens. I wait then put the torch under my fleece
and switch it on, letting a trail of dull light shine round the
room. Arcing the beam around I see another room like a corridor,
about eight feet long and three feet wide with a puddle at the
far end. I can lean against one wall and easily touch the other.
There is no window. I pull the torch out to get the benefit of
the full beam. I tap the walls. Three of them look the same,
old stone, with newer plaster holding the render together. The
fourth wall, the narrowest one, sounds hollow. There is water
at the bottom, the full width of the room, where the floor dips.
It reminds me of the old footbaths at the public swimming
pool, no way through without getting your feet wet. I keep
clear of the water and lean forward, putting my ear against
the slab. I can hear the noise of water running, above me,
under me. But it sounds louder the lower I get. I run the beam
of the torch along the floor, a deep dark trough of water. A
stream of clear, fresh water is gurgling along a low channel

to disappear under the wall. Eric is fond of his little tricks. And his water. The wall in front of me looks solid. I bet it is not. I step forward into the puddle. My foot disappears into the deep blackness and I fall on my backside. Pulling my soaking leg out, I sit and think then I roll up my sleeve and stick my hand under the concrete slab. If I lean my cheek against the flagstone floor and stretch further, I can reach fresh air on the other side. Then I sit back on my haunches.

This is another water door. I try the same trick as I did before – hands underneath and heave. The concrete bites into my fingers and it's difficult to get purchase at arm's-length. I try to push it up, it gives and lifts, accompanied by that familiar sound of volumes of water running, and the channel beside me becomes a mini-tsunami. The door gets heavier. As it stops, the water stops. I lift it again and it gurgles back to life. But I see light, dancing diamonds reflected on the surface of the water. The slab has stopped moving. It will lift no further. I lie down on the floor and look along the top of the water. I can see stairs on the far side as warm air floats out towards me. Again I get the feeling that there is something alive down here. And I think it might be Sophie. This partition must communicate with the room beyond this one. It is logical that this is the door, so why does it not open high enough to let me step across the water and get through? I stretch out my arm again to make sure that I can feel fresh air on the other side.

All I have to do is get underneath. The gurgling noise comes and goes with a promise, but the water level has dropped a little. The dogs might not be able to find me down here, but when Eric comes back to the house and notices that the torch is missing, he will recall showing me the water clock. And he will put two and two together. I have only bought myself some time. Billy will appear with the cavalry – well, maybe Grandpa Cop, in a mood, no doubt. He's a friend of Eric's, I will need proof. Something that cannot easily be explained away.

There is no going back now.

I watch the water level drop. Six inches, seven, ten. It reveals a step. I saw matching stairs on the other side. I take my

phone out of my pocket and throw it across the top of the
water just under the slab. I hear it fall on to a hard surface
without a splash. I check the rubber torch is waterproof. I
think if I slide down into the water feet first, my feet will hit
the bottom and all I have to do then is dip my head under
the partition and I'll be on the other side, no drowning
required. Just full body immersion in bitter cold water for a
minute. In the end I stick the torch into the waistband of my
trousers and hope it will hold. I slide off the edge of the
flagstone. The icy water steals my breath. It bites at my flesh,
and my Rohans suck at the skin of my thighs as I let myself
drop deeper. There seems to be no bottom, my feet kick
against nothing. I stretch my legs down, suspending myself
upright like a living specimen in a jar, hanging in formaldehyde.
I feel myself go down, down, down. I expect my feet to touch
something . . . but nothing . . . it's an abyss. I place my hands
against the flagstone on my right and push hard; my body
floats across, under the slab. I dip my head down into the
water to clear the bottom of the partition. Then I grab
the flagstone at the far side and try for a hand hold. My
fingertips touch, then slither uselessly. I feel myself tumble
down into the water, totally disorientated; my shoulders are
above my head. Everywhere is black. I breathe out slowly,
watching the air trickle from the corner of my mouth. Now
I know which way is up. I reach out, stretching with my arms,
my fingers, and touch nothing. I kick with my feet, the torch
stabs into me. I kick again and reach blindly above my head.
My fingers touch the edge of the flagstone; this time I grip
tight, and pull myself up. My body is heavy in the water, my
clothes dragging me down. But I haul myself up and clamber
out on to the dry flagstones on the far side where I sit for a
minute, dripping wet but clean, very clean. Almost clinically.
As was Lorna. I know that she was here, doing this. I'm sure
of it.

If that bastard comes after me now, I will have him.

I wipe the water from my face, the hair from my eyes. This
place looks the same as the other side but much bigger, older.
It goes back for a long, long way, the walls becoming more
cave-like as they recede. The noise reverberates for a long

way too. And below me is a set of stairs which get older and more worn as they go down.

Like a dungeon.

I try to keep calm, scared that I might be right. This place is warm. And it is warm for a reason. He is keeping them here, keeping them alive. Sophie, Gillian and the rest of them. All I have to do is find them.

Calm, calm, calm. I make my way down the stairs. There is a spooky near-darkness, a dull light coming from somewhere so that I can see outlines but not fine detail. The beam of the torch finds another panel in the wall, a section of different stone. It sits flush with the old wall but newer, like an old alcove filled in. There are others, some obviously disused and bricked up. I know how to work this now. I slip my hands underneath and the plaster slab rises, I hear the same gurgle of water from wherever. The weight lifts easily. There is no water underneath this one, just a ray of light that grows into a triangle on the flagstones. I can smell the life beyond.

I slide under the door and let it close behind me. It seems darker in this room with the little orange spotlights glowing from the upper corners. I wonder if Eric is watching me on some kind of security camera, laughing at my attempts to find my way through the water doors and the dark corridors. I slip the torch on to see a low bench, a metal table like a mortician's slab.

That stops me, my heart goes cold.

I feel true fear when I see the far wall, covered by a rack of tools, like the one that Rod has at home on the wall of the garage. A kind of lattice with hooks and catches. I shine the torch closer, and realize these are not tools, they are too small, too shiny, metal, surgical. The same tools and scalpels that I had used during my orthopaedic rotation. Tools and scalpels that could easily excise a dog bite from calf muscle. I think I hear a gentle moan. The big bench against the wall is not solid, but made of metal panels. The moan rises in pitch until it becomes a squeal.

I shine the torch on some bottles on the shelf, now at eye level, and I recognize the name: Amoxicillin.

Eric is a full-blown nutter. He is keeping them alive – more than that, he's keeping them healthy. But there is someone here.

Still alive.

Then I realize that my phone is missing. I have left it behind the first water door. Big mistake.

I will not make another. I pull a long-handled scalpel from the wall and tuck it into my sock. Then I take a hammer in my hand, just to make sure. Very sure. Just in case he brings the dogs.

I hear the noise again, muffled, and kneel down. The upper half of the work bench is divided like a sailor's chest, three drawers then six. But the bottom half is one big drawer, the same dimensions as a coffin. I grasp the drawer handle and pull. The noise inside gets worse, the pathetic little mewling increasing to a blood-curdling shriek. The drawer jams, it's too heavy for me to pull out any further. I put the hammer between my teeth so I can have both hands on the handles. They are almost at the full width of my arm span. I grip hard and heave.

The noise of metal grinding on metal jars my teeth as the drawer judders open. In the vague light, it takes me a while to work out what I am looking at. It's wriggling like it's alive, but smells of rotting flesh and human faeces. It smells dead already.

Something thrums on the bottom of the drawer, the noise echoing round the stone walls. Instinctively I put my hand out to stop it. I touch something familiar: dry, hot skin. A bony shin kicks against my palm. Wide white eyes stare out in sheer, raw fear, the pupils focusing on the hammer in my teeth. The squealing increases and her mouth pulls against the tape that holds her lips closed, saliva seeping from underneath, foaming and bleeding. There is a blood-stained T-shirt over her chest, a pool of urine in the bottom of the drawer, and it takes a minute to recognize the skeletal thinness, the emaciation. Her lower limbs are bare, she has a single metal cuff on her arm; the skin around it is swollen, bleeding and crusted. There is an echo here of the marks on Lorna's leg. The sweet odour of infection floats over the stench of her body fluids. The cuff is attached to a chain, and the chain is welded to the side of the drawer.

When I do meet her eyes, they are windows of sheer terror, staring deep into mine. Not even pleading. Nothing human is left. Just fear.

'You're safe,' I whisper, unable to resist a look over my shoulder to make sure that we are still alone.

She does not hear me and starts kicking, rattling her heels against the metal of the drawer. So much noise will draw attention. I hold her legs down but she struggles even more. When I place my hand on her chest, she tries to writhe from under it. Her efforts to get away from me are intense.

'Stop making that noise, please. He doesn't know I'm here.'

She pauses, slightly; is she trying to register what I said?

'It's over. You are safe.' I keep saying it and saying it until she lies still. Her eyes are still wary, she doesn't trust herself. Or me. 'You're safe. Don't struggle any more. It's over. Can you hear me OK?'

I place the back of my hand on her forehead; she is running a high temperature. 'Can you hear me?' I repeat.

She nods, a quick, panicky nod. Then she pulls her head back, as if trying to retreat back into the drawer. Tears appear in her eyes, she has known pain for too long.

'I'm going to take that tape off your face. I need to speak to you.'

She nods again but her eyes are flitting over my shoulder. Foam is still seeping from underneath the edge of the duct tape at the corner of her mouth. 'Stay still if you can.'

There is a remote gurgle in the water. It echoes in the air around us, the deep rumble that I had been aware of before. The woman kicks again; her eyes dart towards the door and back to me. The noise passes and there is silence again.

'Is that what you hear when he comes to get you?'

She nods in panic. Her face is skeletal, her bones right under the skin, her mouth bony and protuberant. Her eyes flash again, she is trying to warn me.

'If he comes, I will kill him.'

Our eyes meet. She is daring herself to believe me, daring herself to believe that the nightmare is over.

'I need to put this torch in my teeth so I can see properly.'

She nods again, tears flowing now. She is pitiful. I hold her chin in one hand and gently flick up the corner of the tape with the nail of my forefinger. She wheezes in pain, her heels kicking again. The adhesive of the tape lifts the skin, a steady stream of blood starts to thread over her chin. I drop the torch from my teeth. 'Sorry, but if I pull, I'll just peel your skin off. That will have to wait until you're at the hospital. We can dissolve it and it will come off easily.'

The words register with her. The blink of her eyes makes me smile. As if we'll just go to hospital and all will be well. Then she whimpers; she is trying to tell me something. She starts to cry, real proper tears, sobbing, great intakes of breath. Relief? She starts to shake and I recall my medical training. Sometimes touch is the only weapon we have. In the Western, on the night Sophie was attacked, when I sat beside the dying man, a nurse took me to one side and told me to hold his hand. She didn't actually say the words *you fucking moron* but that's what she meant. When I put my hand on his bony, sweaty head, he opened his eyes a little, as if it was some comfort that he was not alone.

I place my hand on this woman's hair, this temperature needs medical help. 'I need to get out now. My friend is away for help. Are there more of you down here?'

She nods.

I take a deep breath. 'Is there someone called Sophie?'

Her eyes widen.

'Is there somebody called Sophie here, a girl? Blonde?' In spite of myself, I stare her down. She blinks, tears running slowly from her eyes, then she moves her head.

She is here.

'Thank you. Thank you . . .' My voice catches in my throat. 'I am going to leave you.' The kicking with the heels starts again, and her skeleton rattles around in her metal coffin. Her whole body jerks like she is having a fit. 'You must be still. I have to leave you and I need to close the drawer.'

At that she goes absolutely ballistic.

'I need to leave and get help, but I will be back.' I add, 'Soon.' I need to get to Sophie.

She starts shaking her head again, trying to tell me something that I am not getting. There is a rumble, and this time it seems high above me. She squirms and wriggles, her heels kicking hard. Her eyes dart behind me to the door, then to me, then to the door. 'Is that him coming now?'

She nods frantically, fear bleeding from her eyes.

'Don't worry. I will see you soon, I promise.' I place the palm of my hand on her forehead. 'Just pretend that this did not happen.'

She looks straight ahead. I know that she's thinking I am a dream. Or a nightmare. Something that her infected brain has dreamed up to taunt her. She thinks that she will wake and know that this never happened. I turn off the torch and close the drawer, leaving her to her own private hell while I go and find my sister.

I move as quietly as I can in the darkness, trying to minimize the slapping of my wet shoes on the flagstones. I don't want to go back the way I came in case I run into Eric. I creep back out into the main corridor, trying to get my bearings, and follow the slight downward path that goes deeper into the earth. There is a warm pipe suspended above the flagstones by clasps hammered into the wall.

There are other women down here.

Sophie is down here.

I pass other water doors, some boarded up, some cemented over. I go on, amazed by how far this underground tunnel goes. There is some engraving on the wall, the date 1943. I can make out the S of Scottish, the HY of hydro. Were these the tunnels built by the prisoners of war? No wonder Eric knew so much about it. It made sense. I pass another door and then another. The tunnel begins to narrow and flatten, I am running out of space and – as if to remind me I am running out of time as well – there is another rumble overhead. I go to the last door. I place my fingers under the bottom of it and it lifts easily. The noise of water running overhead can be heard elsewhere in the system; all Eric has to do is follow the noise.

I feel the warmth inside and light floods out. I look under the door and take everything in. My heart skips a beat with every piece of the jigsaw I see. A side view of a blonde woman sitting in front of a fire, ice blonde. Her hands lie in her lap, her head is slightly bowed. She is clothed, she could be reading a book. She has a padded armchair, the chair is sitting on a rug. A standard lamp shines an amber light over her shoulder; the flex runs up to the ceiling and disappears. She has a small table of books beside her, a glass of orange juice. Then I see the hair, the familiar double plait twisted into a clasp.

'Sophie?' I call under the door. 'Soph.' I don't actually know if I am making any noise. I try again but my breath has been stolen.

And there is no answer.

Sophie! I am nearly sick.

We have come so far.

I try to lift the door further. But there is a rumble, a cough that sounds very close. It didn't come from the room but from behind me.

My brain is screaming at me to run; it has registered something that I have not.

Eric is on his way.

I retreat. The simple act of removing my hands lets the slab fall to the ground. It closes with no noise apart from the gurgle of water from overhead. I retreat into the tunnel. I have the hammer, I have the scalpel; all I need is surprise. I hear no panting or pitter-patter of dog claws.

The passage narrows, it's darker, narrower, colder. It smells damp. It twists slightly left and right. I think that, if I have come in the right direction, I must be under the old ruined croft by now. Where the dogs were kept, underground.

That makes me stop. I do not want to run into them.

I look up. The rough ceiling was hewn from the rock many years ago. I feel up with my fingertips, there's a ledge above my head. It's only a few inches deep but is the full width of the tunnel and above head height. It would be behind Eric if he came this way. Getting up on it is easy; staying up there without rolling off is not. I brace myself against the sides, rotating myself on to my right side. And stay there, the hammer clasped in my crossed arms, the scalpel tucked down my right sock. If he walks this way, I can drop down behind him and kill him. I calm myself, taking comfort in how fit and strong I am. Much stronger than he will think I am. I settle my heart; we are nearing the end of this.

I lie in the stillness.

I have to push my tongue into the back of my teeth to stop myself from crying. Sophie will be coming home.

My heart starts to thud as I hear the quiet slop of Eric's shoes on the flagstone floor come this way, then cease. Is he looking for me or just doing his rounds as a jailor? I do not hear the dogs but I do hear the slab rise and the whoosh of water overhead. The sound is diminished, distant now. I hear him mutter something, the consonants echo on the bare walls. He is impatient rather than panicked. Could he have missed the phone? Could he have missed the torch? No. He knows I am here and he is confident that I will not get away.

That is the frightening thing.

The door rumbles, to its open position I presume, and I hear him go into the room. I hear him say *hello*, and something that might be *How are you doing?*

It seems a quiet conversation, relaxed and casual. I can hear an answering voice, low and measured. They appear to be having a calm chat – I know that cannot be right.

I catch only the odd word of her replies. I am aware my bones are aching, my wet clothes are sticking to me, and my hands and feet are starting to chill. I can't afford to lose the use of them, so I flex the fingers of my right hand and then my left. Right when Eric is talking, the left when Sophie is talking. There is no point to listening as I cannot hear, and the conversation never changes in pitch or volume. It is like a tennis match or a well-rehearsed play.

I don't know how long I have been here for. My joints are getting very stiff and sore. If I don't move soon I am going to roll off my perch.

I resort to counting from one to a hundred and back down again. Then I hear the footfall, a slight click and a rumble. The footfall recedes. Silence, no noise of water being moved around. Where is he now? I don't care. I put the hammer in my mouth and slide down the wall on to the floor, pause, listen, moving my fingers and my toes all the time.

I think about Sophie. I can't leave her here. She looked fit and well, she will help me get out of here and then we can get help for the woman in the drawer.

Sophie will know what to do.

Heart pounding, I go back to the slab. I put my hands underneath but it is harder to open now as there is less water on the other side to cantilever it. But after sitting for a moment I summon the strength and then pull up hard. It lifts slowly; as every muscle strains I see the small groove at the side of the slab that acts as a runner for it to slide up and down. Eric is a fine engineer. I hold it until I am sure that the slab will stay, then I roll underneath, hardly able to breathe because I am about to say hello to my sister. Lizzie and Laura reunited. I end up sitting in front of the slab, cross-legged. Looking at the girl with her back to me, blonde, the hair twisted in Sophie's style. A little voice is nagging at the back of my head – the way she is holding herself. The perfect to and fro conversation. The voice starts screaming but I just whisper, '*Hello.*'

Sophie does not turn round. She sits very still, looking at her lap. She has not moved. She has not moved since the moment I first saw her. I stand up, keeping my back to the rocky walls of this strange room. My brain works logically. There is a small table under the standard lamp, a teapot and a china cup. Orange juice. There are cakes and biscuits. But the figure has not moved. She is not answering. She is not breathing.

'Hello?' I say again, quietly. As her face comes into view, I acknowledge the relief that this is not Sophie. Her eyes stare into the fire, she is extraordinarily beautiful. I think I recognize her.

I wave my hand across her eyes. Again. There is no reaction. Nothing at all.

I stand in front of her, blocking the light from the fire. She remains still as a statue. I lean forward; she does not blink. I touch her cheek. It is hard, cold to my touch.

She is made of porcelain.

The hammer is in my hand.

I smash her to a million pieces.

*   *   *

It's simple now.

Me or him.

I roll back under the door and begin to run down the corridor back to the big water gate where I had left the phone. I am going to get out.

As I near the wider part of the tunnel I move more carefully, keeping myself against the wall, pausing every now and again to make sure that there is silence. I am getting used to the noises of the water above my head, reading the signs that he is moving.

I get to the large water gate. The water in the trough is higher and the slab that bisects it is lower.

And I cannot see my phone so Eric must have picked it up.

He knows I'm here but he's not looking for me. That suggests I am trapped. This time it's a swimming job to get out, and he might be waiting for me on the other side.

I need to rethink. The woman in the drawer. Sophie? So I turn back. There is another slab here, right at the front. It looks the same as the one where the drawer woman was, with the similar new plaster. I put the hammer between my teeth. I have no idea where Eric might be and I want to be prepared.

The slab goes up easily, with the usual slight rumble. I slide underneath and into the darkness with the torch still in my teeth.

I keep my back against the wall, waiting for my eyes to adjust to the lack of light as I hold the torch in one hand and the hammer in the other. This room is different. I can smell it.

There is fresh air. My eyes start to pick out shapes and shadows, so there is light, but I don't sense anybody moving.

But I can hear someone breathing.

Eric? I press my back to the wall.

I wait for a few minutes but nothing changes, except I begin to see some shapes. I hold the torch out to my side so that if Eric takes aim he will miss his target by an arm's length. I turn it on and direct it to the source of the breathing.

I lower the beam slightly. There is no kicking or trauma, no panic at me coming into the room.

A woman is lying on a makeshift bed, curled away from me. She looks like a naked child in the darkness, waiting for dawn to break. She moves slightly on her thin, stinking mattress, lifting her weight off the festering sores I can see on her back.

'Hello?'

'I haven't turned, I haven't turned round,' she says, struggling to control her voice.

'Hello?' I say again. 'I'm here to help you get out.'

She lies very still. I wonder how many times he has let her think that she can go free. Is that what he told Lorna? Then sent the dogs after her?

'You can turn round.' I touch her shoulder.

'You're not Eric,' she says. As she turns her eyes hold similar terror as the other woman's. She starts to shake.

Recognition. 'Gillian?'

She makes a sound, a spluttering cry.

'It is you, isn't it? Your mum hired us to find you.'

She looks confused; her head shakes, her nose starts to run, her snot joins her tears. 'You won't get out! Oh no, you'll never get out.' She sobs as she grasps my wrist; her fingers are bones covered with paper skin. 'Have you seen my girls?'

'Only in the pictures in your mum's house.'

'My mum's house. My mum's house,' she repeats; this helps to steady her.

'You need to help me get out of here,' I say. 'Then I can get help.'

The grip on my wrist tightens. 'You can't get out. He'll kill you.'

'He won't.'

'He will.'

'Is there a girl here – Sophie?' I brace myself for the answer.

'I don't know. I don't know how many . . .' She starts to cry inconsolably.

'So tell me about the water. Does he only come when it rains?'

She nods, her face streaming with tears as she fingers the small gold dolphin hanging on a chain round her neck.

I point at it, aware that my fingers are blue and shaking, their covering of black hair dried into horny little spicules. I must seem barely human. 'Did he ever want to send that back home?'

She rubs the dolphin a wee bit harder. 'No. So they are still looking for me? It's been so long.' She wipes her nose on the back of her forearm.

'Of course they are.'

'I thought they might forget.' She raises her fist to her mouth, as if that might stop the tears.

'They would never stop looking.'

She raises her chained arm. Her voice becomes rushed with memory. 'There was a girl, I could hear her screaming at him, screaming that she was going to get out. I heard her counting – it came through the pipes or the vents. She was keeping fit, she wasn't going to be weak when the time came. The time for getting out. Then, one day, the noise stopped.' She stares at me. 'Did she make it?'

'She got out.'

I am sitting on the bed with her now. We're talking quietly in the half-light of the torch. It is calming me as much as it is calming her. She starts to cry again.

'Please don't. I don't want any sign that I have been here, so no red eyes, no great emotion. Tell me things about him. The more I know, the more power I have.' My words come out hard. The tears start. I need to move on. 'I'll kill him if he comes near you,' I say simply.

'Are you for real?' she asks, the first touch of humour.

'Yes. If he comes back here, I will kill him.' That worked with the other woman, and it has the same effect on this one.

'Well, you would scare me.' She smiles tentatively. 'We're not quite there yet, are we?'

'No.'

She looks at the wall; the stones are wet and glistening. It is raining inside her underground prison. She pulls the heavy chain over her, arranging it curled like a cobra on the mattress, and then she starts drawing patterns on the dampness. She flicks her bony fingers over it, feeling the coarseness being smoothed by the water. I think she has done this many times; this has been her comfort. 'I hear water move, like hearing the sea through a sea shell.' Then she looks up at the ceiling as the water starts to drip.

She has drifted off somewhere. She has curled up a little

more, turned into the wall. I can see a bite mark on the back
of her bare leg. It has healed but it's still red and angry-looking.
It must have hurt a lot.

'Is that where the dog attacked you?' I ask her.

Her voice is almost a whisper, 'It all happened so fast. I
was in so much pain. He will set the dogs on you, and they'll
kill you.' She is drifting off.

'Gillian,' I said. 'I will be back.'

She turns away from the wall and looks at me. There is pity
in her eyes, but she smiles a wan smile. 'God speed,' she says.

I slide out of the room, doing the same trick with the door,
then slip into the water of the big water gate. I tread, preparing
to dip under and come up at the other side of the partition
which is sitting lower now. I stick the hammer in the waistband
of my Rohans, and am about to start feeling around under the
partition so I can gauge how deep I'm going to go down. I
drop into the water then use the bottom of the partition for
momentum to get me up the other side. I have no idea if Eric
is waiting for me to reappear but he has no need to. All he
needs to do is sit on the front step with those two dogs and
all this will be over.

I come up and wipe the water from my eyes. The little
stairwell is in darkness, all is still. I climb out and stand in
the dark corner dripping and wiping the water from my head
and face, thinking about what to do next. I have to find help,
while avoiding those dogs. They will follow my scent. Lorna
had been forensically clean; if that was because she had been
through that water door then I too would be clean and maybe
have no scent. But I don't know enough about dogs to bet my
life on it.

I go back up the stone steps to the slab at the back of
the cellar of the house proper and get through it. I am now
in the hall, hidden from view by the scaffolding. I need to
be invisible to those dogs. I need to smell like Eric so I
dash back to the front door to the coat rack laden with his
outdoor clothes. One quick search and I lift a pair of waterproof trousers, an old woollen jumper and his jacket from the
hook and slip outside into the fresh night air. It is dark and I

realize how much time has passed, how hungry and tired I am. I nip over to the Land Rover and stand behind it, out of sight of the windows. I pull off my trousers and put his on, turning the waistband over twice. I pull off my T-shirt and fleece then put on his jumper and Barbour jacket. I transfer the hammer and the scalpel. I stick my clothes under the Land Rover, up under the chassis somewhere. Hopefully he will drive away and the dogs will follow the scent all the way to Glasgow.

I run from the Land Rover as fast as I can with the big Barbour jacket on, circling back to the house, past the outside water clock in his front garden. I am trying not to hurry, trying not to breathe too deeply, trying to ignore the noise Eric's clothes are making as I run. There's no sign of anyone coming with help, no lights on the track, nothing. I lean against the wall of the house right next to the front door letting the rain fall on my face. The smell of sweat and dogs rises up from his jacket, it should confuse the dogs a little. I have a plan to get in the house and find a phone. The sky is dark and low, heavy with cloud. That does not bode well for a mobile phone signal. I need a landline.

Then I see a movement through the murky darkness, I catch the sound of a sniff and I freeze. I see a tail, a low tail moving slowly, back and forth. Then another. The dogs are on the path, pulling at something large and bulky lying on the ground. I hear a familiar tune as their tugging makes it roll slightly.

I recognize the tune.

Plinky-plinky-plink-plink.

Billy's phone.

That mass is Billy.

The dogs have got him.

I try not to be sick as I walk backwards slowly, keeping my eyes on the dogs all the time. Their eyes do not leave their feast. I open the door behind me and slip back into the house. There are lights on. There weren't any when I was outside.

Eric is in here somewhere.

I nip under the cover of the scaffolding and wait for him to make a move. When he does, I will hear him. So I wait.

There is a slight noise upstairs but it is the old house creaking, groaning under the onslaught of the weather it has had to suffer over the last few days.

The game has not changed.

Me against him.

I go down the stairs in the cellar, through the slab door and down the steps to the water gate. I get down on the floor and put my arm across under the partition slab; the water has remained high. I will have to go deep again. I pull off the Barbour jacket, slip into the water and take a deep breath; it seems a long way down to get under the partition. I bend my knees up, curling my body to cross under the lower edge, and realize that it is falling on me. If this contraption closes all the way down, it will cut me in two. I have to jack-knife my body to get out the way, pulling myself clear.

I open my eyes under the water.

I see an outline above.

Eric.

Waiting.

I coil back in the water. He has me trapped. He is following my shadow. I feel down to my sock and pull out the scalpel then float to the surface slowly, so that only my eyes are above the water. He is standing there, hands on his hips, looking down at me. He says nothing, he just places his foot on my head. I just get a breath of fresh air before he grinds me under. This time I know where he is. Under the water I slip to the side, reaching up to grab his trouser leg. He bends down to pull my hand off but I stab his wrist with the scalpel. He cries out, probably more with surprise than pain. He kicks, his toe catches me on the side of the head but I don't let go. He is now so off balance, it is easy to pull him in. I feel the impact of his body on top of mine. He expects me to fight to get away from him but I hold him close and take him down with me, right to the bottom of the falling partition. The grinding sound is loud through the water, mixed with the giggle of air bubbles escaping from my lungs. I hold on to his collar, refusing to look at his face. Gravity does the work, I just guide him down, down and down. Then I hook my foot underneath the partition and pull hard, very hard. I feel the concrete graze my face, I twist my shoulders. I keep my grip, catching him under the partition and holding him as it descends.

The water in front of my eyes streaks red with wavering blood, like scarlet seaweed drifting. Then I let go.

Going back into the hall the bitter cold air hits me. Blood is streaming down my face, chilling my skin. I pull Eric's jacket back on and try to think logically. I need to get out and follow the dirt track to the road. If I run wide, I can keep away from the dogs. I can't even convince myself that this is a good idea.

I take my shoes off, rubbing my socks to get some of the excess water out. As I lean on something in the hall that is covered in old rags and blankets, I notice a slight vibration. It is a freezer, an old chest-type freezer. I lift the lid; it's full of huge chunks of raw meat, unwrapped and badly cut. I close it again.

I look out the front door. The dogs lift their heads, watching but not moving. Then the one with the black face starts sniffing the air. It takes a few steps towards me so I close the door a little, just enough gap for me to see them. They snuffle at the door, then leave, purposefully trotting away round the corner of the building. I don't know where they're going but they seem to. They know something I don't. I hear a patter pat of claws behind me.

Right behind me.

The back door was open, hence the sub-zero temperature in here. I move slowly backwards, towards the freezer, and open it up without turning my back on the dogs. They regard me with an intense stare, ears pricked. I rummage behind me, ignoring the biting cold, and pull out a joint. I don't care what it is, I fling it into the kitchen and watch the dogs follow. Then I close the kitchen door, making sure it is secure. Just in case Blackface gets any clever ideas.

I find the side door and close it behind me, locking them in.

It is raining so hard now, it is almost blinding. It is very dark up here, no light pollution, no starlight, just an ongoing empty sky. I see a pile of something lying in the dirt track: Billy.

I want to stop, go over. But he would want me to get away. So I run.

As fast as I can. The big jacket hampers me; it is not cold, the wind has fallen. Then I feel the storm in my legs and slip the jacket from my arms and I am flying. Sailing through the air; my feet barely touch the ground. I have no idea how long I run for. I feel like I am on top of the world. I am invincible. I am free, alive and flying. I will get help. I will get help for Gillian, for the woman in the drawer, for Sophie.

Then my breath is gone, the air is pulled from me. A vice grips my chest and I am on the ground, the heather prickling at my face. I roll as I fall. I can't help it. Lights drift in front of me, foggy drifting lights, and I see two feet floating in the fog, slowly coming towards me. Walking like a teddy bear.

It is Eric. The light gets brighter, he is coming straight for me.

It is over.

THURSDAY, 21 JUNE

The lights over my head flash past, head-to-toe, head-to-toe, strobing my face as I pass underneath. My heart clicks with a precise rhythm, the back beat provided by the echo in my ears. I am going somewhere else, somewhere warm, somewhere that is easy, and I have left Billy behind, left him on the track with the dogs and the rain and the rats. I see the dogs tug at his skin, tearing at his flesh. It rips open and red spills into the brilliant light. The light overhead starts to strobe red then white then red. Quickly. Quicker.

I am unable to move or breathe. The light is fierce, it blinds me through my closed eyelids, the tape on my mouth constricts my lungs, regulating my airflow while my brain starts reaching around, testing itself, trying to find sense in it all.

I didn't get away.

Eric came out of the light, walking towards me, taking me by the arm, holding me down . . .

'Stop that, you'll pull the drip out, you silly cow.'

The voice drifts up through my consciousness.

'Lie still, Elvie.'

Not Eric. This is Costello, the wolf in sheep's clothing. I open my eyes, she has a misty outline like a renaissance Madonna. She lets go my arm and pulls her chair closer then produces a notebook and a pen.

'You look like shite,' she says with her usual honesty as she removes a tube from my mouth, picking off the tape that secured it. I am aware of all the tubes on my face, in my arms, up my nose.

'Billy?' The name tumbles from my tongue.

She shakes her head. 'He would have been proud of you, you did a great job. God knows why he got out of the car, looking for you probably, never saw the dogs. We got all the women out and that was all he wanted. Gilly is home and that was the thing that was important to him. And he would want

you to keep going, he would want you to get Sophie back. So
get well.'

If I am crying I don't feel the tears. Figures walk back and
forth past the door, hospitals never sleep. A phone is ringing
unanswered in some distant corridor, there is the sound of a
trolley being pushed around.

Costello puts her hand back on my arm; her skin is warm,
mine is cold. 'Gilly is safe; the other girl is in High Dependency,
septicaemia. She wouldn't have lasted another forty-eight
hours.' She pauses. 'But there was no sign that Sophie was
ever there. Sorry.'

'She is there. You must go back.' I grab her hand. 'Eric was
coming to get me . . . I saw her, she was sitting . . .'

'No, Elvie, Eric died in the watergate. You saw a porcelain
doll of Magda, that's all. Sophie was never there. Do you
remember running? You were wet, cold and tired, you ran
miles on that hill, following the track, and you ran right into
my headlights, frightening the shit out of me. Your heart . . .'

'So where is Sophie?'

She shuffles in her seat. 'Elvie? Do you know what day of
the week it is?'

'No idea.'

'It's Thursday, you've been here for days. A lot of shit has
come down the line recently. We need to talk.' She hesitates
as if struggling where to start. 'Grant is not good, he has had
some kind of psychosis. He's a mess, Elvie. Rod has had to
move back in to look after your mum.'

I nod.

'We are still trying to piece it together. Did you see the
freezer full of body parts, all that road kill, in the hall at Eric's?
You had been in the Land Rover so you noticed the straps
that pinned his victims against the side. Gilly said they were
so tight, she couldn't even kick. Is that how you worked it
out? Is that how you knew?'

It's easier to nod.

'And you had figured out that the link was Eric being the
architect. Courtesy of Parnell's firm, he got to know the movements of the victims, their running schedules. Gilly says she
went out running and was grabbed on the back of the leg by

the dog. Eric pretended to offer her help, a run home in the Land Rover. It was too late when she realized her mistake.

'The clever thing is, she had no idea who Eric was. She had never set eyes on him until that moment. I bet none of the victims had. And that rules out Sophie, doesn't it?' Costello shivers although the hospital is hot. 'Lorna had worked out the door trick. She nearly made it, brave girl. How did you work it out?' she asks.

'I saw the model at Eric's.' My mind is firing around for some semblance of the life I had before. 'Mary?'

'Fine, left the bastard. She was never abducted, of course – you guessed that. She just ran away from him and cut the chip out herself. Alex thought quickly, I'll give him that. He turned the escape into a kidnap. Mary and Eddie had thought it through. She had packed a rucksack with a change of clothes and tore off those she wore as she ran. A few comments about Sophie running away gave her the idea, running from a situation she could not tolerate.' Costello fills a plastic cup of water and offers it to me.

I shake my head.

'She said she was thinking of you as she ran. One of the best feelings she'd ever had. Freedom. Exhilaration. Can't imagine what her life with Alex was like if running over a hill naked makes her feel better. But that Alex is a clever wee shit. He did the demand, he staged his own failed drop at the flashmob. Two of his security guys took the money down and put it in the hut where Eddie keeps the meter. He wanted to get Mary back and make himself a hero. All he needed was you to run with the idea that Mary was taken by the Night Hunter. Your love for Sophie would blind you. He knew McTiernan's record, he knew Matilda would follow the clues, but Billy suspected it was all too easy – the DNA on the envelope, the stain. Billy was a good cop, he was a wily old fox. He said that envelope was a fricking map! Real crime is never that easy. So Alex sent us to bring Mary back and get Eddie arrested. Wrongly. I don't like being used, especially not by that bastard. But he played you brilliantly. You were programmed to be a Lizzie, you had to go and save a Laura. But don't worry. Mary and Vera are giving us enough evidence to charge him.'

The sheets are warm, I am comfortable. But there is no peace. 'Sophie?'

'No sign of her, Elvie. We have carried out a sweep of the land; there are no areas of non-growth that might indicate where a body is buried. So Sophie is not up there. That might be good news.'

She's not convincing herself any more.

'We're going to try something else. It's a technique called plucking at straws. We need your help and we need it now.'

She is a wolf again. I nod. Although I don't want this conversation.

'Let's start with Mark Laidlaw.'

Piney aftershave, in my kitchen, my hand on the weight bringing it down on his head . . .

'I've been chatting to Belinda at the refuge, she knew Mark well.' I can read her, Costello is pretending to be conversational as she baits her trap. 'Belinda says that Mark's wife came to the refuge with a litany of complaints about Mark, just as he was attending hospital with the injuries she had given him, both as bad as each other.'

'Billy thought the kid was drugged.'

She was not to be side-tracked. 'He was right. But we are talking about her dad. And Sophie only ever saw Mark to advise him of his rights. She was helping him through it, he had terrible communication skills and anger management issues. He was the sort of man that likes things black and white, unable to cope with change or subtleties. They were just friends, Elvie. Sophie was only trying to help him. Soph was good with people like him. She had coped with you all her life.'

I am not going to fill this silence. I know the way he grasped my shoulders, I remember the violence in his eyes. He was going to hurt me. He was about to do the wrong thing. The weight was in my hand . . .

I think she is finished but she takes a cup of water for herself and turns a new page in her notebook. 'Do you think he just went up to the reservoir and sat there, thinking about Sophie? I bet she had become his anchor, one person he could rely on. Not so odd that he should sit where her car was found, thinking, not realising he was slowly dying, that little bleed in his brain . . .'

Our eyes meet.

'Then he lost consciousness, the car rolled. There is such a strong echo of Sophie – the car, the reservoir site. But Mark was a violent man; it's not so strange that sooner or later somebody landed a fatal blow on him. He was very fond of Sophie, I think. Genuinely fond of her.'

'So what did happen to Sophie?'

'I need to show you something.' Costello reluctantly pulls a large envelope from her handbag. Inside is a pile of photographs.

'Here is a photograph of your sister. Have a look. What do you see?'

It is the picture from my drawer at Ardno. 'It's Sophie, looking happy. At her party. Before she got upset.'

'She's not happy. She's looking past the camera, to someone over the camera's right shoulder, if you like.' She covers my sister's eyes with her hand. 'That smile is frozen solid.' She flicks that photo to the back. 'This one is a close-up of Soph's eye.' The picture is now Sophie's pupil, dark and swirling like a black hole in the heavens. I say nothing. Patterns in my sister's big blue eyes gather into little diamonds of colour to form an image of the pub curtain, the brass rod, the price list. The reflections on the surface are as clear as looking through a window pane into the rain. More shadows out on the street, people walking by, some looking in. A face is appearing at the window, in a skip cap. It has a slight fish eye distortion from the curve of Sophie's eye.

'You have said yourself that she was a bit different these last few weeks.' Costello does not give up. 'Elvie, this is the picture of the person who put that look on your sister's face. It's the picture of the reflection in her eye.' She shows me another picture, the image bigger, less defined, but the face is up at the curtain, looking right into the pub, right at my sister. There is a beanie hat, sunglasses, a short wispy beard shaved in stripes.

'And we both know who that is, behind those glasses? And that hat?'

I know. I think I have known all along.

'I'm sorry, Elvie.'

I close my eyes.

'I had to show you that otherwise none of this will make sense.' She pulls her hair back, checking that I am OK. Her voice drops. 'When we tested Sophie's dressing gown, we found Grant's semen. It shows that some kind of sexual activity took place much earlier.' Her hand rests over mine.

I open my eyes and look at the ceiling.

'Your mum wasn't as unaware as you think: she knew something was going on. Your mum and Rod tried to keep them apart but they just couldn't separate them. They were trying to protect your sister but Sophie thought she could help Grant and just kept coming back for more.'

'That sounds like Sophie, thought she could solve the problems of the world with her smile.'

'Well, Rod suspected the depth of Grant's obsession. That's why they tried to send him to America, but he made sure that was not going to happen. In the end, he raped her.' She sighs. 'So it's no wonder Sophie ran.'

I keep my eyes on the ceiling, concentrating on the dirt gathering in the corner of the light fitting. This is all wrong.

'Rod was doing his best, Elvie, whatever that was. He's sorry if he got it wrong but he had no idea what to do. He followed her around, making sure that Grant was not where she was. And Sophie, she must have been terrified that Grant would walk into her party and declare his undying love for her. Sophie had no real place to go, so she ran. Rod sent us the ankh to keep us focused on the misdirection. The whole Facebook campaign was a . . .'

I ignore her, hearing Sophie. Her words slam into my head. *I think I'm going to have to disappear. I have to go away.* I shake my head, and the pain in my cheek rattles through my skull. My mum saying, *Can't you leave Sophie alone?*

Costello is missing the point. I stare into her cold grey eyes.

'So where is my sister?'

The doctor comes in and smiles in that way we were taught to when we are about to give bad news and someone is looking.

She is thinking about sitting down but Costello has nicked the chair. The pasty-looking nurse slides into the corner behind her like a forgotten schoolchild.

'Miss McCulloch. Can I call you Elvira?' The doc tilts her head on one side. She has very shiny brown hair and that healthy-looking olive skin that means she never has to try too hard. I think that if I was some poor bugger up on the cancer ward, vomiting rings round myself and devoid of my hair and my dignity, I would kill the bitch.

'You can call me Elvie. Are you going to tell me how long I can keep being called Miss?' That'll wipe the smile from her face.

Her professional concerned smile does indeed vanish, to be replaced by a small, girly twist of the lips. 'We were thinking either you had a very poor sense of self-awareness or your medical training had gone badly wrong. But then your GP confirmed he had taken bloods and given you medication to see you through until the appointment with the endocrinologist. An appointment you never kept. You haven't been taking the medication either. Your testosterone level is through the roof for a female. Why are you not taking it, Elvie?'

'I've had other things to worry about.'

She purses her lips, a flick of the file.

'I like things in black and white. So tell me, please. Straight. Say something like *you have a tumour, Elvie.*'

'You have a tumour, Elvie. Not untreatable, though.'

I lie back and look at the ceiling.

'There are tests we still have to do but you are well, peculiar . . . You have two types of DNA. This is difficult to explain . . .'

'No. So I am two people. If I have two types of DNA, then I had a . . .' I run through the options. There are not many, and only one that I would not already know about. 'Heterozygous twin?'

'That's what we think.'

'That is rare.'

'Maybe not as rare as you think. But the fact the twin is exerting itself now? That is very rare, so much so we're keeping you our little secret. There are some doctors at Edinburgh

Royal who are doing a study on this and here you are on their doorstep. I have phoned them, for best treatment protocol.'

I take this in, trying to think logically. 'So in utero I was a twin. The twin that became me absorbed its sibling into my body. So I have their tissue as well as mine. And it was a he. I'm male as well as female – is that it?'

'Indeed.' She gives me a well done smile; she'll be patting my head soon. 'Your cells multiplied at a normal rate and his did not. As you put it, you absorbed him. But some of his cells remain and have now started to multiply; they're producing testosterone and that is causing you the problems.' She is very pretty, she is lovely. We both have sallow skin and big brown eyes; we both have strong features. She reminds me of how I used to be. She looks at her clipboard. 'It's the presence of these cells that is giving you the acne, the muscle bulk, the hair growth. But you know all that.' Her fine fingers touch her smooth jawline, where I know my own has too much dark, downy hair. 'The treatment isn't difficult; we have you on a hormone drip as you can't be trusted with oral meds.'

'What about this?' I pat my head.

'You had a slight concussion. More worrying is the damage to your cardiac muscle, but once the testosterone and adrenaline are down to normal levels it will cease to be under so much pressure. And keep away from stress, no more running round hills.' She glances at her clipboard again. 'You need to get some rest now. I'll see you on my rounds tomorrow. We'll talk through your options then.'

She slides out of the room and takes her soft-soled little pal with her.

ONE MONTH LATER

It feels strange to be lying in Sophie's bed back at Mum's house. I've been in hospital for nearly a month and I am supposed to be better. The shiny doctor thinks that what I need now is more time with my family. She is off her head. It's three in the morning, I am still not sleeping.

The game might have changed but it is not over.

I have to keep my eye on Grant, he is not in a good place. Mum and Rod go round on tiptoes. Their story is that Sophie has run away because she needed to be free of Grant. But her liberation has been my incarceration. What Sophie suffered at the hands of our brother is unclear but the police have their hands tied, there is no complaining witness, just a missing person. Costello agrees with Rod, Grant needs treatment more than anything else. Mum, Rod and I, we are all trying to deal with it.

I wish Billy was here, he would have a plan, even if that plan was making it up as he went along.

I hear a familiar noise – Rod going to the loo, no doubt. He doesn't sleep well either. But the horror of the past few weeks is slowly winding down. I do regret Mark's death, but he gave me no option. If I was put in that situation again, I would do the same thing. It's not him I am losing sleep over. Lorna has been laid to rest. Gillian's family has been reunited. Magda, still beautiful and enigmatic, had been found living in London, alive and well. Some PR guru has signed her up; her looks and her story are a titillating combination. The blonde in the drawer was talking; she was a Norwegian student called Carla Holmen and her family had flown over from Trondheim to be with her. She had asked to see me before she left hospital. No hurry there, she will take a long time to heal.

Nobody knows anything about Katrine, the Girl on the Hill. Somewhere there might be a sister looking for her. I think that disturbs me more than anything, because I am back at square one. I still don't know where my sister is.

The creeping round the house goes on. Whoever it is, they're going along the landing to my old room, the one that is now an office. I think I hear them go down the stairs but I hear no noises from the kitchen.

I get up and glance out over our back garden and into Eric's. The first light is tingling on the horizon and I can see his garden is getting overgrown now. When Eric was down here working away, building fountains and water clocks, those women were going through hell locked up in the dark, terrified that he would return. Terrified that he would not. They were alone, naked, waiting for food and water, grateful for any little morsel that came their way.

Yet Sophie was here in the family home, enduring some hell of her own.

I look over the bottom of the garden, wondering what will happen to it now that Eric has gone. The house is up for sale. The lower flower beds are crowded with growth, the water in the ornamental pool is shimmering in the darkness. The four upper flower beds are symmetrical – almost. I notice that one of them is almost bald, bare earth. Did Eric have other plans for it? The last time I recall it was as lush as the others. But when did I last look out of this window?

Four flower beds.

One devoid of growth.

I see a movement in the lower end of the garden, bloody Grant again. He has sneaked out the side door; he's doing his weird sleepwalking thing again.

I watch as he walks into the middle of the lawn, naked. I expect him to sit down and cry as he usually does, but he keeps moving, walking in his strange way – arms at his side, his legs moving with a languid drift as if he is not on the ground at all. I lean my forehead against the glass to watch. He climbs over the gate into Eric's garden and is hidden from view by the wall before he reappears at the flower beds up at the ornamental pool. I get an uneasy feeling about what he is about to do.

But still I watch him.

This is like watching a train wreck.

He walks to the side of the water with the grace of an angel.

He is quite beautiful in the moonlight. Standing between the two marble pillars, his body becomes a perfect sculpture, and the moonlight catches the fine features of his face. He steps into the water, then kneels down and looks up to the sky. Clasping his hands in prayer, he leans forward until he is lying face down in the water. He stays very still, floating with his arms out now in supplication.

I start to count. By a slow count of thirty he has not shifted.

By a slow count of sixty I am beside him.

I step into the cold water, in my bare feet. There is no reaction.

I think my brother is dead, that he has given himself the peace that he desires. I reach out to touch his shoulder; my wee brother's skin is cold and wet to my touch. Then, suddenly, his shoulders rise towards me as he straightens his arms; the power takes me by surprise as he punches himself free of the water. He stares at me. We are inches apart.

It seems like a good time to ask. 'So, how did you kill Sophie?'

His voice is clear, clearer than I have heard it in ages. 'I think you mean, why did I kill Sophie?'

'No, I mean how? You have no justification for it.'

His eyes flick to the raised flower bed, then my wee brother is back, his intelligence is sharp in those blue eyes. 'She rejected me. It was always just her and you, fuck's sake. Never looked at me. So I snapped her.' He clicks his fingers.

I try to process what he has said, where he looked.

'I really hate you,' he says in good humour. 'And I really loved her. But she had to die. Why are you still here, you sad, ugly fuck? Why did you not just move out and leave us alone? That's what we wanted. That's what Sophie wanted. Why did you not stay in your flat? Out of our lives?' I don't see his fist come up, but I feel the pain in my chin as something fractures, my teeth rattle and I taste blood. I try to spin round but he learned from the same book I did and catches my ankle, flipping me on to the wall of the pond. I feel a blow on the back of my head, and the stars dance. My mouth and nose fill with grass as I am hauled backwards, then I feel my knees scrape concrete. He is dragging me into the pond. I put my arms down to stop my face going under, bracing myself against the silt at the bottom of the water. Then his foot is between my shoulder blades.

He stamps down hard.

He is standing on me, with his full weight.

I am pinned down, my face is on the bottom of the pond, my cheek against the plastic lining. I try not to breathe in the silt. The small plants jag at my eyes as I struggle to get my arms free to push myself up, but Grant just presses harder.

My pulse pounds in my ears; I try to get my adrenaline, try to fight, but there is nothing. My eyes are ready to burst, my throat burns, my lungs explode. I trickle air out the corner of my mouth; it bubbles lightly through the murky water, weaving through the fronds of the plants in a pretty dance. My next breath will be my last.

I try one more time, dragging every bit of energy together. My body does not respond. No ice in my veins, nothing.

Then I let go.

I feel myself drift, my face is skewered into the bottom of the pond, a pull on my hair, my face slammed back into the silt as Grant's foot stamps the back of my head. I feel the cartilage in my nose give. The pressure eases, I twist my neck and think I see a shadow fall over me. The darkness is complete.

Then I am sick, relentlessly sick. In the grass. Lying. Solid ground.

Rod stands up. He was either checking Grant's pulse or holding his head under water. Either way my brother is not moving, just floating.

I know Rod heard.

I know that Sophie is here.

Rod tries to hold me back as I crawl across the grass. 'She is here.' His grasp releases me. I am slipping in the grass, blood in my eyes, blinding me, but I know.

I climb up to the raised flower bed, devoid of flowers – things cannot grow where a body has been buried. My bare hands scrabble about in the earth, Rod's hands join mine. Then he stops me, pointing to a sliver of silver catching the moonlight. Sophie's locket.

Rod collapses beside me. 'She never left, she never got away . . .' He is crying now, his arm round my shoulder.

As I cradle his head I lie back and look at the heavens. White fluffy clouds race across the indigo sky but I feel no wind on my face, the night air is warm and still. And peaceful.

In the hushed garden, the words float into my head. I hear them, I can hear Sophie's voice.

> *Must your light like mine be hidden,*
> *Your young life like mine be wasted,*
> *Undone in mine undoing,*
> *And ruin'd in my ruin . . .*

EPILOGUE

It's nearly midnight, the deep chill in the air bites into my bones. Icy stillness hangs all round me. I am a living statue amongst the other statues that are already grey and cold. The trees of Eric's garden are now bare; skeletal twigs stretch out into the night, birdless, lifeless.

The death of night, the endless sleep. This is my routine now that I have Sophie back.

I sit down, pulling my jacket under my thighs, resting my feet on the wall of the raised garden opposite. The bricks are peppered by diamonds foretelling an early frost. Autumn has already bowed out, winter is now centre stage.

I settle myself, wrapping my fingers round my mug of strong hot coffee. It is the one coffee I am allowed in a day and I savour every sip. In the dark I can make out the heap of rubbish near the back door of the house. Drawers, doors, and the old Belfast sink, which is now full of frozen rainwater and rotting leaves. Eric Mason's kitchen will be in a skip tomorrow.

I am alone here. Mum and Rod are away cruising somewhere hot while I sort out the builders. I'm not sure how Mum felt when I suggested selling our house to buy Eric's. I'm sure the neighbours thought it odd, buying the house where your only son drowned in the garden. But Rod told the guy across the road that it was a sound economic decision. Eric's house was run down and cheap because nobody wants a house that belonged to a serial killer. Rod's own interest was the big garden. Mum said that Grant had loved this garden. She didn't want other people living where her only son had died.

I never realized what a good liar my mum can be.

They agree now that Eric's house already seems like home. This garden is the right place to be. Good for reflection, contemplation and conversation.

I usually come out here at night. I started the habit when I was trying to make sense of it all. Just as I had felt Lorna guiding me on the hill, I feel Sophie talking to me as I sit here.

I now know that my brother killed my sister the minute she walked out the door, hiding her up in the long grass in Eric's garden. It was Grant who drove her car to the reservoir and then ran back across the fields. It was Grant who forgot to adjust the car seat back to where it was.

My brother had a full hour to find a hole in Eric's garden, easy in a garden full of ongoing landscaping. As the minutes slipped by, Sophie was later and later and Mum began to cry, Rod paced the floor. Grant pretended to go out to look for her and came back dirty from digging my sister's grave, sweating from digging the hole that hid her.

I know all this now. But we have Sophie back with us, nobody is taking her away. Mum has stopped drinking. Losing Grant and finding Sophie have both eased her troubled mind. It has eased mine. I know that Sophie can hear me now, talking about my day.

'We had the lunch today, Soph, it was awful,' I say, my breath billowing into the steam from the coffee. 'I thought it was Mary who wanted to meet me but when she walked through the door, there were two other women with her. Guess who?'

I sip my coffee. 'Vera was there. Dressed up and looking ten years younger. The other one I only knew by the double plait in the hair. The hairstyle you nicked although you'd never admit it. But it was Magda, or Mags as she calls herself. She was kind of in disguise. She's keeping out of the way of the press until the price is right. I read you that bit from the *Mirror* last week, didn't I? Cow!' I sniff; the night air is making my nose run. 'Then it got difficult. Mary gave me an awkward hug, Vera tried to do the same, but Mags just summoned the waiters to pull the seats out for us.'

There is no comment. I sip my coffee again.

'I read it all wrong, Sophie. They were celebrating. Mags ordered champagne. They were celebrating Mags being free of Eric, Vera being free of Alex, Mary for being with Eddie. She says the fiscal is throwing the book at Parnell. I hope it's a big book, hope it kills him.' I pause. 'But Mary kept giving me funny looks. That lunch was not her idea. I'm not sure she has forgiven me for dragging her back. And you know, Sophie, I'm not sure I care.

'But good God, they wanted all the details, the horror of the tunnels under the hill. But I didn't tell them anything. Mags doesn't need any more fodder for her tabloid exclusive. Exclusives? Can that be plural?' Sophie remains quiet on the subject. 'She wants to interview me for more details for a book deal she's been offered. She had approached Costello, who told her where to go.' I smirk. 'Mags is a pain. I think I preferred the porcelain version with Eric doing her voice. At least he got a word in.'

I look at our own statue at the top of the flower bed; Rose, we call her. She too is being dusted with frost as she holds her harp, looking over her shoulder like someone might nick it.

'What I never realized is that Mary and Mags have known each other for ages. Why did I not see that? We'd never have known if it wasn't for that copy of *Catch-22*. I thought we were good at secrets, but Mary beats us hands down. You'd have rumbled her straight away.'

I sigh.

'I asked Mary about Charlie. All she managed was "he's well but he's . . ." before Vera starts on about her Charles. The half-brothers are in competition already. Vera will get some money out of this, won't she? You'd know about the legal side of it. I was zoning out when Mary slips her palm on mine and passes me this wee card, secretly. Like I say, good at secrets.' I pull the card from my pocket. 'It's a drawing of me in a white coat wearing a miner's hat. I have a huge head and a hairy face. This is what Charlie the Coco Pops kid thinks a doctor looks like.' I show it to Sophie before folding it up.

'But they never mentioned Lorna, Katrine, or Gilly or Carla. They are too wrapped up in themselves. What kind of celebration of life is it that forgets the dead, or celebration of freedom that forgets the incarcerated? And the missing. They never mentioned you. Never mentioned Billy. Never mentioned what he did for them, what he gave . . .'

Sophie seems to contemplate this.

'What did Rossetti say . . . *Pleasure past and anguish past, Is it death or is it life?* It's all past. I said I needed to go to the loo, took my jacket and left. I sat in the car outside and wished I was meeting Billy for chips and cheesy sauce. I wish you had met him, you would have hated him.' We share a giggle.

It is starting to rain now. The garden comes alive with pitter-pat noises, and the surface of the pond starts to dance in an echo of the Goblin Market. I can't help but shiver when I think about the pond, the water, the noise of my nose breaking, my cheekbones shattering. I lift the mug to warm my face. But the injuries, the bruises, the water in my lungs made Costello's job easy. Not that she was totally convinced about the self-defence, less convinced when she later spotted Sophie's silver locket round my neck. She doesn't miss much but I get the feeling she didn't push as hard as she could have. Those cold grey eyes of hers see the bigger picture.

I kick the wall with my toe as if I'm shaking a bed to wake a sleeping friend. In this case it is a flower bed. Rod has reseeded it, some flowers that might bloom in the early spring. Might.

I sip at my coffee. 'If Mags and Vera are the alternative then I'm glad I am as I am. But why did they never mention you, Soph? Not even once?'

The silence intensifies, as if she's thinking about it. The rain is streaming down my face, joining the tears. The surface of the coffee is spotting with raindrops.

A vulpine cough breaks the silence. In the night air it sounds like somebody stifling a laugh. I smile at Sophie, glad we are here, close by, still together. Glad that she never left. Glad that she never got away.

> *Then joining hands to little hands*
> *Would bid them cling together,*
> *'For there is no friend like a sister,*
> *In calm or stormy weather . . .'*